The apparition was waiting for him in the same spot it had first appeared. After the shock of recognition subsided Tom took a deep breath and walked boldly to the far end of the pool and stood beside his nemesis. He tried not to stare but couldn't help himself. He was looking at Eric Hall . . . and Eric Hall had been dead for two years.

But it could not be anyone else. He had waited too long for this moment to be intimidated. Like the substitute Brooks Brothers clothing he had bought in his college days, Tom had found a reasonable facsimile and nothing was going to stop him from sampling the bargain.

VINCENT LARDO

The Prince and the
PRETENDER

Boston • Alyson Publications, Inc.

to Dorothy Sayers

ACKNOWLEDGMENT

The author wishes to express his thanks and appreciation to Robert K. Massie, whose book *Nicholas and Alexandra* (and meticulous research) provided the historical background necessary for *The Prince and the Pretender*, and whose sensitive retelling of the story of the last Czar and his family compelled me to refuse to allow them to perish in the basement of Impatiev House in Ekaterinburg, Russia.

This is a paperback original from Alyson Publications, Inc., PO Box 2783, Boston, MA 02208. Distributed in England by Gay Men's Press, PO Box 247, London, N15 6RW.

First edition, September 1984   5 4 3 2 1

ISBN 0 932870 53 8

1

Thomas Bradshaw arrives at what he affectionately calls the O.V.C.A. (Old Voyeur's Christian Association) every Tuesday and Friday at six p.m. He enters its portals, when feeling mean, like a general leading an invisible army into the fray or, when feeling magnanimous, like the Prince of Wales visiting an orphanage. Shoulders squared, head erect, eyes veering neither to the right nor left, he marches to his locker to the inaudible cadence of a hundred virile tenors belting out "Stout-Hearted Men."

As he nears his locker the strains of "Stout-Hearted Men" give way to the muted trumpets of "The Stripper". His audience can't hear the music but it is the performer, not the song, that draws their undivided attention. The O.V.C.A.'ers are all eyes, and all of them are glued to Thomas Bradshaw.

But the band plays on in Tom's head as shirt buttons pop under his agile touch and the garment is removed with a masculine flourish not unlike Clark Kent's maneuver in the tight confines of a phone booth. The t-shirt is a gleaming white, the material stretched across hard pecs and broad shoulders. A flash of firm belly is momentarily revealed as the t-shirt is yanked free of the trousers.

The tempo of the music changes, becomes relaxed, undecided. He brings one foot up on the low bench and bends to undo a shoelace. This action causes his pants to separate from the rear of his waist and those with front-row seats can see the white band and the letters JOCKEY imprinted in black around and around and around the one-inch elastic.

Shoes and socks gone, he rises and with arms crossed he pulls the t-shirt over his head in one quick motion. His chest is hairless except for a fine line running down its center and curving delicately under each breast. He pauses for a brief moment. The orchestra he conducts, perfectly attuned to his every mood, breaks into a military air. A marine waving the white flag of surrender. His audience is on the verge of bursting into applause.

Now he does an about-face, back to the locker, making himself accessible to those who are in back as well as the lucky ones to his right and left. His sense of *noblesse oblige* knows no bounds at the O.V.C.A. He runs a hand through his hair which immediately falls back into place. Tom Bradshaw has that kind of hair.

The lights seem to dim and a single spot, amber and diffused by the heat of twenty pairs of smoldering eyes, engulf the star. Then the wail of a saxophone; the steady beat of a drum; the hand unlatching the belt buckle; unhooking the top button; parting the zipper. If a feather were to fall to the floor of the West Side Y.M.C.A. at this moment its impact would be like the explosion of a firecracker in a tunnel.

The pouch of the Jockeys is a proud arc. His hand glides the pants downward over a pair of perfectly matched legs. The thumb of his right hand, barely, touches the arc.

He picks up the pants, turns once again, and hangs them by the back belt loop on a hook within the locker.

A roll of the drums preludes the brass section's outbreak into a pure honky-tonk, low-down and dirty burlesque overture. He digs his thumbs into the elastic band of the shorts and pushes downward. The music swells, the hips sway, just so, in perfectly acceptable male fashion.

First the mat of tamed pubic forest. Then the base of a thick, white birch appears, as if growing out of the moss. His hands are buried inside the shorts as with a slight forward thrust the Jockeys go down, one knee goes up and the birch proves to be a mighty oak supporting a giant acorn and resting contentedly upon a billowing mound of flesh.

The air in the locker room stirs as twenty baited breaths are released in unison. Tom takes his jockstrap from the locker and dangles it from one finger as he turns, contemplating the ceiling. With his back to the locker, this sense of *noblesse oblige* goes just so far, he bends and steps into his jock.

Next he dons his swim trunks and then, almost angrily, slams shut the metal locker door. "Stout-Hearted Men" is reprised and, with shoulders squared, head erect, and eyes veering neither right nor left, he exits to the pool area.

A silent ovation accompanies his departure.

⊠

Thomas Bradshaw loathed the West Side Y.M.C.A. but being in reduced circumstances was forced to use its facilities to keep his weight of one hundred sixty-five pounds perfectly proportioned throughout his six foot, one inch frame. Having read Gide's *Corydon* in his freshman year at Yale he knew that the trick of a successful life was not striving, hopelessly, to cure our ills, but learning to live with them. Being a natural exhibitionist, he simply applied Gide's principle to his twice-weekly visits to the Y and not only learned to cope but also acquired a following among the members of what connoisseurs of the chase consider the best man-made hunting ground since Louis XV's Deer Park.

Tom liked nothing better than to show others all the good things in life they would never possess. He wasn't mean, he was just retaliating. This was how life had always treated him and while passing it on did not cure, it somehow helped him to live with it.

Besides the body, Tom was endowed with a face that would make a Norman Rockwell drawing of the all-American boy look ethnic. His hair was that almost blond shade that commercial rinses and tints promise but never deliver. His eyes were truly brown, his jaw square and his teeth white and even. If one insisted on looking for a flaw it could be found in a nose which tilted, ever so slightly, toward heaven. At twenty-eight Tom was not above using all of his considerable assets to ease his climb up Mount Success. No one at the West Side Y.M.C.A., however, was going Tom's way.

The members of the fashionable Yale Club in New York had already arrived at the destination Tom so desperately wanted to reach, and being himself a graduate of that school he could have taken his exercise there and rubbed shoulders with those he considered his peers. It wasn't the club's modest membership fee that prevented him from doing so. He had learned from painful experience that "arriving" was easy, but running with the pack when in reduced circumstances was a trick not even the venerable André Gide had learned to master. If he didn't keep up socially he would be snubbed — or worse, pitied — and Tom couldn't financially afford the upkeep, nor emotionally endure the put-down.

Tom had, not by accident, allied himself with the richest young men at Yale. Here he broke with Gide and tried desperately to cure, by association, what ailed. Keeping up then had been easy because being broke has always been a common ailment among students.

But what had been acceptable at college was totally unacceptable in the real world, a fact all of Tom's formidable endowments could not overcome. He had gotten to Yale on a scholarship and was now a minor executive with a major bank. Those he called his friends had paid full fare at school and were major executives with firms their families tended to own. Tom worked to sustain life. They worked to fill the gaps between dinner parties, long weekends in Southampton and longer ones in Palm Beach. But Tom preferred to be associated, however dimly, with the Haves rather than sparkle with the Have Nots. Hence the snub of his fellow Y members, made infinitely easier by the shape of his nose.

Tom had also managed to fall in love with the richest of his rich classmates. Eric Lindenhurst Hall was not only the richest man at Yale, he was probably the richest young man in America, if not the world. Tom had told himself that money had nothing to do with what he felt for Eric, but whether the cause of Tom's affection was of the heart or the wallet had made no difference to his suffering. He had never gotten to first base with Eric and knew that five minutes after graduation Eric Lindenhurst Hall forgot that Tom Bradshaw ever existed.

He dove into the pool with the ease and precision of a perfectly aimed arrow ejaculated from a sturdy bow, leaving hardly a ripple as his long, sleek body shot toward the tiled floor, arched, and made his way to the surface of the pale green water. He began to swim with long, well-paced strokes and as he did so all the cares and worries of Tom Bradshaw's life were washed away by the beads of foamy water which caressed, retreated and quickly returned to administer their special solace. The tepid water was a gigantic womb and Tom eagerly surrendered himself to its comforting security.

Tom was born under the sign of Aquarius, the Water-Bearer, and astrologers would say that this was the reason he bore that element like a cloak of armor. Within its depths he felt invulnerable. Swimming was the only exercise he enjoyed and the only exercise he indulged in. He found repugnant the thought of lifting weights or being shoved about by intricate pieces of machinery. The results were too often grotesque caricatures of the human body: bulging muscles that were never meant to bulge, mounted on frames not constructed to bear them.

Swimming was a constant cleansing, while every muscle was exercised at the same time and to the same degree, making the whole a perfectly proportioned oneness. Nothing was forced, therefore the end result was a completely natural look. Perfection and straining were to Tom a contradiction in terms.

When he started his sessions at the Y Tom had counted each lap he took, increasing the number with each succeeding visit. Now he swam until he was exhausted, not coming out of the pool until his arms and legs refused to obey the commands of his still willing mind. Then, hands pressed to the marble ledge, he pulled himself out of the water with his last bit of strength and sat, feet dangling, chest heaving, eyes closed and at peace. The smell of chlorine, the echo of voices and laughter in the vaulted room and the water gently lapping at his ankles had all become familiar and strangely comforting sensations. Now, his heartbeat returning to normal, he opened his eyes and wiped the water from them as he focused in on his surroundings.

The first thing he saw was a young man at the far end of the pool, poised to dive. Tom instantly became alert. At first he thought it was someone he knew but quickly discounted the idea; no one he knew would be caught dead swimming at the West Side Y.M.C.A. But liking what he saw, he continued to stare through chemically irritated eyes at the slim, finely-muscled, dark-haired diver. Though he couldn't see from such a distance Tom knew, almost instinctively, that the young man had blue eyes. This fact caused an eerie chill to crawl up Tom's spine and before he could rationalize the cause of this strange reaction the young man plunged into the pool.

It wasn't a very good dive. The timing was off and chest rather than head entered the water first. Tom watched, still somewhat bewildered, as the young man made his way directly toward where Tom was seated. His swimming was no more impressive than his dive and he moved across the water with more bravado than skill. When he reached Tom's end of the pool he lifted his face from the water and found himself staring directly at Tom Bradshaw. Their eyes locked for one second and then, using his feet, he pushed himself away from the marble wall and like a torpedo began to make his way back up the length of the pool.

9

"I was right, his eyes are blue," was Tom's first thought. Then, his gaze fixed on the retreating mass of white foam, his heart once again began to race under his chest and the chill which had invaded his body moments before returned with an overwhelming intensity; but now he knew with devastating certainty its cause.

He had just seen Eric Lindenhurst Hall... and Eric Lindenhurst Hall had been dead for almost two years.

St. Petersburg, Russia — 1884

She had red hair and blue eyes which were now opened wide as they beheld with awe the splendor and pageantry of the scene being enacted in the ornate chapel. Her strict Protestant upbringing had in no way prepared her for the pomp and ceremony, the overt audible and visual rites of the Orthodox church.

The long-bearded priests in robes of silver and gold chanted endlessly and swung their smoking, incense-filled censers to and fro, flooding the chapel with an exotic aroma and creating a filmy haze between altar and spectators as they sent their prayers upward to the frescoed dome and, hopefully, to even higher echelons. The chapel itself was in sharp contrast to the stained glass windows, wooden benches and bare altar of her own Lutheran church. Here, every place her blue eyes roamed they encountered a statue painted a vivid red and blue, icons encrusted with priceless jewels, heavy gold chalices and crosses ablaze with diamonds.

The congregation was dressed as if in competition with their surroundings. The women's gowns of silk and velvet and brocade cloth spun with threads of gold exposed more powdered flesh than they concealed. The exposed flesh, as well as the gowns, was adorned with diamonds, rubies, emeralds and pearls that absorbed and reflected the pink, pampered skin they decorated.

The men wore brilliantly colored uniforms which fit their tall, muscular bodies like a second skin; their chests were covered with medals of gold and silver and, in many cases, even these military adornments were encrusted with precious stones.

The overall effect was that of a gaudy, multicolored tapestry designed to illustrate the pages of an elaborate edition of a book of children's fairy tales.

He was slim and handsome with dark hair cut close to his head and he wore the simple gray tunic of the Russian soldier. He was used to the sights and sounds which now filled the chapel and his eyes, once they had spotted the girl with red hair and blue eyes, never left her face as she turned now this way, now that way, as if trying to memorize all that was happening around here before it too evaporated before her eyes like the gray smoke on its way to heaven. He waited patiently, knowing that sooner or later their eyes would meet and when finally they did he smiled directly at her and she, taken completely by surprise by this friendly gesture amid such alien surroundings, smiled back.

Then, the ornate chapel, the ceremony being performed within its walls and the bedecked and bejeweled congregation dimmed and all that stood before her blue eyes was the boy's handsome, smiling face. Befitting the fairy-tale tapestry into which they were woven when their eyes met for the first time, they had fallen in love at first glance and had sealed their troth with a smile. And what could be more apropos than that she be a princess and he be a prince?

They were not destined to live happily ever after.

This was the first encounter between the czarevich, Nicholas Romanov, and his future bride, Princess Alix of Hesse. The occasion: the wedding of Alix's sister, Elizabeth, to Nicholas's uncle, the Grand Duke Serge.

2

When anyone called Tom Bradshaw a bastard, in jest or in the heat
of argument, his response was always the same. "You're right, I
am." And he was a bastard, a fact he would never forget thanks to a
gray-haired old lady who passed herself off as a God-fearing
Christian.

Emily Bradshaw was a fundamentalist who didn't have to be
born again. She was born that way the very first time. Her husband
died — from boredom, Tom was certain — at an early age and she
raised her only child, Tom's mother, in true fundamentalist fashion. The only book in her home was the Bible, the only song in her
heart was "Rock of Ages."

Mercy Bradshaw long suspected that she was a constant reminder of her mother's one sinful act, giving in to her husband's
lust, and responded in true Freudian fashion. What her mother
cherished, Mercy despised. What her mother called the sin of the
flesh, the offspring elevated to the status of a fine art. Mercy's bible
was *Forever Amber*, a book she told people she had rescued from
the ashes of a pile put to the torch by her mother's church vigilantes
after a midnight raid on the public library; the only song in her
heart was "Let's Do It." The trouble was, Mercy didn't know how to
do it and neither did the young boys she was occasionally allowed
to see.

But all the boys practiced the sin of Onan and before Mercy
was thirteen she was doing it, on a regular basis, for the boy who
passed around the offering plate at Sunday evening services. As her

expertise grew so did her reputation, which preceded her entry into high school where she was known as Onan's Angel.

An itinerant farm worker finally showed Mercy how to really do it and she followed him right out of Nebraska and was not seen or heard of again until two years later when she arrived at her mother's doorstep carrying Tom, age one month, in her arms. Emily Bradshaw did the Christian thing; she took the baby in and tossed the sinner out.

So Mrs. Bradshaw was once again stuck with a constant reminder, this time of her daughter's sinful ways, and lost no time in passing the burden of guilt on to her grandson. Tom learned the story of Mercy at his grandmother's knee and for years thought it was a Biblical epic. When he was old enough to realize that Mercy was his mother and that he was a bastard, the usually happy boy withdrew from the world in general and from his grandmother in particular. His young mind reasoned that because he was different he had to be smarter than everyone else if he wanted to survive, and Thomas Bradshaw, age ten, not only wanted to survive but was determined to triumph.

Always bright in school he now became something of a phenomenon, excelling in everything from academics to sports to being the best dancer in the tenth grade. He read everything the small town library had to offer and when he wanted something they didn't have, his winning smile could usually charm the librarian into ordering it for him.

But the whole town knew that Tom Bradshaw was a bastard. Most of his friends' fathers had been administered to by Mercy Bradshaw. They were too polite to ever mention the fact, but they knew it and Tom knew they knew it. Seemingly extroverted, he was in reality a loner, befriending everyone, confiding in no one. Puberty arrived before he was thirteen, but long before that he was aware of being far more mature than other boys his age. Masturbation was a joy because it was something physical and pleasurable he could do all by himself. The first time, just before sunrise on a cold winter morning, he shivered in the afterglow and taking hold of his wilting penis he whispered, "I don't know who your father was, but he must have been a big son of a bitch." Tom Bradshaw had one hell of a sense of humor.

It was a foregone conclusion that Tom would be offered a scholarship from a good college but even his biggest boosters never dreamed the offer would come from Yale. Tom knew such a scholarship was in the offering before he entered his senior year at high school and he worked like a demon to get it. He had but one goal: to get out of the town he grew up in, but unlike his mother he had every intention of leaving in glory and for greener pastures. To a small-town boy, no pasture was greener than the campus of Yale University.

When the scholarship was announced Emily Bradshaw shook her grandson's hand and said, "I've done my duty, now it's up to you... and God." She was the only family Tom had and in all fairness she had done well by him. He wanted to tell her this, and he wanted to add that his mother's sins were not his and that he was sorry he was a bastard but one day she would be proud to tell people he was her grandson. Instead, with a lump in his throat he answered, "Thank you," and knew he would never see Emily Bradshaw again.

Tom was a very good-looking young man, but in small American towns good-looking men are something of an embarrassment. Men aren't supposed to be attractive. But even in small American towns someone as handsome as Tom Bradshaw does not go unnoticed. He had gotten appreciative looks from many a housewife, and dozens of high school girls. In fact, a surprising number of boys in the locker room, where the talk was always of sex or the lack thereof, had intimated that they were more than willing to "experiment" with a buddy like Tom. He would have no part of any of them. He knew too well the story of Mercy and had no desire to star in a sequel.

On the train from Omaha to Chicago he couldn't help but notice the friendly smiles he elicited from his fellow coach passengers. It made him slightly uncomfortable but more than a little proud. In the club car a man bought him a beer and Tom went from proud to cocky. When the man started talking about all the empty compartments on the train and how easy it would be to slip into one and really get comfortable, Tom fled and then hated himself for what he considered his small-town timidity. It was a long, frustrating ride to the Windy City.

On the train from Chicago to New York, Tom encountered a fellow on his way back to Columbia for his second year. The sophomore not only had his own private compartment; he also had, or so he said, a car, a charge account at Brooks Brothers, a girlfriend who put out and more money in his wallet than Tom had ever seen in one place at the same time outside of a bank. Tom graduated from beer to martinis and the comforts of a private compartment before leaving the state of Illinois.

And after his second martini Tom Bradshaw fell in love. Not with his benefactor but rather with an illusion — an illusion of sophistication, wit, charm and breeding all neatly packaged within a wad of crisp twenty-dollar bills.

His host, with very little trouble, introduced Tom to sex. It was a very one-sided affair; all Tom had to do was lay back and enjoy. "Look, Ma, no hands," he kept thinking. After a few more martinis, Tom not only reciprocated, he actually initiated the second round. He had been away from home for less than forty-eight hours and was already experiencing his first taste, so to speak, of sex and society. For the next four years Tom would have a great deal of difficulty separating one from the other in his otherwise sharp mind.

The thought didn't occur to him that he should be doing this with a young lady until he was someplace in Pennsylvania, and when it did he passed it off as fundamentalist propaganda, roused his companion, and Yale attacked Columbia from the rear for the second time in one evening.

In school Tom sought out the types he thought the boy from Columbia represented. They were easy to find but certainly not as accessible. Those he encountered did indeed have girlfriends who put out and they preferred it that way. But Tom was a quick learner. He got himself a girlfriend who didn't put out, a fact no one believed, and because he had to work in the school library he told his new friends he was into research, which was a lie no one believed.

He couldn't afford Brooks Brothers' clothes but found a shop that sold reasonable facsimiles at half the price. What he did have was good looks and he played them for all they were worth. Among the young they were worth a great deal. After his first semester he managed to position himself among the Haves, peripherally to be sure, and considered himself on his way. To where? was a question that never entered his attractive head.

Then, in English Composition II, he found himself sitting next to a fellow student with blue eyes, dark, straight hair and a smile that made Tom feel as if he were the only person those eyes beheld. Then the smile spoke. "Hi. I'm Eric Hall."

🞖

Tom sat in his living room wrapped in a terrycloth robe and stared into space. He had been sitting this way for a long time. His apartment in the West Seventies, just off Central Park, was small and comfortable. A huge maple tree grew in front of the limestone building and comprised the view from his second floor walk-up. It became his personal calendar, a reminder of time passing, as it changed from green, to flaming red, to bare, snow-lined and then, always unexpectedly, the first green buds appeared to complete the cycle.

Tonight, glistening in the rain which had started falling as he walked home from the Y, and swaying in a late September wind, the branches took on the appearance of tentacles which threatened to enter his cozy nest and engulf him in a slimy embrace. He could have closed the blinds but refused to surrender to a fear precipitated by thoughts no rational person would entertain for a single moment.

The tree was a tree and the person he had seen swimming in the pool of the Y.M.C.A. was not Eric Hall.

Tom lit a cigarette, something he seldom did, and relived again the moment when he had stared into the eyes of the — what else to call it? — apparition. Once the initial shock had passed and he was again able to think logically, he had told himself that the swimmer was someone who resembled Eric; the rest was a result of a tired mind and, perhaps, wishful thinking. He wanted to pull himself away from the edge of the pool and head for the showers, his locker and home, but something held him to the spot. Rigid and shivering, his eyes followed the bobbing head of the swimmer as if it were a tiny crystal dangling from a hypnotist's chain. He would stay until the young man came out of the pool and thereby dispel once and for all any idea that he was watching Eric Hall swim. The man would be too tall, too short, hirsute, bowlegged, walk with a limp, any-thing... anything to prove he was not Eric.

Tom didn't have long to wait. When the swimmer emerged from the pool, at the far end from which he had entered the water, Tom snapped out of his trance, rose, and quickly walked around the perimeter to meet the young man head on. If Tom thought the en-counter was going to relieve him of his anxiety, he couldn't have been more wrong. Eric had been about five feet, ten inches tall. The young man now walking rapidly toward Tom was just that height. Eric's body had been hairless except for a very fine down that cov-ered a good pair of masculine legs. This young man's body was also hairless, except for the hair which covered his legs — which were not bowed; nor did he walk with a limp. Eric's body had been slim, hard and finely muscled. The body Tom had seen dive into the pool

16

lost none of these qualities on close inspection.

When they were two feet apart Tom stared, hard, and knew he was looking at Eric Lindenhurst Hall. But the young man breezed past Tom without the faintest glimmer of recognition in his strikingly blue eyes.

Now, Tom stood up and walked barefoot to his tiny kitchen. He poured a glass of white wine from an economy-sized four-liter jug. When he had come home he had put a T.V. dinner in the oven before undressing. The next time he thought about it was when he smelled something burning. Dumping the mess into the garbage he had poured himself a glass of wine. He was now working on his fifth — or was it his sixth? — glass.

"Should I have said something to him?" Tom spoke to the jug. "But what? Excuse me, are you an old friend of mine who's dead?" He shook his head. He had heard some inventive opening lines but that was certainly not one of them. The corners of his mouth twitched into a wry smile. His sense of humor wasn't going to get him out of this one.

He carried his fresh drink into the bedroom, and kneeling he pulled open the bottom drawer of his dresser. From it he drew out a large cardboard box and placed it on the floor as he sat, legs crossed, like a boy about to explore a hidden treasure. He opened the box and began, very deliberately, to rummage through it. What he picked up, scanned and discarded for the next item were news clippings. Some large, some small, some with wire photos, but all pertaining to one subject. . . Eric Lindenhurst Hall.

"Eric Lindenhurst Hall, grandson of Ambassador Eric Lindenhurst. . ." or "Eric Lindenhurst Hall, son of the former Erica Lindenhurst. . ." were the lead sentences in most of the news items. What followed were accounts of Eric dining at the White House, graduating from prep school, traveling through Europe with his parents or grandparents, dancing at the newest and smartest disco, skiing in Aspen or Switzerland and even one, with photo, snapped unawares as he basked on the beach in Southampton.

Tom had started the collection a few weeks after meeting Eric. He had been so thrilled to see someone he knew, however casually, worthy of mention in the *New York Times* ("Eric Lindenhurst Hall, now at Yale, accompanies his grandfather Ambassador Lindenhurst to a special screening of. . .") that he had clipped the item and saved it. After that he began clipping every news item Eric appeared in. The thrill never lost its bloom. It became first a hobby... then an obsession. Tom graduated from current to past, going to libraries in New Haven and New York and actually pilfering newspaper items that mentioned Eric Hall.

He read everything he could find, which was surprisingly considerable, on the Lindenhursts (American) and the Halls (English). He probably knew more about Eric's life than Eric himself could remember. Tom mentally adopted the Lindenhurst-Hall clan. They became the family he never had. At eighteen, on the train from Chicago to New York, he had fallen in love with an illusion. At Yale he fell in love with the genuine article.

Eric Hall had it all. Tom had invented the slogan and would often repeat it to himself like a litany. The four B's was another secret catch-all phrase he used to describe Eric. Bucks, Breeding, Brains, Beauty. Eric Hall had it all... and Tom Bradshaw wanted it. He never got it.

Under the clippings were the personal photos, most of them taken at school. Eric in the dorm wearing a pair of jockey shorts, a top hat and waving a Yale pennant. Eric on the basketball court. Eric, flashing a smile, his middle finger raised in the air, toting a pair of ice skates over his shoulder. Eric, among a group which included Tom, taken on the steps of the library building. All were looking at the camera except Tom. He was looking at Eric.

Tom felt himself growing hard and put his hand under his robe to move it to a more comfortable position. It was a natural reaction when going through his private collection of Eric Hall memorabilia. For years he had masturbated while perusing the news clips and photos. And then the dream, which had one chance in a million of ever coming true, lost even those improbable odds. Tom picked up the clipping from the bottom of the box.

"Mr. and Mrs. Anthony Hall and their son, Eric, were reported drowned in a boating accident off Montauk Point, Long Island, late yesterday afternoon. The Coast Guard reported that Mr. Hall was piloting a yacht from Montauk Point to Martha's Vineyard, with only his family aboard, when a squall, not unusual in that seaway, engulfed the craft. Hall radioed an SOS to the Coast Guard station at Montauk Point, but when help arrived, some fifteen minutes later, only pieces of the wreck, identified as Hall's yacht, were found on the now calm sea.

"A search for the bodies of the passengers was conducted late into the night and continued today. However, seamen familar with the area expressed doubt that the bodies would ever be recovered due to the erratic and strong water currents which prevail off the Montauk coast.

"Mrs. Hall was the former Erica Lindenhurst, daughter of the late Ambasador Lindenhurst and Mrs. Lindenhurst, 75, now the sole surviving member of a family whose wealth and service to their country are legendary.

"The President has sent his personal condolences to Mrs. Lindenhurst and has issued a public statement calling the accident a great tragedy and a loss to all Americans."

Tom dug into his robe pocket for another cigarette.

Who had he seen swimming in the pool of the West Side Y.M.C.A.?

St. Petersburg, Russia — 1889

The next time Nicholas and Alix met he was twenty-one and she was seventeen. The czarevich had fulfilled his promise of becoming a handsome young man. Nicholas would never be very tall but seated on his white horse and dressed in the perfectly tailored uniform of an Imperial Russian officer he looked every inch the dashing prince of a nineteenth-century operetta. Nicholas adored uniforms and soldiering and never tired of parading and reviewing his garrison on the vast grounds of Tsarskoe Selo.

At night, in full dress, he attended the opera or ballet and frequented the fashionable restaurants of St. Petersburg. During the season he was invited to every ball and missed few. Nicholas Romanov enjoyed all the privileges and comforts afforded a czarevich of Russia but he was never allowed to forget one inescapable fact that was an integral part of the rank he so enjoyed. One day he would assume the autocratic rule of the largest and most backward nation in the world.

But Nicholas's father was young and healthy and the day that the burden of ruling one-fourth of the world's population would fall on his somewhat fragile shoulders was a long way off.

Princess Alix had grown into a beautiful young woman. Her red hair was now the color of polished copper, her blue eyes bright and alert and her skin flawless. She was in St. Petersburg to visit her sister and brother-in-law and during her visit to Russia the czarevich found innumerable reasons to call upon his aunt and uncle. Nicholas escorted Alix constantly during her visit to Russia and although Alix was perceptive and intelligent she was somewhat shy and the czarevich's young friends mistook her timidity for aloofness. More of a problem was her strict upbringing which caused her to view the boisterous, and often rowdy, young Russian nobility with awe and even fear. This they mistook for disapproval and it gave them even more cause to dislike the "German girl."

With Nicholas, Alix was at ease and the czarevich knew her for the charming, intelligent young woman she was. The man fell in love with the princess as quickly and as deeply as had the boy five years ago.

"You are different when you are alone with me than when we are together in a group," Nicholas told Alix.

Alix flushed. "Are you saying I'm a prude?"

Nicholas shook his head. "No. Only that you are very English."

"But I am German."

"No, my dear. You and your sisters and brothers and uncles and aunts and cousins are all English. Your grandmother, Queen Victoria, has seen to that."

"Perhaps. But is that so bad?" Alix teased.

"Only when it makes you do foolish things."

"Like refusing to kick my legs in the air when I dance?"

"No, my dear Alix, like refusing to acknowledge that you are in love with me and that you will one day be my wife."

Alix's face turned the color of her hair. "You must not say that. You know it is impossible."

"I am the czarevich. I can have whatever I desire."

Alix's German blood and English rearing forced her to answer boldly and realistically. "You can have whatever you desire, Nicholas, so long as the czar desires it, too."

Czar Alexander III was six feet, four inches tall, a bear of a man whose natural speaking voice was a roar and whose roar could be heard throughout Tsarskoe Selo and, some said, clear to the Chinese border. Nicholas loved and respected his father but also feared him. It was Nicky's mother, the Empress Marie Fedorovna, who had raised and pampered and disciplined the children and, when necessary, had protected them from the wrath of their father. The small, seductive and often flamboyant Marie Fedorovna was the only person Alexander loved and obeyed. The bear of Russia was a cub in his own bedroom.

It was only natural for Nicholas to seek his mother's advice regarding his intention to marry Princess Alix of Hesse.

"Your father will not like it," Marie Fedorovna told her son. "A German princess."

"She is not German, Mama. She is from Hesse."

"Nicholas, don't talk like a fool. You know it is only a matter of time before Germany gobbles up Hesse and all the other small Germanic principalities. The girl's uncle is the Emperor of Germany and the Germans are a constant threat to our European border. It is not a good match."

"Her other uncle is the Prince of Wales and your brother-in-law," Nicholas reminded his mother.

Marie laughed. "I am aware of that fact, Nicholas. You see, we are too inbred. With the Pretender's daughter we have no family ties and France is our ally. The French have been very good to Russia, my son."

"The Comte de Paris," Nicholas hissed. "You know, Mama, that the Bourbons will never again sit on the throne of France. Pretender to what? And his daughter Hélène is a bore. I am allergic to French perfume, have you not heard?"

"Stop it, Nicholas. I will not have you talking like a fop. An alliance with France would be very advantageous."

"Not for my heart, Mama."

Marie Fedorovna touched her son's handsome face. "When you are chosen by God to rule as we were chosen, it is not always possible to follow your heart. I love you, my son, and want you to be happy. But the throne, Nicholas, nothing must come before the throne — not even your heart."

Nicholas took his mother's hand in his and looked into her eyes. "Did you follow your heart, Mama?"

The Empress nodded and tears filled her eyes. "You know I did, my son. I was lucky."

"Then you know how I feel, Mama. Speak to him for me, please," the young man pleaded.

"I will, Nicky, but I promise you nothing."

Nicky was overjoyed. "He will not refuse you," he answered.

Marie Fedorovna shook her head. "It is not my petition, it is yours. And remember the throne, Nicky. First comes the throne and then his empress. Don't ever forget that."

3

Saturday morning was indistinguishable from Friday night within and without the second floor walk-up. The rain was still falling, the tree still glistening and swaying, and Tom awoke with a dull ache in his heart, a longing for something he could not identify.

This sadness, this depression of mind and spirit, was not new; Tom had awakened to it for as long as he could remember. "I am empty," he had often thought to himself when he was a boy and had learned, as children will, to pretend he didn't care. People couldn't see what he felt, therefore he was safe from its effects. He began to fill the emptiness with personal achievements and for brief periods these little glories were able to banish the depression. But sooner or later the moment passed, the emptiness returned, and as hard as he listened he never heard the splash that could determine the depth of the well within him. "I am a bottomless pit."

Masturbation eased the pain, and since that cold winter morning when he had first achieved orgasm by stroking the erection which had found its own way out of the fly of his wool pajamas, he used it to allay the frustration, not for sex, but for he knew not what. Every morning to banish the ache and every evening to fill the void of his empty house, its silent rooms and the old lady who spoke only to or of God. His body tingling with excitement, he soon began to anticipate the pleasure. He dwelled upon the act long before he was able to safely lock himself in his room and indulge his passion. Then, stripping bare, he would caress himself in a variety of positions; standing, sitting, lying, substituting left hand for right, and even inserting himself between bedspring and mattress to attain his goal. Outwardly, like his gregariousness, it was pure abandonment, but the images which accompanied the lewd act were only mildly erotic.

The boy lay wounded and was comforted by a strong pair of hands which stroked his chest and belly, moving slowly downward with each caress. The boy shivered with cold and was drawn into a warm embrace and held tightly against a body which accepted with a reassuring sigh the hardness which throbbed between them.

The need was the motor, his hand the accelerator, his mind the brake. He drove with consummate skill, accelerating to the brink, applying the brake, refusing to allow the joy of endless anticipation to give way to the momentary pleasure of release.

"To fill myself, I have to empty myself." It was a paradox he never tired of putting to the test.

As he matured so did the images which aroused him, but always there was Tom, taking, the faceless benefactor, giving. Always there was the need, and always more had to be given to achieve satisfaction.

He kicked the bed covers off his naked body and lay staring at his bedroom ceiling and listening to the rain. He was alone in his bed, alone in his room, alone in the world. He was fully aroused and reached down languidly — habit, not passion, was in the driver's seat — to touch himself and at that moment the wet face of Eric Hall, looking at him from above the green water, filled the screen in his mind. Then, the previous evening came back to him in detail and he abandoned what he had hardly begun.

He sat up, planted his feet firmly on the ground and shook his head. "It's all some crazy illusion and I'm not going to think about it any more. " Resolved, he went into the bathroom, relieved himself, turned on the shower and stepped under it. Soap and water erased all traces of a restless night and too much wine on an empty stomach. He shaved and examined his face in a round magnifying mirror. He liked what he saw and smiled at his overblown reflection. "Consternation must be good for the complexion."

In the kitchen he plugged in the coffee maker and was rewarded with an aroma that reminded him he had not eaten the night before. He was suddenly ravenous. Juice, eggs and toast calmed his stomach, but once the bodily needs were satisfied the apparition again began to taunt him. He moved quickly from kitchen to bedroom, slipped into a pair of jeans, donned a flannel shirt which he didn't bother to tuck into his pants, and stepped into a pair of loafers. Without pausing he pulled a hamper from the rear of his closet and emptied it onto his unmade bed. He separated shirts from everything else and stuffed both piles into two pillow slips. The pillow slip with the shirts had the honor of being washed and pressed by the Chinese laundry on Columbus Avenue. The other bundle was destined for the laundromat where, for one dollar extra, a very fat lady separated white from colored and washed and dried both loads for the standard fee.

He also had to go to the drugstore, the supermarket, the liquor store and suddenly decided to shop for wallpaper for the bathroom, a chore he had procrastinated for weeks. The apparition could stay in the apartment or come along, but the essentials of life would be attended to. Five minutes later he found himself on the street in the pouring rain without raincoat, rubbers or umbrella. He had the uneasy feeling that if he looked up at his front windows he would see Eric Hall looking down at him... laughing. He began to run, a bulging pillow slip under each arm, toward Columbus Avenue.

⊠

Tom never lacked for a Saturday night invitation, or as many during the week as he cared to accept, and that evening he went to the Carrs' dinner party. After graduation his crowd tended to socialize in groups, paying scant attention to who was escorting whom, and the men, more often than not, outnumbered the women two to one. Popular restaurants, the theater, and house parties in the Hamptons were always collective situations. Bills, when presented, were equally divided. It was simply an extension of their undergraduate days.

Then suddenly he found himself attending weddings more than any other social function. Jim Carr became the Carrs. Ken Brandt became the Brandts, and Dicky and Amy, who were always just Dicky and Amy, became the Culvers. Tom was amazed at how quickly his classmates had assumed what he called the corporate image. The young executive, upwardly mobile, complete with attaché case and pretty wife. Their social milieu now consisted of formal dinner parties — couples only — and reciprocation was expected. This tended to bring the same people together constantly, making each occasion duller than its predecessor. Tom was good looking, charming, well educated, and a good mixer, in short, the perfect odd man — an expression which always made him wince — for these functions.

24

The girls he was paired off with were sometimes pretty, some-times intelligent, but almost always rich. But rich girls, contrary to romantic novels, seldom marry poor boys. With someone like Tom they were more than willing to engage in a one-night stand, or even an affair, but Tom, always perverse, tantalized to the limit but never gave them more than a goodnight kiss. If he couldn't have it all he wasn't interested in any of its parts. He classified them in the same group as his O.V.C.A.'ers and wished like hell he could dan-gle it in front of them, too.

The men he met at those affairs fell into two distinct groups: straight and closet cases. He preferred the former. The latter he knew very well, and when they didn't amuse him they annoyed him. All their affairs are quickies and once attained, their momen-tary partner is shunned for life. Tom, having never given in, was a constant target for these strange young men. And for them, with great joy, he dangled it. . . in public restrooms or, better still, at crowded parties. He would watch one of them head for the john and then, just before the door closed, slip in and. . . "Mind if we share it? I can't wait."

Flushed with embarrassment, unable to urinate *à deux*, eyes bulging, they were forced to watch Tom sigh with relief, shake it more than was necessary, receive a pat on the shoulder and a "Thanks, buddy," when it was all too soon over. For the rest of the evening they would follow Tom around like a lap dog and Tom treated them exactly as they would have treated him once they had had him. He completely ignored them.

It didn't cure, but it helped him live with the resentment the type inspired.

Tom was happy to note that Dicky and Amy Culver were not on the Carrs' guest list that evening. Dicky Culver had been Eric Hall's closest friend and in his present mood Tom feared he would be unable to stop himself from telling Dicky about the apparition. The two shared a mutual dislike of one another and Tom could imagine Dicky looking askance at the mention of the West Side Y.M.C.A. and losing no time in telling their mutual friends that Tom Bradshaw was crazy. And the first person to hear this news would be Amy Culver, an even bigger snob than her husband, who would immediately state, "Nonsense. . . Eric's ghost would appear only to us, naturally."

Amy's imagined, but accurate, statement was the true reason Tom wanted to keep the apparition to himself. Eric Hall had been the richest, the most respected and sought after member of Tom's class. Dicky Culver had been Eric's best friend. The others, if not in the same category as Eric and Dicky, were certainly in their social league. It was Tom Bradshaw who was the odd man out. But now Tom knew something pertaining to Eric that no one else knew. Either Eric had never died, or Eric's clone was alive and well and living in New York City. Whatever the case it was Tom's secret and for the first time he felt slightly superior to all his supposed friends. He intended to savor the feeling and keep his secret for as long as he could, or at least until he knew just what he was privy to.

The odd man's dinner guest this particular evening was an odd young lady who had gone directly from Vassar to social work. She had a special interest in third world nations and wondered, vocally, why there were no blacks present at the Carrs' gala.

"But there are," Tom assured her, "at least two in the kitchen."

The lady, as intended, was not amused and completely ignored Tom throughout the remainder of the meal which enabled him to contemplate his apparition while acknowledging with a nod or a one-word response the chatter that passed for polite conversation. Someplace between the salad and dessert he decided exactly what he was going to do to resolve the problem. He was going to pursue the apparition.

He would haunt the West Side Y.M.C.A. until the apparition appeared again, and when it did he would talk to it. He would learn all he could about this Eric Hall look-alike and when he did. . . . Well, one step at a time and the first step was to be there when and if it reappeared. If it didn't Tom would pass the incident off as a figment of his imagination, a dream while awake brought about by exhaustion, and forget it ever happened.

Having set a course of action he immediately felt better and for the first time that evening turned his full attention to the company the Carrs had gathered together. He had lost his dinner partner to the man on her left so he flashed his most dazzling smile at a closet case he had been toying with for months. The man, somewhat cautiously, responded in kind and Tom's spirits rose considerably.

▨

Tom began his vigil the next day, Sunday, at four in the afternoon. He reasoned that this would be the perfect time to catch the early crowd before they left and the evening group as they arrived. By seven he was waterlogged, tired and disappointed. The apparition did not show itself. But what did show up were a surprising number of faces he had assumed were strictly his Tuesday and Friday night regulars.

Many of them appeared again on Monday night. The apparition did not, and Tom wondered if they came to the Y every night while they, in turn, wondered if Tom had joined their ranks and dared to nod and smile as they passed him in the locker room. In retaliation, Tom undressed as surreptitiously as possible leaving his audience perplexed and not a little angry.

Tuesday, his regular night, he hardly swam a stroke but spent most of the time sitting at the edge of the pool staring at the entranceway and trying not to look like he was doing what everyone thought he was doing.

All day Wednesday he argued with himself about whether or not he should go to the Y after work. He was tired, he felt foolish, and he was by now convinced that the person he had seen in the pool last week existed only in his mind. By five o'clock his rational self won and he decided to go straight home from the office. But as he walked up Central Park West from Fifty-Ninth Street he was drawn, like a magnet, to the portals of the West Side Y.M.C.A. He stood, looking at the entrance like a real estate agent mentally composing an ad that would attract a buyer for the building; finally he turned and walked away, but before reaching the corner decided that he would never forgive himself if he didn't complete at least one full week of his vigil and retraced his steps.

He entered, not like a general or a prince, but like a man resigned to his fate. To add insult to injury his regulars hardly looked at him and he felt like an actor suddenly labeled box office poison. He had committed the unforgivable crime of the gay cruising circuit: overexposure.

The apparition was waiting for him in the same spot it had first appeared. After the shock of recognition subsided Tom took a deep breath and walked boldly to the far end of the pool and stood beside his nemesis. He tried not to stare but couldn't help himself. He was looking at Eric Hall; it could not be anyone else. And as he looked he could sense the O.V.C.A.'ers eyeing him and nodding knowingly. "So that's who he's after," silently thundered throughout the hall. *Fuck them all*, Tom thought. He had waited too long for this moment to be intimidated by what others were thinking. Like the Brooks Brothers' clothes of his college days, he had found a reasonable facsimile and nothing was going to stop him from sampling the bargain.

"Put your head down." The sound of his own voice surprised him. These were probably the first words he had uttered to another person inside the Y.M.C.A. in all the months he had been coming here.

The apparition, about to dive into the water, jerked upright and looked at the speaker. Tom was reminded of a frightened fawn.

"Put your head down," Tom repeated. "Rest your chin on your chest and just fall over so that you cut the water with the top of your head and not pound into it with your belly."

The young man nodded and smiled and Tom was transported back to Yale and his first day in English Composition II. His spine tingled and his mind expanded to a high no known drug could ever induce. He wanted to stretch out his arms, grab Eric and shout, "You beautiful son-of-a-bitch, it's me, Tom Bradshaw...."

A voice deep inside of Tom's head, disguised as Eric Hall's, responded... "Who the hell is Tom Bradshaw?"

Wounded, but not fatally, by his own retort Tom stood with arms folded across his chest as the young man pressed his chin against his chest, bent from the waist, and literally fell into the pool. He clearly overcompensated and this time the back of his neck, quickly followed by his behind, made the initial splash. When he surfaced he looked up at Tom and laughed. "You can't say I didn't try." Then he turned and swam away before Tom could reply.

The voice... that was the final crucial test. Was it Eric's voice? "You can't say I didn't try." Repeating the words Tom recalled the voice that had spoken them. A British accent? Eric's father had been English and Eric had spent innumerable vacations in England since childhood. But Tom was grasping at straws and he knew it. Eric's clone did not have Eric's voice but the mouth speaking the words diminished the fact.

Tom dove into the water with his usual expertise and quickly caught up with the other swimmer. Slowing, he paced himself to keep up with the other and together, a few feet apart, they made their way up and down the length of the pool. Occasionally the young man glanced Tom's way and smiled shyly. Tom grinned back and at one point shouted, "Kick your feet. Don't drag them." Playing instructor had given him his opening, and he decided to stick with the same guise. At once the young man began to kick his feet wildly as he swam. *You can't say he doesn't try*, Tom thought, liking the man for his courage if not his style.

Five minutes later the young man was hoisting himself out of the pool and Tom, still at his side, did the same. "I was just warming up," Tom offered.

"I'm not a pro," the other answered.

"Neither am I... it's just a matter of practice." And then the hack line he hated to speak but had to. "Do you come here often?"

"As often as I can. Well... thanks for the lesson." And he began to walk away.

"I'm usually here on Tuesday and Friday after work, and the lessons are free." Christ, he was making a pitch and felt himself blush at the thought.

Again he got the shy smile and the frightened fawn look. "I'll try to make it." And again he turned to leave.

"My name is Tom," he quickly blurted to the retreating figure.

The fawn stopped and turned his head. Tom held his breath and could feel his heart pounding in his chest. "I'm Nicky." Then he was gone.

Nicky! Holy shit. "Well, what did you expect him to say? I'm a ghost."

◫

He had talked with the apparition and was still not convinced that it was not Eric Hall. In fact his brief encounter with Nicky had not solved but rather had compounded the problem. And something else was now bothering Tom. Now, when he thought about Nicky he felt slightly euphoric without associating Nicky with Eric Hall. "No." Tom shook his head. "No way. Complications I don't need."

He knew what he had to do next but didn't know exactly how to go about it. He had to talk to Dicky Culver. Not to tell him about Nicky, but to find out anything he could about Eric's death without arousing Amy Culver's naturally suspicious nature. That wasn't going to be easy, nor was setting up a date with Dicky who had always resented anyone who dared intrude upon his relationship with Eric Hall and Tom was the only person, however feebly, to dare do so. When they met now it was when both were invited to the home of a mutual friend. But Tom did have one slight in and he was ready to use it. Amy was an avid bridge player and Tom, as Amy openly admitted the first time she played against him, was the only player she knew who could challenge her skill.

He called, suggested a game and, as he hoped, was rewarded by an enthusiastic Amy who set a date for the following Saturday evening. Tom could imagine Dicky frowning when he got the news

and the image brightened his day. He went to the Y on Friday but
Nicky wasn't there. He was disappointed, went through his swim-
ing routine with little enthusiasm and never even noticed if the regulars eyed him or not.

⊠

"Tom must find the view more interesting than our company."

Tom quickly turned from the window and faced the three people now staring at him. "I'm sorry, I was . . . I was thinking about
Eric."

The living have a great respect for the dead and Tom's response
to Dicky served a dual purpose. It made Dicky feel a little foolish
and it opened a conversation Tom had been trying to broach all evening. They were sitting in the Culvers' den which overlooked Central Park, having a nightcap, and what Tom had been doing while
not paying attention to the company in the room was trying to pin-
point his limestone across the vast expanse of the park. Now, he
turned his full attention to his host.

"He's dead, isn't he?" Nancy Maron said.

She was the social worker from Vassar whom Tom had all but
snubbed at the Carrs' last week, and he couldn't believe his bad
luck when she turned up as Amy's fourth for bridge. He had silently
wondered why Amy had dug her up but five minutes into the game
and he knew. Nancy Maron was as good a player as Tom, perhaps
better, and Amy, in her inimitable style, had ferreted out the best
for her beloved game. Together, Tom and Nancy had taken the Culvers for seventy-five dollars at a tenth of a cent a point. Amy was in
a foul mood.

"Rich, wasn't he?" Nancy added to fill the silence which followed her pronouncement.

"I miss Eric," Dicky said, staring into the glass in his hand. He
had changed little since his school days and one could imagine
Dicky Culver being laid to rest looking very much as he had looked
the day he turned sixteen. Small, wiry, his horn-rimmed glasses as
much a part of him as the thinning hair which had been threatening
to leave his head since his prep school days. His intense and
slightly effeminate manner had misled more than one opponent on
the squash court where he was a formidable player. "He aims for
the balls and never misses," someone had said of Dicky Culver at
college, to which Tom had unkindly added, "The faggot is one
tough cookie."

"Why were you thinking about Eric?" Amy asked in her usual
matter-of-fact fashion. She could respect the dead for just so long

before her curiosity about the motives of the living took precedence.

"Being with you and Dicky, I guess," Tom shrugged as he spoke, giving the impression that the matter was of little importance. "And that picture of Eric," he added, pointing to a torso shot of Eric Hall which stood framed and sitting on the Culvers' grand piano.

"It didn't seem to distract you during our game," Amy responded with a smile that was at odds with her tone.

Amy Culver looked more like Dicky's sister than like his wife. Indeed, their parents, rich and social New Yorkers, were great friends who had raised their respective son and daughter like siblings; the subsequent marriage was more a foregone conclusion than a romantic event. She was as openly demonstrable as Dicky was seemingly retiring. Amy had worn glasses since childhood, hated them, and donned contact lenses as soon as she was old enough to make the choice. When glasses came into fashion she bought a pair of the biggest, boldest horn-rims she could find and, like one who has triumphed by persistence, was never seen without them. At Barnard she had been a good student not because she was naturally bright but because, like everything else Amy did, she applied herself to the task at hand. She approached life like a hunter, relentlessly pursuing her prey until it was cornered, killed and devoured.

And Amy hated Tom Bradshaw. "He's not one of Us," she announced soon after meeting Tom but not before she had heard about him from Dicky. Amy's statment translated to the fact that Dicky was jealous of Tom's brief friendship with Eric Hall, and Dicky had never been jealous of anyone's friendship with Amy. If Eric's death was not a tragic event in Amy Culver's life she never let anyone know it. . . especially her husband.

"He was drowned, wasn't he?" Nancy, feeling ignored, got back into the conversation.

Dicky nodded. "In a boating accident along with his parents. You know, it's been almost two years and I still can't believe it. Sometimes I find myself looking for him at parties or thinking he'll walk into a room, singing, the way he used to."

And I could make it happen, Tom thought, feeling like a genius surrounded by a group of incompetents. "Do you visit the family?"

"Family?" Amy raised an eyebrow. "There is no family except for old Mrs. Lindenhurst."

"I've been there a few times," Dicky said, used to his wife answering for him but always managing to get in the last word. "But it's pathetic. She sees no one, goes no place and lives in the past. Sometimes she refers to her daughter and Eric in the present tense."

"And what a vibrant woman she was," Amy lamented. "Closest thing we've ever had to royalty." She sat upright in her chair as she spoke, as if contending for Mrs. Lindenhurst's vacated position.

"And all that money," Nancy sighed. For someone interested in third world nations she was certainly keen on first world capitalists.

"Was that picture taken at school?" Tom asked, pointing to the piano. If the photograph looking back at him wasn't of Nicky he would eat the frame.

"No," Dicky answered before Amy had a chance to. "It was taken just before the accident. I had it blown up from a small one Eric gave me." He walked to the bookcase which lined one wall of the room and pulled out a photograph album. "Some of you in here," he said handing it to Tom, "and all the old crowd from school."

Tom opened the album and began to flip through the pages.

"Dicky was a very close friend of Eric's," Amy was explaining to Nancy Maron. "In fact both my family and Dicky's were very friendly with the Lindenhursts."

While Amy was impressing Nancy and Dicky went to mix a fresh drink Tom spotted the small replica of the photo on the piano and gently inched it out of its plastic cover and then quickly slipped it into his pocket.

"Another drink, Tom?" Dicky asked.

"No . . . no thank you. I think I'll be on my way." He carefully replaced the album from where Dicky had removed it. He turned to Amy. "When are you going to try to get your seventy-five bucks back?"

"You'll hear from me," Amy shot back and Tom was sure he would.

"Can I give you a lift, Nancy? I owe you a taxi ride from last week." It was the first reference all evening to their previous meeting.

Nancy giggled. "You'll have to keep owing. I live next door."

Naturally; where else would a social worker live but in a posh Fifth Avenue apartment building? Tom's spirits descended with the elevator and as he stepped onto Fifth Avenue he felt the first chill of autumn in the night air. "I learned nothing," he thought as he started walking down the avenue. Then he stopped abruptly and said, almost aloud, "Wrong... I learned there's nothing about Eric's death I don't know... and that old Mrs Lindenhurst is senile." That last thought stayed with him all through the long walk around the southern perimeter of Central Park.

Saint Petersburg, Russia — 1889–1894

Marie Fedorovna spoke to her husband and, as she had feared, the czar would not even consider his son's request.

"And," the empress told Prince Nicholas, "I have even more disquieting news for you, my boy."

The czarevich looked sadly at his mother. What could be more disquieting than what she had already told him?

"The English ambassador," she continued, not looking at her son, "told Papa that the Prince of Wales's oldest son, Albert, has asked for the hand of the Princess Alix."

"But he is her first cousin," Nicholas shouted.

"It is not unheard of," his mother answered.

The mild-mannered czarevich, when his passions were aroused, could and often did act on his own behalf. Now he went directly to his father. "If she refuses Albert," Nicholas asked the czar, "may I ask for her hand? If she refuses me I will not speak of the matter again and will consent to whomever you choose for me."

It took the czar a brief moment to consider his son's offer. What girl in her right mind would refuse an offer to marry a future king of England and sit on the throne of the mightiest empire in the world? "I accept your proposition," the czar told his son.

Alix's reply to Albert was brief and to the point. "I do not love you and therefore cannot marry you.'"

The czar immediately sent Prince Nicholas on a world tour which did not include a visit to the duchy of Hesse-Darmstadt.

In 1894, ten years after Nicholas had first smiled upon his princess in the chapel of the Winter Palace, Alix's brother, the grand duke of Hesse-Darmstadt, was married in Coburg and Nicholas Romanov represented Russia at the royal wedding. But Nicholas did not journey to Coburg solely as a wedding guest. He went as a lover, determined to return to Russia with a bride.

The only drawback to Alix's joy was the fact that as Nicholas Romanov's wife and future Empress of Russia she would have to convert to the Orthodox church and leave the more simple and secure Lutheran faith. Since her first visit to Russia she had been fascinated and awed by Orthodoxy but, at the same time, afraid of the mysterious and almost pagan rituals of the Eastern church. But her love for Nicholas was such that she felt conversion to Orthodoxy was a small price to pay for the joy of marrying her prince.

Prince Nicholas and Sonny (the family pet name for Princess Alix) spent some time in England, first at the home of Sonny's sister, Victoria of Battenberg, and then with the queen at Windsor Palace. The newly engaged couple were much in the company of their cousin Charles, heir to the throne since his brother Albert's death, and his wife May. Besides being very close friends Nicholas and Charles bore a remarkable resemblance to each other and thanks to Nicholas's perfect command of the English language the czarevich, on more than one occasion, was mistaken for the heir to the throne of England. During this visit Nicholas and Sonny participated in their first family ceremony together. They were godparents to Prince Edward, the first child born to Charles and May.

The idyll in England ended abruptly and on a depressing note when Nicholas received word that his father, the czar, had been taken ill and had moved to the warm Crimea to recuperate. By the time Sonny arrived to join Nicholas, the czar was on his deathbed.

"I am afraid," Nicholas confided to his future wife.

"Your father is dying and you are his heir. You must take charge of all that is going on here. You must tell your father's doctors and ministers and aides to report directly to you, not to your mother. You must make them all understand that until your father is well or... you must make them understand that all decisions, from now on, will be made by you and you alone."

And so for the first time, but certainly not the last, the German princess tried to wean Nicholas Romanov from the protective arms of his mother.

In November of 1894 Alexander III died and Nicholas Romanov became Czar Nicholas II of Russia. The dead czar's body was borne back to St. Petersburg and the new czar's incipient wife entered the city for the first time as its future empress behind a funeral cortege. It was indeed a harbinger of things to come.

A week after Alexander III was laid to rest Nicholas and Alix were married in the simplest ceremony possible for one of his rank and Princess Alix of Hesse became the Empress Alexandra Fedorovna of Russia. The newlyweds moved in with his mother and like all such arrangements, in and out of fairy tales, friction soon arose between mother and daughter-in-law. Nicholas was a mama's boy and Mama was a recently bereaved widow so what could be more natural for such a young man than to spend more time with his mother than with his bride? But it was not the time Nicholas spent with his mother that irked Sonny; it was the fact that the dowager empress, through her son, was ruling Russia.

And so a tug of war, which could last for years, began between the empress and the dowager empress of Russia with the czar as pawn. The younger of the two would eventually win but by then it would be too late for Nicholas's wife to save either her husband or his throne.

But nothing could overshadow the joy the young couple felt at finally being man and wife. In their private apartment in the palace Nicholas discarded all the cares and pomp and ceremony that were part of the life of a czar and he and Sonny, dismissing all the servants, played at being simply a man and woman very much in love.

"I am Mr. Nobody and I have just returned from work."

"So, I must prepare your dinner."

"Then why don't you?"

"Because my husband, Mrs. Nobody does not know how."

Then they would fall into each other's arms, laughing with joy at their own foolishness and make love in whatever room of the apartment they happened to be.

"You must not touch me there," Sonny would tease, "I am an empress."

"Then tonight Mr. Nobody will ravish an empress and teach her delights unknown in even the greatest of palaces."

Nicholas was fully experienced in the ways of sex and his wife, naturally, was not but the young czar was amazed at her eagerness to learn and please and at the almost wanton passion he could so easily arouse in her. "You English never cease to amaze," he whispered in her ear at the most intimate of moments.

"But I am German," she never tired of correcting him.

"And now I will fill you with the seed of Russia."

4

Tom heaved himself out of the pool and sat next to Nicky. "You're fantastic," Nicky exclaimed. "Almost twenty-five minutes, nonstop."

"I told you it was just a matter of practice," Tom panted. "Besides, I was showing off."

"For me?"

"Why not?"

Nicky's eyes were on another swimmer as he answered. "I didn't think you would show up tonight."

"Why?"

He still refused to look directly at Tom. "Because I didn't, that's why."

"You don't look like the type who's used to being stood up."

Nicky grinned. "I've never been stood up because I've never had a date."

"Bullshit."

"It's the truth." Now he looked at Tom like a hurt child. "You're the first person to ever ask me to meet them at a certain time and in a certain place."

Tom waited for an explanation but none was forthcoming. "Your diving is improving," he finally said.

"Now who's bullshitting?"

Tom laughed because the vulgarism did not fit the image of the man who spoke it. It was obvious that Nicky had never used the word publicly before, and he was sure Nicky did so now only in imitation of Tom. This was their second meeting and Tom was beginning to feel a little uncomfortable. The flesh and blood was stranger than the apparition.

"Are you just learning to swim?"

Nicky shook his head. "No... I learned when I was a child, in England, but I didn't keep at it so it's like starting all over."

England... well, that was something. "Are you English?"

"Born and raised."

"I thought you had a slight accent but you don't sound like a native."

"The people who raised me aren't English."

Again Tom waited and again in vain. Was Nicky an orphan? Tom didn't want to constantly ask questions, to probe like some sort of inquisitor, but Nicky left him very little choice. Not that it mattered, because all Nicky's responses were short and to the point. Nothing was offered that was not specifically asked for, and too often even his one-sentence answers only paved the way for another question. Tom shrugged inwardly and tried again. "Are you going to stay in America?"

"I hope so. I feel much freer here."

Freer... what had he been in England, a prisoner? And why did he hope so? He was an adult and could do what he wanted. Don't push, Tom thought. He's a fawn and when fawns feel threatened they flee. If Nicky never showed up at the Y again Tom would lose him forever. "By the way, my full name is Tom Bradshaw."

Nicky smiled and blushed at the same time. "Mine is Nicky Three." And suddenly he stuck out his hand and Tom took it into his, happy to find Nicky's grip strong and enthusiastic. Like a little boy, Tom thought, trying to act like a man.

"Three? That's the strangest name I ever heard. Don't tell me it's English."

"No, Russian."

"Russian? You're playing with me."

Nicky was now very serious. "I wouldn't do that, Tom. It's a Russian name which was shortened and Anglicized. I'm really Russian."

And I'm a monkey's uncle. English... Russian... orphaned, and on his first date. He is psychotic. No, Eric's double couldn't be crazy. He had to be perfection. Tom felt slightly sick and, an all-time first, at a loss for words. They sat side by side, feet dangling in the water, everyone around them in motion, and looked everyplace but at each other.

"If you don't talk we'll sit like this till it's time to leave."

"I beg your pardon."

"I mean," Nicky said, "I'm not very good at making conversation. You know, small talk."

Tom shrugged. "Small people make small talk. We're giants."

Nicky beamed. "Thanks. What I'm trying to say is I've never had many friends. I'm sort of a loner."

"I have a lot of friends," Tom mused, "and there is no one lonelier than Tom Bradshaw. The word 'friend' has many meanings, not all of them complimentary."

Nicky stared at Tom in the manner of an uninhibited child. "With your looks you can pick and choose."

Finally, Tom thought, we are on solid ground. A pass perhaps, but with him, who knows? "You're not the Elephant Man, and don't tell me the regulars around this place haven't noticed you." Tom played his ace and waited to see what Nicky would lay beside it.

He grinned and looked at his feet, wiggling his toes under the green water. "If they have, I haven't noticed."

Tom felt as if he were back in high school and the feeling was not unpleasant. "You noticed me."

Nicky looked at Tom with his clear blue eyes in that special way of his that made Tom feel naked. It was disconcerting but not unpleasant. Then Nicky trumped Tom's ace. "No, Tom, you noticed me."

He might be crazy, but he's not stupid, Tom thought. And well educated, which was something else Tom was eager to learn more about. "How can you help but notice someone who belly-wops into a goddamn swimming pool. Besides, you remind me of someone I used to know."

"Who?"

"A friend."

"Why don't you still know him?" Here again Nicky's sharp mind became evident. His childish demeanor certainly didn't reflect what was going on behind those blue eyes.

"Not important," Tom shot back and then quickly added, "How about a beer and burger? I'm starved."

Nicky looked at the clock. "I have to go."

"Where?"

"Home."

"Are you married?"

Nicky looked startled. "No. What made you think that?"

"You said you had to go home. Only married men have to go home. Come on, it's my treat."

Nicky stood up and Tom followed. "No, Tom, thanks, but I really have to go. I live with my aunt and uncle and they worry about me. They're very old and I don't like to. . . give them a hard time."

"Are they the couple who raised you?"

Nicky nodded. "They're brother and sister, not a couple, and they're not really my aunt and uncle. . . but they're just like my parents." Nicky looked as confused as his statement. He seemed to want Tom to understand something that was completely unexplainable.

Here we go again, Tom was thinking. Five minutes of the rational and then back to the incomprehensible. "Do you live near here?"

"Not far. West End Avenue. Will I see you again?"

Tom put his hand on his naked breast. "Every Tuesday and Friday, as regular as Old Faithful." Nicky turned to leave but Tom wasn't about to let him go without setting up a definite meeting. "See you in a few days, Nicky."

Nicky stopped and turned around. "You don't have to if you don't want to. I'll understand."

"Shit," Tom almost shouted, then looked about and lowered his voice. "Why did you say that?"

"Because I'm a bore."

"You are not a bore. You're a lousy diver and a mediocre swimmer. . . but you're not a bore." Tom pointed to the tile floor as he added, "And be here Friday at six. Okay?"

Nicky's handsome face glowed as he stared, almost unbelievingly, at Tom. "Thank you. . . and I'll be right here." Then he was gone.

Tom waited a respectable length of time before he made his way back to the locker room. He wanted to be sure Nicky had left the Y, certain that another parting scene would only be embarrassing for both of them. Had he gone too far? If he had, Nicky didn't show any signs of being turned off. On the contrary, Nicky seemed completely in awe of Tom. And why should someone who looked like Nicky Three be in awe of anyone, and why had he turned down Tom's invitation for a drink and dinner? Certainly not because he had to check in with his parents who weren't his parents, or his aunt and uncle who, likewise, were neither, like some teenager. Maybe Nicky was being kept by a rich old man — or woman — who kept him on a very short leash. Now here was something Tom could fully understand but it didn't help his dilemma, it only made him jealous. But of whom. . . the rich old man or Nicky Three?

It wasn't until he was dressed and on his way out of the Y that Tom realized he had been speculating about Nicky as an individual, and not as Eric Hall's clone. This evening, as he had gradually gotten over the striking resemblance between Nicky and Eric, he knew for a fact that Nicky was not Eric Hall. This reminded him of twin brothers he had gone through high school with who were so identical no one could tell them apart. It was common knowledge that one often attended a class in which the other was registered and even rumored that they had screwed each other's girlfriends without the girls knowing the difference.

Mrs. Haskell, the twins' mother, could never understand these deceptions. "Why, they are as different as night and day," she would exclaim. "I can tell one from the other from a distance of one hundred feet."

She was speaking of course of nuance of personality and character which are indeed individual trademarks, but meaningful only to someone as closely associated to the person as a mother who has raised and been in constant contact with her offspring. Knowing Eric was dead forced Tom to see Nicky as an individual. If Eric were not dead, or if Nicky were trying to pass himself off as Eric, Tom would be completely fooled.

He froze on the sidewalk in front of the West Side Y.M.C.A. Trying to pass himself off as Eric? What a weird thought.

⊠

Tom Bradshaw was not celibate, nor did his sex life consist solely of a one-to-one relationship with Tom Bradshaw. He had never set foot in a bar, or any other public place, frequented by gay men, and he did not have a circle of "special" friends kept distinctly separate from his crowd. If the visible gay population represents ten percent of the nation's homosexuals, Tom belonged to the other ninety percent, or the bottom of the iceberg. He was not a closet case; had nothing against the tip of the iceberg; and certainly never thought of himself or his sex life as being invisible. When he thought about it at all he placed himself in the species of human being, and the gender of male. He saw no reason for a subheading of this category.

At college he had avoided the obvious places, not because of

40

the stigma attached to them but because the obvious, like everything in life, is mundane. By experiment he learned that the better hotels in New Haven offered exactly what he was looking for: men who were in town on business, or for pleasure, who sought the companionship of other males without pretense or ritual. Many of the men he met were married; others, like himself, preferred a low-key style, and more than once he had encountered a fellow student and friendships had arisen which would not have occurred under ordinary circumstances. These shared moments were physically rewarding; nothing more was offered and nothing more was expected.

When the right one came along Tom would know, as he had known Eric Hall was what he was searching for. That perfect combination of bucks, breeding, brains and beauty. Until another Eric Hall appeared he would find contentment in his own special way.

If the few hotels in New Haven had proved fertile ground, New York offered a virtual Garden of Eden. Men of all persuasions gravitate to what some consider the capital of the world. In Wichita and Muncie and Kalamazoo they are the pillars of their communities; on a bar stool in New York they are on the make.

The bar at the Algonquin, just off the lobby, is probably the smallest hotel bar in the city. A few hours before and after curtain time it is filled beyond capacity. But between the rise and fall of theater curtains it is one of the coziest watering holes in town. Tom ordered a martini. The man seated next to him was drinking beer.

"I drank martinis at a party one night and didn't come to for forty-eight hours." Tom detected a Midwestern accent in the voice of the tall, blond, nicely-put-together stranger.

Tom sipped the ice-cold liquid and felt exhilarated. A slight tingling sensation in his groin told him the chase was on. "I hope you did something you always wanted to do but never had the balls to try." Bar conversation, meaningless to the average listener but pregnant with innuendo to the cognoscente.

"Might have... but I don't remember."

"Well," Tom responded, "the trick is to drink enough to obliterate the inhibitions, but not enough to black out the fun."

"How much is that?" the man asked.

Tom pretended to think a minute before answering. "My capacity is two, but everyone is different."

"I've had two beers," the man offered.

"Then I would see what happens after one."

The man ordered a martini.

His name was Bill and he was from Cleveland and in New York with a convention of home builders. "A construction worker?"

Bill looked offended. "An architect, but I'm not knocking the bricklayers. They make more in a week than I do in a month."

"Are you staying at the Algonquin?"

Bill shook his head. "Americana. But it's full of home builders, including the guy I'm sharing a room with who has seen ten porno shows in twenty-four hours."

"Doesn't leave much time for the convention."

"Wrong... the entire convention is at the porno shows."

They both laughed and Tom felt a strong hand grip his knee. The hand said its owner knew exactly what he wanted. "Another martini?"

"Two's my limit."

"And then?"

"Home."

"Roommate?"

"Me, myself and I."

"Sounds good to me."

Bill paid for the cab. "I'm on an expense account," he said by way of explanation.

"What are you going to charge this to?"

"New business."

Tom opened his front door, turned on the lights and announced, "The mansion."

"I like it."

"That's what they all say. Take off your jacket and make yourself comfortable."

"If I'm going to be comfortable I'll take off more than my jacket."

"Sounds good to me," Tom parodied.

They stood in the middle of the room looking at each other as jackets, ties, shirts and pants fell to the floor.

"Shy?"

"Hell, no."

"Go on."

Bill pushed down his briefs and kicked them off his feet.

"No wonder you're not shy."

Tom removed his shorts and Bill stared, grinning. "I'm outclassed.

"I'd call it a draw."

And then they came together, arms and legs entwining, lost in the pure pleasure of the moment. Nothing more was offered; nothing more was expected.

⊠

Tom was alone in the world, alone in his room, alone in his bed. He felt satisfied, but not fulfilled. "I am a bottomless pit." He closed his eyes and saw Eric... or was it Nicky?

Russian? He had to be crazy. Then Tom smiled and fell into a peaceful sleep.

St. Petersburg, Russia — 1895-1918

In 1895 the empress presented the czar with their first child, the Grand Duchess Olga Nicolaievna. Their disappointment at the infant not being a boy was hardly perceptible in the joy they both exhibited over the fruit of their love. In the next six years Alexandra would give birth to three more children, all girls, who would be called Tatiana, Marie and Anastasia and all would be considered a blessing of God by their adoring parents.

Then, in 1904, the empress Alexandra Fedorovna was once again confined with child and this time the mightly cannons of St. Petersburg salvoed three hundred times and all the city knew that the empress had given birth to a czarevich of Russia.

The boy was called Alexis and not even the unrest of the Russian people which was becoming more apparent and more overt every day could spoil this moment for Nicholas and Sonny. Indeed, they viewed the birth of a son and heir as a joyous omen, a new beginning for Russia and the throne from which they ruled.

But the omen soon proved to be one of horror for the infant and his parents. The czarevich Alexis was born a hemophiliac — his blood would not clot normally and the smallest cut, if left untreated, could be fatal. It was of the utmost importance to keep this fact from the world especially now when a revolution against the autocratic rule of the czar appeared to be more than a possibility. But the czarevich's suffering could not be hidden from his heartbroken parents who would never again know a moment's respite from fear and anguish.

Alexandra Fedorovna had been a reluctant convert to Orthodoxy but, like most converts, once she had converted she entered the faith with a zeal more passionate than those born into it. When a monk, said to have extraordinary powers, was brought to the empress's attention she immediately invited the holy man to Tsarskoe Selo and once there she allowed him to administer to her son, the czarevich.

For reasons unknown to medical science the monk, Rasputin, had a remarkable effect on the hemophiliac Alexis. The man was able to calm the boy's fears, alleviate his pain and even reduce the unsightly swollen joints caused by internal bleeding which were all symptoms of the czarevich's disease. From the moment Rasputin performed his first "miracle" on Alexis he became an intimate member of the royal family.

Gregory Rasputin was not a holy man. The monk was a leech, a womanizer and an opportunist. The more power he derived from the empress the more flagrantly he used and abused it throughout St. Petersburg. Perhaps Alexandra did not know of Rasputin's excesses or else refused to believe the rumors concerning them or, most likely, she simply did not care. He was a holy man, sent by God to cure her son. This was all she knew and all she cared to know.

The revolutionaries used Rasputin as a weapon against the royal family. The nobility, unwittingly, fearing the monk's power over the czar and his wife and growing power over all of Russia, did the same. Together, this most unlikely of alliances spread the most vile rumors regarding the relationship between Rasputin and the empress of Russia.

Nicholas knew all that was being said but was powerless to stop either the rumors or his wife's dependency on Rasputin. He also knew that Rasputin was able to do more for Alexis than all the doctors in St. Petersburg and Europe. He would not banish the monk.

Nicholas II was not, nor had he ever been, callous to the cries of his people. His problem was that he had never heard them cry. Tsarskoe Selo was not only the village of the czar, it was a village removed from the whole of Russia and very often from reality itself. What Nicholas knew about the Russian people he learned from ministers and deputies whose only goals were to perpetuate the autocratic rule of the czar which in turn would perpetuate the spoils they derived from that rule. Nicholas Romanov's tragedy was that he obeyed those he loved and trusted.

He obeyed his ministers who told him to use force against the malcontents.

He obeyed his mother who told him he must never concede

one iota of his autocratic rule. "Give them an inch and they will take your throne."

He obeyed his wife who pleaded, "Rasputin is our salvation. Because of him our Alexis will live and be well."

It came as a surprise to no one, except Nicholas Romanov, when he and his family were arrested and detained in the Alexander Palace at Tsarskoe Selo. Nicholas's mother and most of his other relations were allowed to flee Russia. But the czar, his wife and children represented all that the revolutionaries opposed in Imperial Russia and they would never be allowed to go free until they had paid for their crimes against the people.

The czar and his family were kept prisoners for over a year during which time communications between St. Petersburg and Nicholas's and Sonny's families in London and Berlin were kept open and the Romanov relations tried desperately, but seemingly in vain, to free the czar, his wife and children.

Then, quite suddenly, Nicholas and his family were moved to the town of Ekaterinburg in eastern Russia. They were housed there in the home of a rich merchant who himself had fled from the ever advancing revolutionary army. By now the royal family had been stripped of all power and possessions. All hope of being saved by the ruling families of England and Germany was abandoned.

Then, in July of the year 1918, Czar Nicholas II, his empress Alexandra Fedorovna, their daughters Olga, Tatiana, Marie, Anastasia and their son Alexis, were assassinated by firing squad at close range, in the house that had become their prison in Ekaterinburg, Russia.

Or so the news reports said.

5

"This is good," Nicky said, picking up a chicken leg and biting into it.

"It's not caviar, but it ain't bad," Tom agreed.

"I don't really like caviar," Nicky answered, looking very serious.

Tom's eyes widened. "I've never had enough of it to acquire a genuine dislike." He waited a moment, as usual, for Nicky to expand on the theme, and, as usual, nothing appeared forthcoming from Nicky who now picked up his glass of beer and downed almost half of it in one long swallow.

They were sitting in O'Neal's, just opposite Lincoln Center, the current "in" place for opera buffs, out-of-work ballet dancers, aspiring composers, musicians, actors and tourists on the lookout for celebrities. The price was right and the food was good; those attributes coupled with a reputation for attracting an arty crowd had made O'Neal's instantly popular. Tom thought it the perfect place to take Nicky for their first confrontation outside the walls of the West Side Y.M.C.A.

Arriving at this moment had not been easy for Tom. After a month of seeing Nicky at the Y almost twice a week, and extending an invitation each time they met only to be refused, had exasperated Tom to the point of intimating that one more refusal on Nicky's part would end their friendship, if their relationship could be called that. Nicky had looked so hurt by the insinuation that Tom could have kicked himself for having spoken the words.

"Look, I wasn't serious."

"Yes you were."

"Okay, but it's only becaue I like you and I would enjoy your company outside of a fucking swimming pool. You know I've never seen you with clothes on."

Nicky grinned. "You hate my body."

"No, Nicky, I like your body, but I don't like sharing it with ten thousand gallons of water and fifty gawking faggots."

Nicky hadn't blushed. He had become accustomed enough to Tom's picturesque phrases to avoid that reaction but he did smile his little-boy smile and had answered, "Next Friday night. I promise."

Tom attacked his fried chicken-in-the-basket, sipped some wine and then, with an inaudible sigh, asked, "How often have you had caviar?"

"We used to have it every night before dinner. Uncle Alexis loves it."

Tom put down his fork which, at the moment, was halfway between his plate and his mouth and stared at Nicky. "Every night?"

Nicky nodded as if acknowledging a commonplace occurrence. His clear blue eyes were bright, alert and deadly serious.

"Real caviar?"

Now Nicky paused, fork in midair, and looked questioningly at Tom. "Is there such a thing as fake caviar?"

Tom rolled his eyes toward the ceiling. Sophisticated enough to nosh on caviar every night and naïve enough to never have heard of lumpfish. A ghost, Tom was certain, would have been easier to deal with. "Yes, Nicky, it's called lumpfish."

"What does it taste like?"

"Caviar... but it's dyed black and the dye tends to stain the eater's lips and tongue. Class will win out."

Nicky stuck the tip of his tongue out between his lips. "See, it's not black. I had real caviar."

"The stain is not permanent, you nut. It goes away."

"Ah... then I'll never know for sure."

Tom laughed. "You are a nut. But a charming one. Now, why did you stop having caviar? Did Uncle Alexis's money run out?"

"No, his health. High blood pressure. Salt is a no-no."

"So, Uncle Alexis goes salt-free and Nicky, in his prime, does likewise. I think Uncle Alexis is a shit."

"Don't say that, Tom, he's like my father."

47

"I don't care if he's like your mother. He can't eat the expensive fish eggs so he cuts you and Aunt... what's her name?"

"Aunt Marie."

"You and Aunt Marie off. I think he's a shit."

Nicky looked torn between the desire to defend his Uncle Alexis and the need not to antagonize his new friend. The result was the frightened fawn look complete with glassy eyes. He solved his dilemma by finishing the beer that still remained in his glass.

"Another?" Tom asked. Nicky nodded and Tom signaled the waiter, pointing to both of their glasses. Their silence was audible.

"Look," Tom finally sighed. "I didn't mean to offend you or, God knows, Uncle Alexis. I expressed an opinion and if you don't agree with me just say so, but don't pout."

"I'm not pouting."

"You are pouting. If you think I'm a prick, say it."

"You are a prick. But a charming one."

And Tom laughed; what else could he do? It was as impossible to stay mad at Nicky Three as it was not to spoil an adorable two-year-old. "Level with me, Nicky. You had to plan on coming out with me tonight. I mean you had to give him some excuse for not coming directly home after your swim. Right?"

"Right."

"What did you tell him?"

"That there was a lecture being given at the Y and I wanted to stay and hear it."

"And he asked the subject of the lecture." It wasn't a question, but a statement of fact. Tom was beginning to know Uncle Alexis very well.

"Naturally."

"And you said...?"

"A lecture on the Golden Age of Royalty."

"Holy shit. And he fell for it?"

"Uncle Alexis loves royalty."

"And caviar. Uncle Alexis is presumptuous, let me tell you. Nicky, you're a man. You've got to be my age, at least—"

"I'll be twenty-eight in February."

The fragile wine glass Tom had just picked up almost shattered as he clenched his fist about its narrow stem. Eric Hall would have been twenty-eight in February. The same natal month as Tom and a fact he was not likely to be mistaken about. Until this very moment Tom had not once thought of Eric but the gods, whoever they might be, refused to allow Eric to be forgotten. The rich are indeed different, even in death. Eric's birthdate had been the seventeenth but Tom would not ask Nicky what his was. He was actually afraid to do so. Slowly, he brought the glass to his lips and sipped from it. The wine helped to steady him and hoping Nicky had not noticed the momentary lapse he continued to lecture.

"You're an adult, a full-grown man, why the hell do you have to account for your time to anyone?"

"He raised me, Tom. If it weren't for Uncle Alexis and Aunt Marie I don't know where I'd be now. I owe him something."

"Sure you do. . . your gratitude, but certainly not your life."

"It's not as bad as all that," Nicky countered.

"No. . . I think it's worse. Do you always have to lie when you go out socially?"

Nicky hesitated before answering. Tom knew his friend was debating with himself between answering honestly or fabricating a plausible explanation for life with Uncle Alexis. If he did not speak the truth Tom would know it at once. Nicky Three's face was an open book. He was too unworldly to get away with anything but the exact truth.

"I've. . . I've never gone out socially. This is the first time."

Tom stared at his dinner companion. Nicky was telling the truth, but it was the last thing in the world Tom expected to hear and the last thing any sane person would believe. "You're not kidding, are you?" Tom whispered.

"No, I'm not."

"But in twenty-eight years there must have been someone. . . someone you. . . what about school? You couldn't go to school and not speak to a living soul."

Nicky took a deep breath. "I never went to school."

"But that's impossible," Tom almost shouted. "You had to. . . Christ. . . Uncle Alexis arranged private tutors."

Nicky nodded at the small pile of chicken bones on his plate. He refused to raise his head and look directly at Tom.

"It can't be true," Tom exclaimed.

"It is."

"I refuse to believe it."

Nicky shrugged his wide shoulders. "Whether you believe it or not doesn't change anything. It's still the truth."

"And you never talked to anybody. . . like this. . . before? Why me?"

Nicky managed a brave smile. "Because I have no one else to talk to."

"I don't know if I should be flattered or insulted."

"Flattered, I hope."

"Oh, sure." Tom waved his hand over his head. "I won out over all the competition."

"I like you, Tom."

Tom was beginning to melt, and when he answered his tone belied his words. "Fish like water. . . I mean what choice do they have?"

"I read a lot," Nicky said, "and I go to the theater and the films and I watch television and I do live in this world. I've never had a friend but I know something about people and life. Christ, I'm not a fool. I know when I like someone."

"But why me?"

"Because you spoke to me and befriended me and tried to teach me how to dive. And I know it wasn't easy because I didn't know how to respond. I wanted to run and stay at the same time. You know that first time you spoke to me I thought about nothing but you for days. I even prayed that I would see you again and when I did I still didn't know what to say or do but you did it all." Nicky looked imploringly across the small table. "Don't leave me because I'm different, Tom. Please don't."

Nicky Three had finally opened up. He wasn't answering one of Tom's questions and he wasn't trying to make small talk. He was showing Tom something of himself, the man behind the frightened fawn façade and the almost childlike eagerness to please. It wasn't much, but it was a beginning and it proved one thing beyond any doubt; Nicky Three was not an apparition but a very real and unhappy human being.

Tom was overwhelmed. Had they been alone he would have taken Nicky into his arms, held him as one would a frightened child and assured him that everything was going to be all right. But under the circumstances all he could do was stare at Nicky, feel his pain and try desperately to assuage the guilt which Nicky's uninhibited words had evoked. Tom had not pursued Nicky. He had pursued Eric's clone. He had not talked to Nicky. He had talked to Eric's clone. He had not befriended Nicky. He had befriended Eric's clone.

Had Nicky not looked exactly like Eric Hall, would Tom have struck up a friendship? Or, if Eric had never existed in Tom's life

50

would he have befriended Nicky? "I don't know," Tom thought. "How the hell could I know?"

"I'm aware of what it's like to be different, Nicky," Tom finally answered.

"Tell me about it."

"You first."

Nicky tried to laugh. "You want the story of my life?"

"Just the highlights. Sooner or later we have to give up this table."

"There are no highlights. Just one bloody bore, believe me. Are you sure you want to hear it?"

"Try me," Tom smiled. What Nicky Three needed more than anything else was to let it all out. Tom knew the feeling well and was ready to be a sympathetic listener. Besides, he was sitting where he was now under false pretenses so he owed Nicky something. Or would he do the same if he owed Nicky nothing? He looked into those clear blue eyes and thought he saw his own reflection in them. Yes, he would, whether he owed Nicky or not.

There was nothing remarkable about Nicky's parents except for the fact that during the chaos which engulfed Europe following World War II they were able, with the help of Alexis Romaine, to flee Russia and settle in England.

Tom held up his hand. "Alexis Romaine is Uncle Alexis?"

"Yes, he was related to my parents, distant cousins or something like that."

"And he was already living in England?"

"Yes. He and Aunt Marie got out of Russia before the revolution."

"What?" Tom exclaimed.

Nicky, now acting the part of the teacher, looked at Tom patiently. "The Russian revolution, as Uncle Alexis never tires of telling me, is not ancient history, Tom. As history goes it's a very recent event. Just think, World War I vets are still alive and kicking and marching in parades and the revolution was born when they were adults, and Uncle Alexis was just entering his teens."

"You're right, of course. Go on, I'm sorry I stopped you."

Still unremarkable, but sad, was that Nicky's mother died giving birth to him and his father was killed in an accident in the factory where he was employed before Nicky was a year old. The boy was legally adopted by Alexis and Marie Romaine and here the unremarkable beginnings of Nicky Three become very singular.

51

Nicky lived all his life in the country home of the Romaines, was schooled by private but very good tutors, and was literally never let out of the sight of either Alexis or Marie Romaine. They accompanied him wherever he went, which was never very far, discouraged even the idea of any social life for Nicky as well as themselves, leaving books, newspapers, films, television and the theater as the boy's only communication between himself and the world around him.

Yes, a ghost would have been easier to deal with, an exasperated Tom Bradshaw thought as he listened to Nicky's tale. One could define a ghost. How did one define Nicky Three?

"Then, about two years ago Uncle Alexis came to America and six months ago he sent for Aunt Marie and me."

About two years ago, Tom now thought. Uncle Alexis appeared just about the time Eric Hall disappeard. No, forget that line of thinking there is no connection — just a remarkable resemblance. Then aloud, "Okay, bread and butter."

"What?"

"Bread and butter," Tom repeated. "How do you all live?"

"Oh, that. Uncle Alexis worked for the British Foreign Office. He's retired now, of course."

"The Foreign Office. Nicky, grow up. You don't eat caviar every night and live in the country home you described on what the British Foreign Office pays you. There is money, real money, someplace."

"There is some sort of trust fund" Nicky acknowledged. "A check comes every month from a bank in London, but it stops when Uncle Alexis and Aunt Marie die. I mean I don't come into anything. They told me that."

Tom, his sense of humor intact, smiled inwardly. Enter Tom Bradshaw, exit the trust fund. Nicky was Eric's clone but two of the essential B's were missing. Breeding and bucks. Could a bastard from Nebraska find happiness with just brains and beauty? The bastard didn't think so.

"I never wanted for anything," Nicky was saying. "And Uncle Alexis and Aunt Marie aren't crazy. They're just. . . different."

"That's putting it mildly, my friend. Why the recluse bit? I don't get it."

"I have a theory." There was a note of excitement in Nicky's voice.

"Good, because I don't. Let's hear it."

"Uncle Alexis worked for the Foreign Office. I think he was a double agent."

Tom looked startled. "You mean he was acting on behalf of Russia and England?"

"Not exactly. I think he was pretending to help the Russians, feeding them false information, but really gathering intelligence from them for the English."

"How do you know it wasn't the other way around?"

"Because I know Uncle Alexis. He hates the communists and lives for the day they'll be overthrown. I mean he really hates them, Tom."

"He would like to see England, or America rule Russia?"

Nicky was looking at his plate of chicken bones again and mumbled something Tom could not distinguish. "The Golden Age of Royalty," Tom suddenly shouted. "Christ, he wants to restore the czar to the throne of Russia."

"You've got it," Nicky said.

"And you're telling me he's not crazy. He's certifiable, Nicky. And the Romanovs are all dead. Weren't they shot in a basement or something like that?"

"Uncle Alexis says there's no proof they were and Aunt Marie screams at him and says they're all dead and that's that."

Tom let out a low whistle. "You've led some life, baby."

"But doesn't that double agent thing figure, Tom? He couldn't want himself or his family to be even remotely noticeable which accounts for the way we live and those monthly checks could come from the Russian government, or the English government." Nicky once again sounded excited and Tom wondered if all this was the result of too many adventure novels and films and too little of the real world. "It also accounts for why the money stops when my uncle dies."

"No it doesn't. They told you it stops after they both die. That means Aunt Marie collects after Alexis is gone. Then it stops. And don't tell me she's a spy too. And... why are the checks still coming? You think he's playing double-oh seven on West End Avenue?"

"He's too old for that now... and sick." Nicky looked defeated. "Besides, those are just details. What I think is the only logical explanation."

"Nicky, there is nothing logical about Uncle Alexis. And why don't you ask him? You told me you're just like a son to him."

"I did ask him."

"And what did he say?"

"He said the less I know the better off I am. Doesn't that mean something?"

"Sure. It means mind your own business. Did you question Aunt Marie too?"

Nicky nodded. "She said pretty much the same thing."

Tom now sat upright in his chair and leaned toward Nicky across the table. "They're very old and the money stops with them. You're very young and what the hell happens to you when they leave this vale of tears?"

"That's what Aunt Marie keeps preaching. I have to get out, meet people, get a job, learn to fend for myself. If it wasn't for her I would never have started coming to the Y. In England I was always out, horseback riding, playing tennis, even ice skating in the winter, but in the apartment I was beginning to go to seed. Uncle Alexis finally agreed to the swimming. God, he had to."

"What does he say about your getting a job?"

"He says he needs a little more time."

"He needs a little more time? What the hell is that supposed to mean? A little more time and he'll be dead and you'll be stuck."

Nicky looked miserable. "Not if you help me, Tom."

"I'm not rich," Tom pleaded.

"I mean help me meet some people and find a job and . . . and shit, I don't know what I mean."

"Easy, Nicky, easy . . . it's going to be okay," Tom lied. "Do you mind if I ask you a rather personal question?"

"Why not? I just gave you the story of my life. What's left?"

"*Sex,*" Tom answered, "as in *fucking.* That's what's left."

Now Nicky blushed. "I have a strong right fist."

"Don't we all, and don't bullshit me. What about it?'

"Nothing . . . I swear . . . just me and my buddy." He extended his palm toward Tom.

"You mean . . . you . . . never . . . ."

"No, Tom, I never."

An embarrassing silence followed, relieved somewhat by the waiter who came to clear their table. They avoided looking at each other as plates, glasses, forks and knives moved from table to carrying tray. "Anything else?" The waiter asked.

"The check," Tom said.

"I'll pay." Nicky began reaching for his wallet.

"No you won't. You can't afford it."

"I'm not poor."

"Not yet, but just wait."

"Thanks for the vote of confidence."

"Someone in your life has to be practical and I think I'm it. Let's face it, Nicky, the Romanovs are not going to recapture Moscow and when those two old people die you are going to be up shit's creek, as we used to say in the sixth grade."

"Any suggestions?"

"I have the solution for one of your problems."

"Which one?"

"Come home with me tonight and I'll tell you all about it."

Nicky tried not to look astonished and succeeded in looking twice as surprised as he actually was. "I can't, Tom. You know I can't. I have to get back."

But Tom wasn't about to let him off the hook. "If you didn't have to get back would you come?"

Nicky grinned, his face lit up and he managed to look devastatingly handsome. "You know I would, Tom."

Tom felt himself relax. He wanted to giggle, shout or jump out of his chair. Instead he winked at Nicky and said, "Don't worry. We'll work something out."

"I trust you, Tom."

"Don't... I'm a real bastard."

Outside the restaurant Nicky hailed a cab and just before he entered it Tom touched his arms and said, "I was born in February too. The fifteenth. What's your date?"

"You're two days older than me. Mine is the seventeenth."

Ekaterinburg, Russia — 1918

It was still hours before sunrise when the train, which had been standing in the old depot for three days, moved slowly from the station and into the dark, summer night. Its departure was as quiet as Ekaterinburg itself. The train's whistle did not sound nor did a conductor wave a lighted lantern from the moving steps of the end car. Only a cloud of smoke, the steady clack of the steam engine and the fact that train and station were no longer one would have announced to an observer, were there one present, that the train was actually departing.

The engine pulled only two closed box cars and, between them, a single coach. Inside the coach three passengers, alone in the dirty, hot car, sat close together as if the carriage contained a horde of invisible riders. A man, a woman and a boy. The man was handsome, bearded and bore a remarkable resemblance to England's George V. The woman was pretty, if too thin, and stared out of vacant eyes down the length of the empty coach. The boy who sat between them was in his early teens and now sound asleep, his head resting on the man's shoulders.

When the train was clear of the depot the man sighed and spoke without looking at the woman. "It is all over, Sonny."

"English," she responded quickly, her eyes glued to the dirty glass of the car's door as if she expected it to part, like a curtain, and uncover a mystery long sought after by the observer. "We must speak only English."

The man smiled a weary smile and careful not to disturb the boy he turned and looked at the woman. "English, French, Russian. It makes no difference. In any language it means the same thing, my dear. It is all over."

The woman finally broke her gaze and turned slowly to look into the eyes of her companion. "Are you sorry, Nicky?"

The man stroked the boy's soft, dark hair before he answered. "No, only relieved. We're alive, Sonny, all of us, and soon we will be together, a family again with nothing to fear and only each other to look after. For a long time I feared. . . ." He allowed the sentence to remain unfinished and once again touched the head of the sleeping boy.

"I know, Nicky," the woman answered and tears welled in her clear blue eyes.

The boy moved fitfully in his sleep and immediately the attention of his parents was directed solely upon him. "We have disturbed him," Sonny whispered.

"The tension of these past few days has given the Prince nightmares."

"Do not use that word," Sonny cautioned, trying to sound forceful while not daring to speak above a whisper.

The man's eyes flashed with anger as he strained to keep from shouting. "He is—"

"No, Nicky. You are not and I am not and Alexis is not."

"Alexis will be—"

"He will not be," his wife broke in again, "and you must keep your voice down or you will wake him. We made a bargain and to break it would mean our ruin." Reaching out to touch the sleeping boy as if to make clearer her meaning she added, "All of us."

56

Nicholas sighed and resting his head aginst the back of the hard seat he closed his eyes. "Mr. and Mrs. Romaine."

Sonny smiled and her clear blue eyes lit up as if they suddenly beheld a scene as far removed from the shabby coach as was the pale moon which looked down upon the train's snail-like progress through an endless landscape of black forest. "Do you remember, Nicky, when we used to pretend that we were Mr. and Mrs. Nobody?"

Nicholas, his eyes still closed, smiled in spite of himself. "I remember, Sonny. But pretense and reality are two very different things. It is easy to pretend but difficult to accept the reality." He opened his eyes and looked at his eerie reflection faintly outlined against the dark window of the moving train. "And now I am nobody. I am not even myself."

"You are Mr. Romaine," she answered, her blue eyes once again dull and lifeless. "Those were your cousin's terms. He had no other choice."

Nicholas looked at his wife out of the corners of his eyes, the hint of a grin beginning to form above his dark beard. "He is also your cousin, Sonny, or has the new Mrs. Romaine so soon forgotten her past?"

Sonny smiled and came as close to laughing out loud as she had in a long, long time. "No, I have not forgotten. And our German relations—"

"No, my dear, your German relations," he quickly corrected her. Now they both laughed and then, suddenly remembering the sleeping boy, they stopped themselves and for a long while only the clacking sound of the iron wheels rolling over iron tracks filled the dreary carriage.

Finally, Nicholas whispered, "What are we going to do, Sonny?"

"Mr. and Mrs. Romaine and their children are going to grow old together, in complete obscurity... that is what we are going to do."

More than forty-eight hours later, late in the afternoon, the strange train reached its destination, a small seaport town on the Baltic Sea. Its arrival was as unheralded and ghost-like as was its departure from Ekaterinburg. Once again the train stood in the depot with no one disembarking or approaching it until later in the evening when a car arrived at the station. The three passengers, like actors trained to respond to a cue, suddenly appeared at the

57

door of the coach, descended to the platform and made their way to the waiting car. The boy, supported by his parents, walked with a decided limp. No one, except the man, woman and boy, was visible on the dark set. They could have been the only human beings on the planet, the last of their species, and in a sense that is exactly what they were.

From the depot they were taken to a deserted dock where they boarded a small craft that carried them over the dark water until, like an apparition emerging out of the fog, a British man-of-war appeared, towering above the small harbor boat as it made its way alongside the warship and the weary travelers once again transferred for the final lap of their journey.

6

Tom began to wonder what had occupied his mind before Nicky Three entered his life. Now it seemed that his every waking moment was given over to thoughts of this young man who looked enough like Eric Hall to be his twin, who was unworldly wise and impeccably educated, who carried himself like a prince and often acted like a child, who had been reared in what amounted to an isolation booth and who had fallen out of the sky and landed in the swimming pool of the West Side Y.M.C.A.

He had heard the story of Nicky's life, or what there was of it, and if Tom knew one thing it was that he knew nothing about Nicky Three. If all of Nicky's short, terse answers to Tom's probing questions had prompted another question, Nicky's life history begged for a volume of footnotes.

The twin theory arose, naturally, as Tom had watched Nicky's cab pull away from the curb after their dinner at O'Neal's. "You're two days older than me. Mine is the seventeenth." The shock had been buffered somewhat by the fact that Tom had been almost certain what Nicky's answer would be. From the moment he learned that Nicky's natal month was February he knew that the date would be the same as Eric Hall's. True, countless thousands shared a common birthdate, but how many of them were exact images of each other? Only twins... but twins had more than just a face and body in common. They shared the same parents and the same place of birth. Nicky's mother was a poor Russian émigré to England who had died giving birth to Nicky. Eric's mother was a very rich, very prominent American who had lived in the limelight until her untimely death two years ago. Nicky was born in England, Eric in New York.

At this point in his reasoning Tom paused. He had no proof of where either Nicky Three or Eric Hall was born. Nicky had told him he was born in England and Tom had always assumed that Eric had been born in New York. All Nicky really knew about his origins was what Uncle Alexis had told him. But Nicky had traveled from England to America; for that you need a passport and on the passport, in no uncertain terms, is your name, date and place of birth. What Uncle Alexis had told Nicky and what Nicky had passed on to Tom was corroborated by that passport. Tom had not seen the passport but he knew Nicky well enough to know that Nicky was not a liar. What Nicky had told Tom was all fact.

But even if Nicky and Eric had been born in the same place — which they obviously had not — it would still not mean anything. People like the Lindenhursts, or the Halls, do not sire twins and immediately give one away. The thought was too ridiculous to even dwell upon. And the reverse was also true: the Lindenhursts would not adopt a child and keep it a secret. When the very rich perform a noble deed they see that the world knows about it.

Finis the twin theory.

So where did all this leave Tom? Once he had abandoned the twin theory his thoughts were completely dominated by the final moments of his and Nicky's first dinner together. Tom relived those moments over and over, word by word.

"If you didn't have to get back would you come?"

"You know I would, Tom."

This resulted in intermittent periods of Tom's being giddy, remorseful, overwhelmed with joy, and unaccountably depressed — and always, in the background to each mood swing, was a nagging doubt that the proposed date would ever become a reality. Tom found himself thinking about Nicky and smiling broadly until the stares of fellow office workers or strangers on buses brought him back to reality. Never had he remembered being so horny but reluctant to relieve himself in the usual manner or visit one of his hotel bars where his batting average was as high as any major league hitter's, albeit in a somewhat different category. Tom was willing to sacrifice momentary pleasure in expectation of many better moments to come. He shunned his friends, fussed about the apartment, laid in a supply of beer and several varieties of liquor just in case, and told himself that everything he was doing had to be done and had nothing to do with Nicky's expected visit.

In short, Tom Bradshaw was in love.

But with whom? Was this a continuation of what he had felt for Eric or was it related solely to Nicky? "I don't know. How can I know?" was all Tom could tell himself. To add to his dilemma, he refused to even consider any long-term relationship with Nicky Three. "No way," Tom kept repeating. "No fucking way." When Tom had lost Eric he vowed that he would settle for nothing less than another Eric Lindenhurst Hall. Someone who would take care of Tom Bradshaw. Someone who could magically wipe away all traces of a poor bastard from Nebraska and endow him with all the trappings of respectability; elevate him to the status of the Haves and enable him to replace Dicky Culver's condescending attitude with one of respect, and even awe.

And last, but certainly not least, someone who would finally put a face to the comforting body and strong arms of that mysterious hero of his youth.

Nicky Three could fulfill none of these prerequisites. On the contrary, it was Nicky who needed all the help he could get. And Tom would help him in any way he could. But if Tom could get laid as part of the bargain... well, why not? It was a give-and-take world. The trick was to give as little as possible and take as much as you could get your hands on.

Then came the nagging doubt. Was Nicky cognizant of the full implication of Tom's invitation?

"You know I would, Tom."

He would what? Pay a visit to Tom's apartment. That was all that had been stated, the rest was pure innuendo. When conversing with someone seated on a hotel bar stool the innuendo is the message. When conversing with Nicky Three... who knew? The guy, for all his education and fine manners, was as naïve as a two-year-old. Did Nicky understand Tom's references to the "regulars" at the West Side Y? Or did he just pretend to do so? Tom recalled his early days at Yale when he had smiled and nodded knowingly at conversations that were completely beyond his ken. Was Nicky's openly childish fascination with Tom just that — a childish fascination — or was there an adult emotion behind those nakedly honest blue eyes?

"Nothing, just me and my buddy." Tom saw the palm of Nicky's hand, turned upward and extended across the small table. Then depression set in.

61

But his memory of the pleading look on Nicky's face and the words — "I read a lot, and I go to the theater and the films and I watch television" — banished the depression and sent Tom's roller-coaster emotions back up to the summit. But where could they go from the top?

And what difference did it all make? Tom had no intention of getting emotionally involved with Nicky. "He needs a nursemaid and I need an Eric Lindenhurst Hall." But Nicky not only looked like Eric, they also shared a common birthdate. "Nicky is Eric. . . Oh, Christ. . . ."

What had occupied Tom's mind before Nicky Three entered his life?

It was little boy time. It was doing it behind the handball court in the schoolyard. It was remedial groping in the cloak room. It was the thrill of discovering the oldest ritual on earth and truly believing it was being performed for the first time. It was sheer delight.

Tom was Peter Pan. Nicky became a child. Together they would soar.

"Next Friday, Tom, instead of coming here I'll meet you at your place."

"Uncle Alexis is duped again."

"Just a little lie."

I hope not, Nicky, I hope not, Tom hummed to himself.

Nicky entered the enchanted forest.

"Your own place." Tom didn't know if his guest was going to laugh or cry.

"Well, what there is of it — three rooms and no view — but if you hang out that window till you think you're going to fall you can see Central Park."

"I want to see the bathroom."

"Why?"

"The wallpaper. You've been talking about it for weeks."

"Oh, the wallpaper. Sure you can see it." Tom opened the hall closet, reached in, and pulled out two rolls of wallpaper. "Here it is."

"Christ, you haven't even unwrapped it."

"I decided I can't do it alone. . . any volunteers?"

"I've never hung wallpaper."

"Neither have I, but after a few drinks who knows what we'll be capable of."

"You're nuts, Tom."

"But charming."

"I think what we both need is more talent and less charm."

"Depends on the talent. There are some in which I excel."

A good white wine, perfectly chilled, is the best tranquilizer in the world.

Tom lit a cigarette.

"I never saw you smoke before."

"I seldom do. Just sometimes in the evening when I'm relaxing, like now."

They had never before been alone with each other and were acting like strangers in a doctor's waiting room. Nicky was seated on the couch, Tom on the love seat which flanked the couch at a right angle. Never crowd a fawn, Tom thought as he assumed this position.

"Do you want one?"

"No . . . thanks. I tried it once and hated it, but I was all alone. It's not much fun experimenting by yourself."

"Nothing is much fun when you do it alone."

Nicky moved slightly in his seat. He was wearing jeans and a polo shirt. The jeans were a perfect fit: they hugged his narrow hips and as he stretched his legs outward his maleness became more pronounced under the buttoned fly. He was looking out the window.

"You even have your own tree."

"In New York, mister, that amounts to an orchard."

Tom went to the kitchen, returned, and poured them both more wine.

"I know one thing that's fun to do alone."

"What?"

"You know."

"Tell me."

Nicky extended his hand, palm upward.

"Tell me."

"Why?"

"I want to hear you say it."

"Jack off. Okay, I said it. Does that make you happy?"

"Yes, but I'd be happier if you showed me."

The fawn flinched. Was he going to flee?

"You've been here a half hour which means you're no longer a guest."

"So?"

"So pour us some more wine."

Nicky, happy for something to do, refilled their glasses.

"I guess you get a lot of company. Friends and things."

"Things?"

"You know... company... people."

"Some, but most of my friends live on the other side of the park. It's called the elegant Upper East Side. I'd rather go there."

"Why? This is a palace."

"Nicky, how would you define a tenement?"

"Do you want to do it?"

"Jack off?"

"Yeah."

"Sure."

The enchanted forest became the petrified forest. Tom looked at Nicky and Nicky looked at his glass of wine. Tom wanted to laugh and even had trouble suppressing a smile. Nicky had proposed doing what he should have done fifteen years ago. It suddenly struck Tom that Nicky was, in all but his chronological age, a teenager. A fourteen-year-old on his own for the first time. And then the smile no longer had to be suppressed for the urge to laugh was instantly replaced with pity. Pity for a handsome, intelligent young man who had been forced to live like a hermit and who now wanted to experience everything life had to offer but didn't know how. "You can't say I didn't try." Those were the first words Nicky had ever spoken to Tom and the latter now knew that was what Nicky Three was all about. He wasn't afraid of anything.

Tom tried to imagine the courage it took for Nicky to be seated where he was now. For an adult to face a one-to-one situation for the first time in his life. He had come determined to share something personal with a friend, his first and only friend, and he hadn't the foggiest idea of how to do it. But he had done it. In quick nervous, sentences, sandwiched between mundane conversation, laughable and sad at the same time... but he had done it. And that was the bottom line.

Tom wasn't about to disappoint his new friend. He reached out and switched off the lamp, leaving the room illuminated only by another lamp opposite to where they were seated. Tom began to open his belt. "Come on, Nicky."

Nicky followed suit, but he didn't look at Tom as he undid the buttons on the fly of his jeans and, moving as little as possible, wiggled the pants off his hips. He was obviously aroused and he pushed his shorts down to his knees where the jeans already rested.

Tom looked at Nicky in the now dimly lit room and discovered that Nicky Three was beautiful all over.

"Look at me, Nicky."

"Do you want me to?"

"Yes."

"You're big."

"So are you... and beautiful."

They stared openly at each other.

"Don't hide yourself, Nicky."

"I'm not."

"You are... and relax... this is supposed to be fun, not a funeral."

"Are you ready?"

"Hell, no."

"I am. I'm really there, Tom."

"Think about something else."

"Like what?"

"Like me."

"I am, that's the problem."

"I want more than this, Nicky."

"So do I."

"Do you still trust me?"

"Would I be here, like this, if I didn't?"

Tom kicked off his loafers and got out of his pants and shorts. Then he took one giant step and sat himself next to Nicky. "First of all, get out of all these damn clothes."

"I thought you were tired of seeing me without clothes on."

"Shut up."

Tom's kiss was almost chaste but his hands explored without inhibition. He could feel Nicky tense under his touch.

"Relax."

"No one ever—"

"Don't you want me to?"

No answer was necessary.

Tom led and Nicky followed, but the latter was less a novice than Tom expected. Nicky was more the diligent student who had done his homework and committed each lesson to memory. His shyness was no match for his desire... his confidence more powerful than his inexperience.

Every sense was catered to and every possibility explored. Both teacher and pupil made a remarkable discovery. Nicky learned that his imagination — until now his only sexual outlet — was pathetically limited. It could act, but it couldn't interact. Tom learned what good teachers have long known. . . they are taught by their pupils.

Together they soared.

⊠

"Shit, it's nine o'clock."

"A.M. or P.M.?"

"Come on, Tommy, wake up."

"No one has called me Tommy since I left Nebraska. . . wherever that may be."

"Come on, I have to go."

Tom woke up. "Go? We've got all night and all Saturday and Sunday."

"You know that's impossible."

"I don't know anything of the kind. All I know is that I want you right here with me."

"I've got to go. I'm two hours late already. What am I going to tell them?"

"Tell them you drowned."

"Don't spoil it, Tom."

"Me, spoil it? What the hell do you think you're doing?"

"I've got to go and you know it."

"When will I see you?"

"I'll try to be here tomorrow."

"Don't try. . . be here."

Tom was alone in the world, alone in his room, alone in his bed. He was furious with Nicky for having left and he was furious with himself for so desperately wanting Nicky. "I don't need Nicky, I need Eric. Why the fuck can't I have them both?" He sat straight up and stared into the blackness before him. "My God. . . *Oh, my God!!!*"

England — 1918

A week later the travelers reached their destination: a house in the English countryside, indistinguishable from its neighbors, neither mansion nor cottage but typical of the homes of the English gentry in the early years of the twentieth century. Its only noticeable characteristic was its remoteness from the village and neighboring estates.

They were met at the door by a tall, pretty girl in her early

66

twenties who rushed out to meet them. "Mama, Papa," she cried. "Mama, Papa, thank God, thank God." She fell into the arms of the man and he embraced her, weeping openly.

"Olga, Olga. You knew we would come. There is nothing to fear now. It is all over."

"Mama, I prayed. We all prayed. We feared. . . ."

Sonny was too overcome to speak. She embraced her daughter and nodded her head knowingly, trying to drown the sobs which rose again and again in her throat.

"Alexis," the girl now turned to the boy and reached out to enfold him in her strong arms.

"Gently, Olga," the man cautioned. "It has been a long journey and Alexis is not well."

"I am fine, Papa," the boy protested, trying to match the exuberance of his sister's embrace but his pale skin and watery blue eyes made a lie of the statement and it was obvious that the boy was in almost constant pain.

"I prayed, too," the boy said. "I prayed as the monk taught —"

"Alexis!" the man shouted in a voice that rang with an authority of one long accustomed to giving orders and never having them countermanded. The soft, gentle Nicky could exhibit an arrogance that was as inbred as his facial features. "I told you never to mention —"

"Not now, Nicky," Sonny quickly cut in, touching her husband's arm, "and not here. Let us go in, quickly, I am anxious to see the girls."

Inside the house two girls, a little younger than Olga, greeted their parents and brother and the reunion, like the one outside, was mixed with joy and tears.

Now the man looked slowly around the room. "And where is Anastasia?"

The three girls looked first at each other and then at their father. They began to move toward each other as if for protection.

"Where is Anastasia?" Sonny repeated her husband's question, unable to mask the fear which caused her voice to quiver as she spoke.

"Papa," the girl called Olga began. "It was not our fault."

"What was not your fault? Where is your sister?"

"She did not come with us."

"What are you saying?" Nicholas shouted.

"Mother of God, Mother of God," Sonny began to chant.

The youngest of the girls, Marie, answered her father. "She ran off with one of the soldiers who escorted us through Poland."

"Ran off. . . like a common. . . ." The man took a step toward his daughters who were now linked arm in arm. "Olga, how could you let this happen?"

"I knew nothing, Papa. In the morning we found a note. . . that was all. Just a note telling us she was leaving with him."

Sonny was in a state of shock. Her lips moved rapidly but no sound came from her throat, and her eyes, as they had on the train stared at something that no one else could see.

"But you knew your sister had to be watched carefully. She is not a well child."

"She is slow, Nicky." Sonny, emerging from her trance-like state with renewed vigor, began to take charge of the situation with an authority born of long practice. "That, I think, is the polite way of stating it. Anastasia is slow and has always been slow. She could not even keep a simple school lesson in her head overnight. There is now no reason to pretend otherwise."

Nicholas began to pace the room as his family, without moving their heads, eyed his every step. "He is at Balmoral. I will go to see him."

"A dead man cannot go to the castle of a king, Nicky." Sonny's voice was strained but strong and clear. Nicholas stopped his pacing abruptly and stood before his wife like a schoolboy called down for being naughty.

"You are dead. I am dead. We are all dead. Even Anastasia is dead. Our bloody obituary appeared on the front pages of every newspaper in the world the day after we left Ekaterinburg. That, Nicky, is the only reality."

"What must we do, Sonny? What must we do?"

"Pray, Nicky," Sonny answered softly, and then in a tone that challenged him to defy her she added, "the way the monk taught us."

7

While the rest of the world revives itself each spring, New York's renaissance occurs in the autumn. The air is usually crisp and clear, the sky a vivid blue and the slow pace of summer is replaced by a burst of energy on the part of natives and visitors alike. Joggers, now as much a part of the landscape as skyscrapers, go from shorts to sweatsuits, and their warmer attire and quickened step seem to reflect the mood of the city. Those who had fled the concrete pavement for shore and country return en masse; June graduates arrive to launch careers; aspiring actors come seeking fame and fortune; even those with no definite goal are swept along by the tide of expectation that permeates the town.

Tom's tree announced the new season by changing its green cloak to one as colorful as Joseph's proverbial robe. The image it evoked in the early morning sunlight, still glistening from the chilly night air, was more reminiscent of a country scene than the cityscape it actually was. Tom paused each morning for a moment before going to work to admire the phenomenon and the picture, framed by his living room window, always left him feeling slightly melancholy. Thanksgiving was two weeks away and after it the Christmas season would begin in earnest.

He wondered if Nicky's strange family celebrated Thanksgiving. He doubted it. He thought about buying a turkey and making a traditional dinner for the two of them but abandoned the idea on the grounds that he had never attempted anything more ambitious than a roast chicken or a broiled steak. He could make reservations at a good restaurant... no, he couldn't... eating out, or just going out in general, had become a bone of contention between the two young men. "Why don't we ever go out?" Nicky was beginning to ask with unrelenting regularity.

"Are you tired of me already?"

"You know I'm not, but I've never been out on my own and now that I have some freedom and a guide I still don't get out."

"Nicky, the only time we have together is when you can get away from Uncle Alexis and I don't want to waste it." Tom left no doubt as to what he meant and Nicky would immediately relent. It was a bitchy thing to do and Tom knew it but nonetheless he continued to use the ploy to keep Nicky from straying on his own. The truth of the matter was that Tom didn't want to take Nicky about because the places Tom frequented were also frequented by Tom's friends, including some who had known Eric Hall. Tom still didn't want anyone who had known Eric to see Nicky Three. He made dozens of excuses to himself for wanting to keep Nicky a secret but refused to face the only reason that mattered to him. He thought that if Eric's friends saw Nicky, and once they had gotten over the shock, they would lionize Eric's double, even turn him into some sort of minor celebrity, and odd man out Tom would once again be just that: odd man out.

Tom was very sure of himself in places like the West Side Y.M.C.A. or seated on a hotel bar stool, but in the company of his rich friends he was as insecure as the boy who had journeyed by train from Omaha to New Haven some ten years ago. Amy was not the only one who knew Tom Bradshaw was "not one of us." Tom knew it better than anyone else.

True, Nicky went out on occasion with Aunt Marie and Uncle Alexis, but from what Tom could gather it seemed that Alexis Romaine was now very ill and seldom left the apartment on West End Avenue. But if friends of Eric's saw Nicky alone it would just be a passing glance which might draw a "he reminds me of Eric Hall" comment. Such things happen very often, especially in a city as large as New York. But if he were with Tom, and they stopped to chat as they most certainly would, and stood face to face with Nicky then the shit would hit the fan as it had never done before. No, Tom would not risk it.

The ploy Tom used to keep Nicky from pushing the situation was a perfect one because it was, for the most part, true. The only time they spent together was the two or three hours, twice a week, when they ordinarily would have been at the Y. Occasionally Nicky could stay an extra hour or two using lectures at the Y as his excuse for being late, and sometimes on Saturday or Sunday afternoon he stopped by when he was supposedly out for a walk. Nicky, a grown man, felt foolish and not a little guilty about these restrictions and Tom played that for all it was worth. Nicky Three would not stray.

Tom had not changed his mind about how he privately viewed his relationship with Nicky. It was still not going to be any long-term deal, but the more time they spent together the more often he had to remind himself of this conviction. Their sex life went from good to better. It hadn't worn thin, as such relationships often do, because their interest in each other went beyond the bedroom. They enjoyed being with each other and they enjoyed getting to know each other which made their intimate moments an extension, not a thing apart, of their relationship.

Thanks to Nicky's age, intelligence and avid reading he was fast becoming not only an apt sex partner but was also teaching Tom the difference between love and sex. Nicky was a true romantic; more importantly his romanticism had never been tainted with the realities of life. While he thoroughly enjoyed hearing about Tom's previous sexual exploits he never gave a thought to experimenting with anyone but Tom. But if Nicky lacked experience he made up for it with enthusiasm and a desire to please. He gave of himself completely and his giving was infectious.

"Would you understand what I meant if I told you you were the first person I've truly had sex with?" Tom asked.

"I'd not only understand, I would agree with you," Nicky replied.

"You're a wonder, Nicky, and now tell me why I feel that way."

"Because I'm the first person you've ever had sex with... and loved at the same time."

"For a beginner you're very sure of yourself."

"For an old-timer you've got a lot to learn."

They told each other everything. Not only in the bedroom but more often, and more significantly, seated in Tom's living room, wearing robes or nothing at all, sipping wine or beer and smoking cigarettes as Nicky now did on occasion. Two souls coming together, naked physically and mentally, nestled in the comfortable room with only their tree as witness. Sometimes one would touch the other intimately while the conversation was as far removed from sex as it possibly could be and the touch said "I understand" more profoundly than the words themselves ever could.

"You're really a bastard?"

"Let's put it this way, Nicky, if Mercy married before I was begot, as the good book says, she never bothered telling my grandmother about it."

"So Bradshaw is—"

"My mother's name."

"Did the people you grew up with know it?"

"Are you kidding? According to Grandma my mother didn't exactly leave town a blushing virgin. Besides, my grandmother's name is Bradshaw and she had one child, a daughter. Grandma didn't even have the good common sense to pass me off as Tom Smith or Jones or even Doe."

"Your mother could have married a man named Bradshaw."

"Nicky, you've read too many novels and watch too many soap operas. No way did Mercy marry a Bradshaw. In fact, no way did Mercy marry. I don't think she was exactly a one-man woman."

"Do you think it was the farm worker she ran off with?"

"Who knows? She ran off with a hired hand, as Grandma called him, and came back with yours truly and no sign of the hired hand."

"If you could have anyone you wanted for a father who would you choose?"

Tom thought about the faceless body and strong arms of his masturbation fantasies. Then he thought about the Lindenhursts and Halls. "I don't know. Who would you pick?"

"Uncle Alexis."

Tom almost choked on his beer. "You're kidding."

"No. Tom, he's really a very wonderful person. So is Aunt Marie. You always make it seem as if they treated me like some unwanted stepson, but that's not true. They've always been very good to me, in their own way."

"You know who Uncle Alexis would pick for a father?" Tom thought aloud.

"Who?"

"The last czar of Russia, that's who."

"You're a bastard, Tommy."

"So what else is new?"

Nicky wanted to know all about the town Tom grew up in, his school friends, his upbringing at the knee of the God-fearing Emily

72

Bradshaw and especially about his life at Yale and his subsequent existence as a carefree bachelor in New York. To one brought up as Nicky Three was, Tom's rather unextraordinary life seemed more exciting than any adventure novel Nicky had ever read.

"I sure would like to meet your friends, Tommy."

"Oh, sure. We'll have a little cocktail party and at ten minutes to seven you'll excuse yourself and leave. Then we might get invited to a dinner party and just about the time everyone is sitting down to dine you'll get up and leave. Even Cinderella had till midnight."

Nicky looked at his hands which rested placidly on his lap and the conversation was ended.

And Tom learned all about Nicky's life with Alexis and Marie Romaine.

The country house in England, for someone with Tom's background sounded like a castle. A tennis court, and horses; a pond for skating in the winter and caviar every night. Nicky had been surrounded with everything a young man could want, except people. He had been given everything one could wish for, except his own life.

"What about sex?" Tom asked. "Did he ever mention sex to you?"

"Never."

"How did you learn to jack off?"

"How did you?"

"Me? I'm the product of the American public school system. You won't find masturbation on any curriculum but along about the sixth grade it's the most discussed extracurricular activity on the agenda. I knew all about it long before I could do it and one little bugger even told me where babies came from. He said you quote stick it in her and jack off unquote and you keep doing it until you put enough in there to form a baby."

Nicky, who was sitting on the floor, began to rock with laughter.

"Then he said the size of the baby that came out—"

"Depended on how much you put in," Nicky finished, rolling across the room and kicking his legs with glee."

"You think I had it easy? Christ, I wonder what ever happened to that punk."

"I don't know, but I bet his wife had the biggest babies ever conceived."

"Okay, you had your laugh on me, now what about you?"

"I, Mr. Bradshaw, had tutors. And very good ones. They told it like it was."

"Doesn't sound like much fun."

"It wasn't, but at least it was the truth."

"Did any of your tutors ever try to put the make on you?"

"No. I think they were afraid of Uncle Alexis. And don't forget, tutors need references."

"How did you know you liked guys, Nicky?"

Nicky shrugged his shoulders. "It wasn't a sudden revelation. Reading, going to the films, looking at magazines... I found myself hung up on the hero or the guy pushing shaving cream all the time."

"Did you think it was strange?"

"No, did you?"

"I'm not really sure I'm gay."

"You do one hell of an imitation, Bradshaw. And on that subject, why did you pick me?"

"I didn't pick you, we just happened to meet."

"You picked me."

"I couldn't resist your beauty and your diving skill."

"You said I reminded you of someone you knew."

Tom looked surprised. "You never forget anything, do you?"

"I don't have very much to remember."

"It was just an opening line, Nicky... just an opening line."

Over the weeks that followed, with no conscious effort, the apartment became as much Nicky's as it was Tom's. A toothbrush for Nicky appeared, a robe for Nicky to relax in, underpants and t-shirts that Nicky could change into if the need arose and jars of peanuts which he never tired of munching on all became a part of the walk-up off Central Park West. Tom even had a duplicate key made for Nicky and very often when arriving home from work he would find traces that Nicky had been there in his absence. A bottle of champagne chilling in the refrigerator or some item of food that Tom especially liked and occasionally a small gift like a tie or shirt that never failed to be just what Tom would have bought for himself.

Nicky had gone from one gilded cage to another, but the new one contained Tom and that made it as big as the world. The rest, Nicky was sure, would come as soon as he was able to break away from Uncle Alexis and Aunt Marie. But it would be nice to meet some of Tommy's friends, even if he could only be with them for just a few hours.

Tom wondered why he had been given Eric, but an Eric bereft of family, friends, wealth. He had "Eric"and old Mrs. Lindenhurst had all that money and no grandson and heir. "Why the fuck can't I have them both?" Those words he had uttered weeks and weeks ago which had acted like an electric shock to his brain had never completely left his fertile mind.

If the gods work in strange ways they had picked the right mortal to entice.

London — 1955

Erica Lindenhurst was not a classical beauty. She could possibly be called pretty but striking would be a more fit adjective for the only child of the American ambassador to the Court of St. James. Erica had red hair, blue eyes, a complexion dotted with freckles when not carefully covered with make-up and a smile an unkind columnist had once labeled predatory. But men seldom noticed the young lady's flaws when presented to the sole heiress of one of the greatest fortunes in America.

Her father, Eric Lindenhurst, was the scion of an old and well-known Boston clan and the name Lindenhurst had long been synonymous with great wealth in America. He had devoted all of his adult life to the service of his country and he considered his appointment to the Court of St. James the crowning glory to a life filled with unselfish achievements.

The tea dance, sponsored by the British Foreign Office, was everything Erica expected it to be and less. But the girl, substituting for her mother who was ill with a cold, did not show the boredom she felt in any way. She drank the offered punch with relish, smiled when a smile was called for, shook many hands and danced with whoever asked her to dance. She was the center of attention and appeared to be loving every minute of it.

Her father was the most important person in the room and Erica adored standing next to him and basking in his reflected glory. Like most young ladies, and especially only daughters, Erica delighted in taking her mother's place beside her father. She felt like a little girl at her first grown-up affair except, in this particular instance, there were no "little boys" present for her to charm and no hearts to conquer. Just as Erica was beginning to wonder when she could make a polite exit a soft, male voice whispered in her ear:

"There is a small bar at the far end of the room where one can get a proper drink."

Startled, Erica turned and faced a man with dark hair and deep blue eyes which stared, unblinkingly, directly at her. He was smiling but in spite of that, or maybe becuse of it, he did not look happy. In fact his manner, immediately noticeable, was that of one in perpetual mourning.

"But I like the punch," Erica answered in a conspiratorial tone.

"Spoken like a true diplomat which means I don't believe you."

Erica laughed. "How right you are."

The man, who was exactly Erica's height, offered her his arm and she took it, allowing him to lead her across the crowded room. She noticed that he walked with a slight limp.

"Is it your job to ply young ladies with booze and extract military secrets from them?"

"Perhaps. Would that make you flee?"

"If I run it will be after I have my drink," Erica answered.

The man smiled. "I thought so. My name is Alexis Romaine."

"Alexis. I like that. How do you do, Mr. Romaine. I am Erica Lindenhurst."

"If I did not know that, Miss Lindenhurst, I would be either a fool or illiterate and I am neither."

"I'm sure of that, Mr. Romaine."

"Please call me Alexis."

"And never Alex."

"No, never that."

The bar was as small and as inconspicuous as a bar could possibly be. The fact that it was intended to serve over a hundred people almost made it a joke. "You said scotch?" Alexis asked.

"I didn't, but I will if you ask."

"And plenty of ice for Miss Lindenhurst," Alexis ordered the bartender.

"Thank you," Erica said when Alexis handed her the ice-filled drink. "You must be a diplomat. Plenty of ice for the American." Erica tried unsuccessfully to imitate Alexis's soft but demanding voice.

"Not really," he answered.

"But you are with the Foreign Office."

Alexis nodded. "In a minor capacity. I translate Russian and French and spot trends in those two countries, whatever that may mean."

Erica took a long sip from her drink, "Russian and French, what a strange combination." She accepted a cigarette from the pack Alexis offered her and appraised the man as he lit it for her. "You look and act very English," she flirted, "but there is a hint of something foreign and mysterious in your manner."

"And you are an over-imaginative child. But there is some truth in what you say. I was born and lived for a while in Russia."

"How did you get out?"

Alexis looked startled for a moment and then, realizing what Erica meant, smiled and said, "I left before the big, bad revolution."

"But you're not that old," Erican blurted in most undiplomatic fashion and then quickly recanted with, "I'm sorry, I didn't mean that the way it sounded."

Alexis shook his head. "I am not offended, Erica, if I may call you that. I am fifty-one years old and why do the young think anything that occurred over thirty years ago is ancient history?"

"Because we believe now is the day we turned eighteen and everything that happened before then is long, long ago."

"You are as bright as you are pretty. So many young ladies today are good to look at and dismal to listen to."

"So are a lot of young men."

The evening was no longer a chore for Erica. She had made a conquest and under no circumstances did she function better or enjoy herself more. And the man who called himself Alexis Romaine was different than any Erica had ever flirted with. It wasn't only his age — over fifty put him in her father's generation — that made Alexis Romaine different. It was his calm self-assurance and his masculinity which, paradoxically, was made more pronounced by his slightly effeminate manner. Romaine exuded a confidence in his role as a male which did not need the overt physical characterizations of the gender to make itself known. He was at once as physical and as ethereal as the smoke which rose from the cigarette poised constantly between his fingers.

The young men Erica knew had been greatly influenced by the recent war. Their idea of romantic love was a grim cross between saccharine Hollywood films and latrine conversation. Her current beau, the Honorable Anthony Hall, was a tall, lanky, handsome and somewhat impoverished member of the English gentry. The young man had managed to take Erica's heart and virginity six months after her arrival in England. The fact that Hall was well connected but poor greatly excited the ever romantic Erica. They were Cinderella and Prince Charming in reverse.

When Alexis suggested they skip the tea dance buffet supper, "Unless you are mad about Spam," and suggested a restaurant he particularly liked, Erica happily accepted the offer.

"But I must clear it with my father first," she told him.

"Has your father ever refused you anything?" Alexis asked.

"No."

"Then why ask?"

"Because it would be rude not to."

Alexis nodded his approval. "That is what I was hoping you would say."

8

Once the embryo of the idea of having Nicky Three become Eric Hall planted itself in Tom's mind, nothing short of a lobotomy could keep him from nurturing it to maturity.

The idea itself was simple. Nicky was Eric's double. Nicky would become Eric. But to pull it off was going to take careful planning and a hell of a lot of luck. Tom was capable of the former and ready to take his chances with the latter. After all, what did he have to lose? Visions of posh townhouses, chauffeured limousines and spitting on the collective eyeglasses of Dicky and Amy Culver filled his mind and dulled his intelligence. What he had to lose, of course, was Nicky, but this thought never entered his mind.

Tom was a dreamer, and a dreamer who truly believed that dreams did come true. This characteristic was the mainstay of his existence; it made his life bearable because he knew that his dream of security, of belonging, would one day come true. When he had met Eric Hall he thought that his time had come, and not until Eric's death did he abandon that dream. But now he had been given another Eric, another chance, and that proved beyond any doubt what his destiny would be. The good Lord giveth and the good Lord taketh away . . . and when He giveth a second time, well, that had to mean something.

When did the idea first occur to Tom? Now that he was actively considering going through with it he realized that it first occurred when he spoke to the "apparition" and was satisfied that it was a breathing, living human being and not a figment of his imagination. When did the idea go from wishful thinking to the possibility of becoming a reality? When he learned from Dicky Culver that old Mrs. Lindenhurst was practically senile and "sometimes refers to her daughter and Eric in the present tense."

When did it go from the drawing board to operative? Each time he saw Nicky, each time he marveled at the resemblance between Nicky and Eric, and each time he waited for that remarkable resemblance to fade with familiarity and each time it never did.

At first Tom's scheme took the form of a daydream, with no basis in reality. He would knock on Mrs. Lindenhurst's door, present Nicky, she would throw her arms about her lost grandson and the three of them would live happily ever after. Sadly, Tom's and Nicky's ever after would be considerably longer than Mrs. Lindenhurst's.

Or, he would tell Dicky Culver he had found Eric. Dicky would take one look at Nicky Three, throw his arms around him, take him to Mrs. Lindenhurst and the scenario would end much like dream number one. It was all pure nonsense and Tom knew it. But gradually the daydream, as daydreams will, began to expand and adapt itself to reality. What could not work was ousted, what could was retained and refined. The daydream became a viable plan. . . .

Nicky Three had no past. . . no friends, no relatives, no former schoolmates or co-workers. Tom had questioned him repeatedly on this point and, impossible as it sounded, Nicky, age twenty-eight, truly had no past. There were the Romaines, but at this stage Tom shoved them under a column in his mind labeled "to be dealt with." There was no one who would come forth and say, "He's Nicky Three." But there were literally hundreds who would say, "He's Eric Hall."

Eric Hall's body had never been recovered. A man with a very public past who was presumed dead, who had never been viewed as a corpse and had never been buried; and his double who, as it were, had never been seen alive. One would become the other. But first, Eric would have to be resurrected. But unlike Lazarus, Eric would be resurrected logically, not miraculously. Not only would Eric's return to the land of the living have to be explained, but a gap of some two years would have to be filled, also logically.

Nicky looked so much like Eric that Tom was certain even a thread of credibility would suffice because at the end of the story a living Eric Hall would appear. The details of how Eric had been saved and had managed to survive for two years without being detected would dim under the awesome light of the fact that Eric was standing there for all the world to see. The story had to be believable, airtight, and within the realm of possibility but nothing more. In this case the end result would prove the means.

Tom would have to school Nicky, naturally, but Tom knew everything about the Halls and Lindenhursts. What he didn't know he would learn from Dicky, Jim Carr, Ken Brandt — anyone he could pump for a missing fact that he thought relevant. But Tom was sure he knew enough to pass on to Nicky, especially if Nicky . . . no, Eric. . . was the victim of amnesia and wasn't supposed to remember very much. Amnesia was an old ruse and Tom didn't much like it but the old which survives is usually the best, he decided — if it weren't it would have been replaced.

Tom was bursting with ideas and energy. . . grasping, discarding, refining and growing more confident each day. He took out his Eric Hall memorabilia nightly to refresh his memory. The picture of Eric that he had pilfered from Dicky's album he kept close at hand as a reminder that the plan would work and to encourage him to iron out any stumbling blocks that seemed impossible to surmount. Naturally, he made a point of keeping it out of Nicky's sight and well hidden when he was not home. He went to the library and made notes on dates, places and events regarding the Halls and Lindenhursts. He was once again obsessed with Eric Hall and his fervor was intoxicating. It would work. . . it wouldn't work. . . he just needed time. . . all the time in the world wouldn't be enough time. He thought about it constantly. He thought about everything connected with the plan. . . except Nicky Three.

Would Nicky want to become Eric Hall? Why not? Who wouldn't want to be Eric Hall? Eric had millions of dollars and there would be more millions when old Mrs. Lindenhurst died. Besides, Nicky would do anything for Tom. Of course, Tom would have to approach Nicky with great care; he had tamed the fawn, but a tamed fawn was still a fawn. He would do it carefully and gently, taking one step at a time. First he would tell Nicky about Eric. Nicky loved to hear about Tom's friends. He would dazzle Nicky with the life and times of Eric Lindenhurst Hall. Then he would show Nicky the photograph of Eric. If Nicky didn't drop dead — please, God, no — he would wait until Nicky got used to the idea of being someone's double and then he would approach him with the *pièce de résistance*.

Who would not want to be Eric Hall? What a crazy idea. But before telling Nicky anything Tom would work out all the details of making his dream become a reality.

And happily, Tom thought, with the exception of his plan another problem that had become more pressing every day would solve itself. No longer would he wonder if he loved Nicky or Eric. They would become one and the same person and then it would make no difference. Yes, Tom Bradshaw was indeed intoxicated.

▧

As it turned out Tom didn't have to snare the fawn. The fawn, nestled in his trap, snared Tom.

Tom was pleasantly surprised to find Nicky waiting for him one evening when he returned home from work. It was an all-time first for Nicky whose comings and goings when Tom was not there were always erratic and, Tom assumed, quick stops to deliver some goodie for Tom or stock their liquor supply. Tom noticed a bottle of champagne sitting on the kitchen counter as he entered the apartment but never gave a second thought to the fact that it should have been chilling in the refrigerator.

"Hi. Nice to come home to someone. It makes me feel almost domesticated."

Nicky was sitting on the couch, in the same spot he had occupied the first night he visited Tom. He looked pale and distracted. Except for a slight turn of his head he hardly moved as Tom entered the room.

"Nicky? Are you all right?" Tom took another step into the room.

"I'm fine."

"No, you're not. What the hell is wrong?" Tom, now concerned, moved tentatively toward Nicky and was shocked to see that Nicky was not only distraught but visibly shaking. Uncle Alexis?... it had to be Alexis Romaine. Tom knew the old man was now very sick, and Nicky was here when ordinarily he would not be. "Is Uncle Alexis—" And then Tom saw it. The photo of Eric Hall, sitting on the coffee table, staring up at Nicky Three. "Oh, my God."

"I never gave you a picture of me."

"Nicky, please, take it easy. I can explain it."

"...and I never had such a picture taken of myself. I never owned that tie and—" There was a frightening note of hysteria in Nicky's voice.

"Nicky," Tom pleaded once more. "Please listen to me."

"I sat down... just for a minute... I do that sometimes when I come by during the day...." He spoke as if he were in a trance. "I pretend... you know... that I live here... that we live here."

"I'm going to get you something to drink. Something strong."

"And then I looked down at the table and... and I saw myself looking up at me. Christ, Tom. Jesus Christ."

Tom took off his jacket and tossed it on a chair. Then he sat on the love seat, positioning himself to complete the picture of their first evening together. He had left the picture of Eric on the coffee table last night and never even noticed it in the morning. He had fucked up royally. Christ, had he fucked up. "Nicky, look at me. Damn you, Nicky, look at me and stop acting like a fucking two-year-old."

Nicky raised his head toward Tom and his blue eyes, usually bright and alert, were dull and looked at Tom from a distance far greater than the few feet that separated them. "It's him, isn't it?"

Tom felt the sweat forming on his forehead. "Who?"

"Your friend. The one you said I reminded you of."

Tom relaxed and fell back into the soft cushion of the love seat. "I'm going to get you a drink."

"I don't want a drink."

"You need a drink, and so do I." Tom stood up, happy to remove himself from Nicky's gaze, and headed for the kitchen. "Think and think quick," he mumbled as he poured two bourbons, neat, into juice glasses and started back to the living room. His mind was racing. "No more lies... it's too late for that... a little sooner than expected but... this is it."

"Here, drink this. It'll make you feel better."

Nicky took the glass from Tom and put it to his lips. He swallowed and grimaced. "It is him, isn't it?"

Tom knocked off half the bourbon in his glass. "Yes, it's him."

"What's his name?"

"Eric Lindenhurst Hall."

A flicker of recognition moved across Nicky's face.

"You've heard the name?"

Nicky shrugged. "Money... I think... a lot of money."

"I was going to tell you about him, Nicky. I swear I was."

"Where did you meet him?"

"At school."

"How well did you know him?"

"We were friends but not really very close friends."

"Is that all?"

"That's all, Nicky."

"But you wanted it to be more, didn't you?"

Tom didn't know if the pain he felt in his chest was for himself or Nicky. He drank more whiskey but it didn't help. "Yeah. . . I wanted it to be more."

Nicky picked up the photo and spoke to it rather than to Tom. "Pictures are funny things. They say the camera doesn't lie, but it does. The lighting, the angle, things like that all make a difference." He was very calm now and this frightened Tom more than the hysterics of a few minutes ago. "Here he looks just like me. . . Christ, I thought it was me. But in the flesh I guess there's just a striking resemblance."

When Tom answered he spoke very quietly, either in imitation of Nicky or because he didn't want to upset the sudden tranquility which now prevailed. "That's not true, Nicky. He looked—"

"Looked?"

"Eric is dead. . . he drowned a few years ago. And it's not that particular picture of Eric that resembles you, Nicky, he looked just like he does there. . . just like you."

Nicky tossed the photo back on the coffee table like a poker player discarding an unwanted card. "So that's it." He wasn't listening to what Tom was saying. He was a million miles from the apartment off Central Park West. He was in a world which only he could reach and enter and which no voice, other than his own, could penetrate.

"What's it?" Tom asked.

"Why you noticed me."

"What are you talking about?"

"Me, Tom, I'm talking about me." Nicky was still calm, almost comatose, and Tom wished he weren't. Tom wished he would scream, break something, hit Tom. . . anything. . . anything but what he was doing. "I'm talking about why you noticed me, why you befriended me, why you fucked me, yeah, literally and figuratively, fucked me. It was never me you wanted, it was him." Nicky pointed, accusingly, at the photo of Eric.

"No, Nicky, I give you my word. At first, yes. But later on, after we. . . after I got to know you, it was you I cared about."

"And you never thought about him?" Again, the finger pointed at the photo of Eric Hall.

"Yes... no... I mean, I thought about him but not like you think I did."

Nicky still wasn't listening to Tom and his finger continued to point, like a dagger, at the photo. "And if I didn't look like that, or if you never knew him would you have spoken to me? Would you have noticed me?"

"I don't know," Tom shouted, breaking the guise of calmness that the two had kept up, like a contest, to see who could be more civilized. "Jesus H. Christ, I don't know. Don't you think I thought about that? Don't you think I thought just that a thousand times over? And I don't know. How the fuck can I know? You do look like him, and I did know him. I can't change that."

"And I thought it was me." Nicky began to laugh, the hysteria returning as if in response to Tom's outburst. "And I thought it was me. The country idiot, straight off the farm, and Mr. Wonderful who wouldn't stop pushing until he got the idiot in the sack. And I thought it was me. What an asshole I am. What a fucking bore. What ever made me think that you... *you*... would be interested in me. I don't have a friend in the world and I actually thought—"

"You have me, Nicky."

"No. Oh, no. *He* has you. Dead or alive, he has you... by the balls, I hope. I don't have a fucking thing." Nicky stood up.

"Sit down, Nicky."

"I'm going."

"Please don't, Nicky," Tom pleaded.

"There's nothing for me here."

"There's everything for you here. You live here."

"Maybe I used to, in a way, but suddenly it's become too fucking crowded."

⌗

Tom was alone in the world, alone in his room, alone in his chair. He hadn't moved since the door closed on Nicky hours ago. He hadn't eaten, he hadn't made himself another drink, he hadn't even lit a cigarette. The tears had dried and caked on his cheeks. Had he shed them for Nicky or for Eric Hall, a second time? "How the fuck can I know? You do look like him, and I did know him. I can't change that."

And when He taketh away a second time, well, that has to mean something, too.

London — 1955

Erica's affair with Alexis Romaine began the next time they

85

saw each other which was early in the week after their initial meeting. They dined at the same restaurant, the only place they would ever dine in public, and then went to his flat.

Surprisingly, Alexis's lovemaking did not live up to the promise of his earlier manner. There were no words of endearment, no foreplay and, afterward, no display of gratitude. He performed efficiently and almost by rote, more in the line of duty than in pleasure of the sport. After Tony, Alexis Romaine was a great disappointment to Erica.

Therefore it was not sex that caused Erica to continue seeing Alexis. It was her fascination with the man himself and, Erica knew, because he reminded her of her father. He often treated her like a child, scolding and lecturing, and was very protective and concerned about her well-being. He never mentioned her relationship with Tony Hall and never questioned her about what she did when she was not with him. Erica often felt their relationship was incestuous and this, naturally, made the affair seem more intriguing than it actually was.

Their first night together Erica asked Alexis if he were going to take precaution before he entered her.

"It is not necessary, Erica. I am sterile."

Erica believed him. Her father would not lie to her and neither would Alexis.

In the time they spent together Alexis learned all about Erica Lindenhurst and Erica learned almost nothing about Alexis Romaine. He had a home in the country where he lived with two single sisters and he kept a flat in London. He worked for the Foreign Office and didn't have a friend in the world or at least not one that Erica ever met. Alexis expressed no interest in meeting her friends and for this Erica was grateful.

"You must promise you will never tell anyone of our relationship," Alexis requested. "I want it to be something very special between only the two of us." It was a romantic notion and one Erica found very stimulating. She was still a child at heart and like all children liked nothing better than a secret, especially where sex was concerned. Erica Lindenhurst would soon grow up.

Alexis's passion for privacy amounted to an almost religious fervor. Once, coming out of a concert hall, Erica ran into friends and after greeting them she turned to introduce them to Alexis only to find that he had disappeared in the crowd, leaving her quite alone. He never reappeared and she had to make her own way home. At that point she had decided never to see Alexis Romaine again.

But after a two-week hiatus in their routine of seeing each other once a week it was Erica, strangely enough, who finally called Alexis. She found that she missed their quiet evenings together, so different from her time spent with Anthony Hall. She missed Alexis's stimulating conversation and, most of all, she missed being treated like Daddy's little girl.

"I told you, Erica," he said when she saw him again, "I value my privacy."

"But it was just a matter of meeting a few people."

"Those few people manage to get their names in the gossip columns at least once a week."

"Is that so bad?" she asked

"For them, obviously not. For me it is." And there the conversation ended.

9

Alexis Romaine was reclining on a couch, his head propped up by a pillow and his painfully thin body covered with a flannel blanket in spite of the stifling temperature of the room. No trace of the handsome man he once was could be found in the drawn and lined face or in the deathly pale complexion that accentuated the deep blue color of his eyes now focused on his sister.

"I knew this would happen."

"You knew what would happen?" Marie Romaine answered without looking up from the delicate and intricate needlepoint canvas she was stitching without the benefit of eyeglasses.

"Nicky. Since he has been going to that place he comes home later and later each night."

Marie Romaine smiled, almost imperceptibly, and continued to concentrate on her canvas. "I'm glad."

"Naturally, you encouraged this foolishness."

"I did not encourage it, Alexis, I insisted upon it."

Alexis reached for his cigarettes, lit one and tossed the used match into an ashtray littered with cigarette butts. "What is this institution called?"

"It is not an institution, Alexis, it is a youth hostel. It is called the Young Men's Christian Association and offers recreation and classes and companionship."

"Do you think he speaks to the others there?"

"I think, Alexis, he has found a friend."

"This is crazy, Marie."

Now she looked up from her work and spoke directly to her brother. "No, Alexis, what we did... what you did... was crazy. This is right."

"Nicky is inexperienced. The boy is—"

"Not a boy, he is a man and we must let him go... now."

"Go where?"

"Anyplace, so long as it is away from us. He is young and we are old and dying...." The sudden pause was too obvious to go unnoticed and, as if startled by the verbalization of her innermost thoughts, she covered her mouth with her hand.

"No... no, Marie, no pretense. We have come too far together for that. I am dying and my doctor is not the only one who knows it."

"I am sorry, Alexis." Now her tears prevented her from continuing with her stitching. Since his birth Marie had been taught to respect and care for her younger brother and in all her long life she had neither forgotten the lesson nor abandoned her duty. She was an intelligent woman and a kind one who, were she born in a different time and place, could easily have made her mark with a career in medicine or perhaps the arts. However, her own narrowly circumscribed world had allowed only for duty: caring for and nursing first her father, then her mother, then two older sisters, all of whom now rested in a small family plot in an undistinguished country cemetery in England. All during those years she had never lost her wry sense of humor, her ability to create a semblance of tranquil domesticity in an old and isolated house. And, for the past twenty years, she had tried to raise a young boy to manhood in as normal an atmosphere as was possible under the most abnormal of circumstances.

Marie Romaine appeared as healthy as her brother was ill. Her face was almost unlined, her complexion clear and rosy and her white hair, pulled back from her face and knotted in a bun in peasant fashion, all combined to present the appearance of an astute, able woman who had not only adjusted to but also triumphed over a dismal fate.

Now, when she spoke she sounded like one long resigned to fighting a losing battle but refusing to give up the fight if even a glimmer of hope remained. "You must let Nicky go, Alexis. The way he was raised and the way you continue to keep him a prisoner is unnatural. What will happen to our Nicky after we are gone?

89

When we die the money stops. We can leave no heirs because we never existed after 1918."

"Yes, I know a decision must be made. But I will not be rushed into doing anything foolish. I need time."

"Time? Isn't almost thirty years time enough?"

"When I came to America I thought things would be different." Alexis Romaine also spoke like one long resigned to his fate but, unlike his sister, there was not a glimmer of hope for himself or for Nicky reflected in his voice.

"You thought the cold war would grow hot. You thought America would engage in war against Russia and when that happened you thought the old ways would be restored. Well, it will never happen, Alexis, not in our lifetime. And if it did there is no chance that you. . . ." Marie sighed, rolling her eyes upward. "First Papa and then you. Isn't eighty years of hoping enough? Wasted, all wasted years. I will not let it happen to our Nicky."

"He knows nothing, Marie, you know that."

"And I will see to it that he never does."

Alexis Romaine crushed his cigarette in the overflowing ashtray and immediately lit another. "You smoke too much, Alexis," his sister told him.

"And isn't almost eighty years of telling me that enough?" There was a slight edge to his tone. "Besides, what difference does it make now?"

They sat in silence, Alexis smoking and Marie returning to her needlework. When Alexis finally spoke he directed his words to the blue clouds of smoke that rose over his head with great effort in the overheated room. "When I sent for you and Nicky I had made up my mind to go to see her." He paused like one in a confessional, uncertain as to whether or not he was ready to bare his soul. "I was ready to admit defeat if she would accept Nicky as her son and heir and then one morning I opened a newspaper. . . and she was gone. They were all gone. And with them went my only hope for Nicky's future."

"And you didn't dare go to the old lady, Mrs. Lindenhurst."

"How could I? What proof did I have?"

Marie shook her head. "That wasn't the reason you didn't go to her. You didn't need any proof. All she had to do was look at Nicky to know he was her daughter's son. A duplicate of the grandson she had lost. No, you were afraid to go to Mrs. Lindenhurst because she is a highly placed woman. She would make inquiries in England. Perhaps even contact our cousins."

"Now it is you who sound like Papa. Our cousins... do you think Elizabeth would know us? Do you think she even knows what her grandfather did to us?"

"Not to us, Alexis, for us. No, I do not know but you couldn't take the chance that Mrs. Lindenhurst would find out more than she bargained to know."

"No, I couldn't take that chance. My Nicky would become a pretender, a public joke like Anastasia."

"Do not speak unkindly of Anastasia."

Alexis pointed an accusing finger at his sister. "Why did you go to see her, against my wishes, when you came to America?"

"Because she is our sister."

"And why did you show her Nicky's picture?"

"Because he is her nephew too."

Alexis put out his cigarette, reached for another but withdrew his hand before touching the pack. He took his frustration out on Marie. "Anastasia is a fool and a clown, and you know it."

Marie smiled her sad smile. "A fool, a clown.. perhaps... but a smashing comeback and an Academy award for Ingrid Bergman."

Alexis grinned and then laughed out loud. "You could always make me laugh, Marie. What would I have done all these years without you?"

"No better or no worse than you have done. And you have nothing to fear from Anastasia. She is old and senile. I doubt she knew who I was. The poor thing does not even know who she is anymore."

Alexis gave up the struggle and reached for a cigarette. "What are we going to do, Marie?"

"We are going to let Nicky go. We will begin by allowing him to get a job so he can learn to support himself. That is most important, Alexis. Our time is running out and Nicky's is just beginning."

"We have no contacts here, Marie. What can the boy do?"

Marie Romaine smiled contentedly and said, more to herself than her brother, "I think my Nicky has made a contact."

London — 1955

Their affair began to pale for Erica when she decided that Alexis Romaine had no secrets to conceal or share. "If I stopped seeing you, would you miss me?" Erica asked one evening.

"Naturally," he answered, seemingly unconcerned at what Erica was hinting at.

"Do you love me?" she continued to probe.

"You are very young, Erica, and the very young find it easy to love and hate. When you get older you will find that relationships are not as simple as all that."

"Why do you see me?"

Alexis sighed. "You remind me of someone who used to be very dear to me."

Finally, Erica thought, a confession. "A past love?"

"In a way. I am talking about my mother."

No, Alexis Romaine had no secrets, except perhaps an unnatural attachment to his mother, and Erica began to find him less and less interesting. At the same time, and for a number of reasons including a strong sense of guilt, she found herself more and more attracted to Anthony Hall. So involved was she with this momentous decision that it was more than a week after her monthly period was due before she realized it had not occurred. Hiding her famous red hair under a turban and using a false name Erica went to a public clinic and two days later a smiling nurse confirmed Erica's worst fear. What could be more natual for Erica to turn to the older, wise and fatherly Alexis Romaine in her hour of need.

"Tony always uses something but I guess it's not foolproof. I've heard of such accidents," Erica confessed to Alexis. "Oh, Alexis you must help me. I want an abortion and I know you can arrange it."

"I am sure, Erica, that the child is mine. And no, I won't arrange an abortion."

Erica was sure she had misunderstood what Alexis had said. "But—"

"But, I told you I was sterile. I lied to you, Erica. I wanted you to have my child and I still do."

The nausea Erica had felt that morning suddenly returned with a vengeance. Who was this cold, smiling man standing before her and what was he telling her? "What are you saying, Alexis?"

"Just what I have already said. I am not sterile and I want you to bear my child."

Now Erica felt dizzy and found it difficult to focus her eyes on the man in front of her. "You're mad... crazy...."

Alexis moved toward her and held her shoulders in a firm grip. "You are getting hysterical, Erica, and that would serve no purpose for either of us."

"Take your hands off me," she screamed, pushing him away. "When I tell my father about this he will see to it—"

"If your father hears about this," Alexis shouted back, "I will see to it that the world hears about it. The Court of St. James will not be amused."

Erica began to laugh and cry at the same time. "The world? You would rather die than see your name in print. I will tell my father and you will never breathe a word of this."

"We must all die sometime and without this child my life is meaningless. It is all the same to me, Erica, so don't force my hand. I will make a public scandal if you don't do exactly what I tell you you must do."

Erica was shocked out of her hysteria. The man was insane and ruthless. He would make a public scandal no matter what the cost to him. She thought of her mother and father and the headlines that would make all they loved and stood for a sham. In one mad moment she could ruin them and herself. She shivered at the thought of the power Alexis Romaine now held over all of them. In the confused jumble that was her mind one sensible, restraining thought kept her from physically attacking Romaine. No matter what it might do to her she would not contaminate her family with what was her own shame. "I will marry you," Erica whispered.

Alexis started to laugh and the sound of his high-pitched giggle, like a woman being told an off-color joke, sent Erica into the rage she thought she had just conquered. Restraint was forgotten at the hideous sound of his triumph and her degradation. Her arms flew out at him, her hands flaying at the air, her long, red fingernails reaching for his eyes. "Bastard. Bastard. Bastard."

In a surprisingly swift and agile move Alexis caught her hands before they touched him. "Don't ever do such a thing." His voice was menacing, his eyes ablaze with fury. "You could hurt me far more than you realize." She thought her wrists would crack under his grip and tried to break away. He pulled her closer to him and hissed into her face, "I don't want to marry you, Miss Lindenhurst."

Only the fear of further humiliation prevented Erica from being sick all over herself. "Then what the hell do you want?" She cried.

Alexis was once again his calm, assured self. Slowly he relaxed his grip on her wrists, freeing her, but never taking his eyes off her as he reached for a cigarette. "I want you to marry Anthony Hall." Hearing the totally unexpected for the second time in less than five minutes almost caused Erica to faint. Her knees buckled under her and again Alexis's quick reflexes went into motion as he supported her with his arms and led her to the couch. Once she was seated he continued to speak as if nothing had happened.

"I want you to go on an extended honeymoon and when your time comes you will come to my home where the child will be born." Alexis struck a match and lit his cigarette. Erica followed the movements of his hands with unseeing, dead eyes. "Tell Hall anything or nothing. The choice is yours. But whatever you tell him, my name must not be mentioned. The young fool's head is spinning at the thought of marrying Erica Lindenhurst and he will believe or do anything you tell him or ask of him."

Erica sat, numb and speechless, staring at the cigarette Alexis held between his fingers. But her mind was as active as a pair of nimble hands fitting in the last pieces of a jigsaw puzzle. *This is not an accident but a carefully planned and executed scheme. From the moment we met, maybe even before we met, this insane man picked me to be nothing more or less than his brood bitch.* And now there was nothing she could do but deliver the litter to the stud.

10

At work, there were moments when Tom Bradshaw believed Nicky Three was, after all, an apparition — a ghost he had conjured up with his fanciful imagination and breathed life into with his almost neurotic desire to bring Eric Hall back to the land of the living. He cringed inwardly with shame at the irrational thought that only he had seen Nicky Three, that he had talked to the empty air which surrounded him at the Y and that all present had thought him a lunatic. Tom had seen people on the streets of New York who talked with, argued with, and even screamed at people only they could see. Had he become one of them? He eyed his co-workers, especially his secretary, in search of a clue to his own sanity. The only information his secretary confided to the girls she lunched with was that "Mr. Bradshaw's been kind of depressed this week. I think his love life is in big trouble."

But at home Tom was surrounded by traces of Nicky which illusion, no matter how real to the beholder, could not have left behind. The shirts and the sweater Nicky had bought Tom. The undershorts and jeans and terry robe Nicky had brought to and left in Tom's apartment. And mostly the bottle of champagne which Nicky had brought the day he discovered Eric's photograph. Perversely, Tom refused to remove it from the kitchen counter where it still stood as a monument to Nicky's departure and Tom's stupidity.

He didn't know Nicky's phone number but he did know something of Uncle Alexis and was sure the number would not be listed.

He checked and it wasn't. He didn't know Nicky's address but he knew the apartment building was on West End Avenue and Eighty-something Street. Hard as he tried he could not remember the exact cross street. So one chilly Saturday morning, amid people toting Christmas trees and hurrying to and from department stores with gaily wrapped packages in their arms, he walked the ten blocks along West End Avenue, from Eightieth to Nintieth, east and west sides of the blocks, staring at every young man he passed.

"Nicky! Good to see you. I just happened to be in the neighborhood. How about a beer?"

"Nicky! What a surprise. . . . "

"Nicky! I've been searching all over this fucking town for you."

"Nicky! I miss you. . . how about coming back home."

It began to snow, a wet New York snow, and still he walked, hatless, up and down the ten-block rectangle until he began to get odd looks from doormen who ordinarily don't give passersby a second glance. He finally returned to his apartment chilled, wet and alone.

Nicky Three, who had fallen out of the sky and into the swimming pool of the West End Y.M.C.A., had gone back from whence he came, wherever the hell that was. "Face it. He's gone."

Gradually, Tom began to resume his old lifestyle, falling back into it as easily as he had fallen away from it.

"Long time no see, Tom. Been away?"

"Yeah. Palm Beach."

"You don't look tan."

"It rained. . . every fucking day for a month."

They were all unchanged: the Carrs, the Brandts, the pretty girls and closet cases, but they now appeared to Tom as flat, two-dimensional people who had said and done all they were ever going to say and do. Had he really found them interesting? No, he never had, he now admitted to himself. They were never real friends, but representations of what he wanted from life. And what did he want? Nicky? Eric? "No, goddammit, both of them."

Amy finally got her return bridge match: herself and Dicky opposite Tom and Nancy. "I hear you've been to Palm Beach, Tom," Amy said, adjusting her glasses before fanning out the cards just dealt her.

"Who told you that?"

"Laurie Carr, I think."

"Well, it's not true."

"Why would she make up a story like that?"

"She didn't make it up. I did."

Nancy giggled. "Tom, you're a nut."

"Are we playing cards or making chit-chat?" Dicky injected, adjusting his glasses.

"What was the bid?"

"Two hearts."

"Christ, don't do that to me."

"I just did."

"If you weren't away then where have you been? I haven't seen you at one party all season." Amy talked like a character out of a Noel Coward play.

"Having an affair."

Like a Greek chorus slightly out of sync Amy said, "With whom?" and Nancy said, "With who?"

"Laurie Carr. That's why she's passing around the Palm Beach story."

"Bullshit." Amy occasionally broke from Noel.

"I can't concentrate," Dicky moaned.

"I've never known a single girl you've had an affair with, Tom." Amy, relentless as always, continued to probe.

"That's because I only have affairs with married ones."

Nancy dropped her cards and laughed heartily. "Very good, Tom. Do you get it, Amy? You said a single girl and. . . ."

"I get it, Nancy, and you're not funny, Tom."

"I don't think I am either, Amy. In fact I'm very handsome."

"Would you cut the crap and play cards. I'm not interested in Tom's sex life."

You were when Eric Hall was around, you stupid little punk, Tom thought as he tossed down a card and trumped his partner's ace.

"Tom!" Nancy shouted.

Amy smiled majestically.

Tom had accepted Amy's invitation not out of a keen desire to see any of those assembled but to return the picture of Eric to where it belonged — Dicky's photograph album. He knew that sooner or later the picture would be discovered missing and that Amy, bless her cold heart and sharp mind, would recall just who they had last shown the album to. Returning it had proved easier than Tom had anticipated. Before Nancy arrived and while Dicky and Amy were busy elsewhere. Tom had been left alone in the den. It had taken

97

less than a minute to replace the picture but, with Tom's mind on other things and in spite of Nancy's usually brilliant playing, it had cost him sixty-five dollars to accomplish the feat.

Amy Culver was jubilant.

Tom finally went back to his swimming exercises at the Y. If a ghost could make love the way Nicky had, Tom thought, then I have wasted a good many years sitting on hotel bar stools — I should have been cruising séances. He thought, briefly, of paying daily visits to the Y in search of Nicky as he had done before but, like his useless canvassing of West End Avenue, he now realized that Nicky knew where to find him and if Nicky was ever going to return, which now seemed unlikely, he would do so of his own volition.

The Y, like Tom's friends, remained unchanged. After his long hiatus the regulars welcomed him back with open eyes and Tom, reckless in his depression, dangled it like he had never dangled it before. Finding himself alone in the showers with a man Tom thought made his home in the shower room of the West Side Y.M.C.A., Tom lewdly pointed to himself and said, "You've been after this a long, long time."

The man froze under the spray of water, wide-eyed and speechless.

Tom cupped himself. "You want it? You got it."

Recovering, the man looked about the tiled room like a rabbit and stuttered, "Not... here... I... I live just around...."

"Here and now, or never."

The rabbit, obviously of little faith, opted for the here and now.

Tom felt ashamed, dirty and degraded. Christmas was a few days away. The tree in Rockefeller Center was ablaze with lights as were the trees along the island in the middle of Park Avenue. Department stores overflowed with shoppers and the streets were crowded with tourists and merrymakers and the sound of brassy carols which only the Salvation Army bands know how to render. The depression that had descended upon Tom since Nicky's departure appeared to want to settle in for the winter solstice. But Tom Bradshaw was a fighter and a good fighter knows, above all else, when to retreat. That time had come.

Tom decided to leave New York: not for a week in Florida or St. Thomas or the ski slopes of Vermont, but away, and far away, forever. There was nothing for him here and he now felt there never would be. He was less than a little fish in a big pond. He was a hanger-on. He moved in a circle that would always regard him as an outsider, the odd man needed only to even off a hostess's dinner table.

It would soon be a new year, so why not a new life to go along with it? He had a few dollars saved to help him get started. He would give the bank their two-week notice and then... Rome, Paris, London. London would be best... no language barrier to overcome. Surely he could find work there. Tom poured himself a stiff bourbon and began to make plans.

London... the Prince of Wales was taken but Charlie had a viable younger brother. Tom envisioned a conversation between the queen and her second son. "But Andrew, my dear, you cannot make Thomas Bradshaw the Duchess of York."

As Tom made plans for a new life, so Alexis Romaine's ended as unobtrusively as he had lived it. Marie knew her brother was dead the moment she entered his room to rouse him for supper. The stillness which met her soft call was not the peaceful quiet of the sleeper but the absolute tacitness of death. Marie Romaine knew it well. She looked down upon her brother who had died, an old man, in his sleep and thought of the screaming headlines which had proclaimed his violent death at an early age many years ago. She heard her father's pleading voice.... "What must we do, Sonny? What must we do?" And her mother's calm response.... "Pray, Nicky, the way the monk taught us."

Marie, with very little effort, sank to her knees and prayed for the soul of a man who was born a prince of the largest nation on earth and died a recluse without a country. Then, her eyes dry and her small figure perfectly erect, she walked down the long passage to a room at the far end of the apartment and knocked gently on the door.

Nicky was sitting in a comfortable chair, his shoeless feet propped up on his bed, reading. He smiled as Marie entered. "Supper ready?"

"He is dead, Nicky."

The young man was stunned as we are all stunned when the inevitable finally happens. The book fell to his lap and he began to get out of his chair. "There is nothing for you to do, Nicky."

"I must go to him, Aunt Marie."

The old woman nodded, knowingly. "Yes. But first we must talk."

"The arrangements. Yes, I must...."

She held up her hand to silence him. "There is nothing for you to do," she repeated. "I am going to take Alexis back to England and put him to rest beside our mother and father. That is what they would want and what he desired."

"But arrangements must be made. If we start now we can be in England the day after tomorrow.'

"I still have some connections in England and I will be back there tomorrow. You will stay here."

Fear showed in his blue eyes. He heard, he understood, but he refused to believe. "I can't let you do this alone. It's my duty—"

"Your duty is to yourself. We have kept you too long." He made a move to get up but she stepped forward and restrained him by placing her hands on his shoulders. "Listen to me, Nicky. Just sit and listen. You are like my own son. No, you are more than that. You are the son I never had. Can you understand that difference? Do you think I want to leave you now . . . especially now when you are all I have left in the world? No, Nicky. No, no, no." The tears she had not shed for her brother now flowed freely for his son. "You must learn to live on your own. Here and now, you must do it. Soon, too soon, I will join Alexis and the others and then what will you do? Now, Nicky, you must make the break now."

"But you're all I have and I love you," he protested. "I loved him, too . . . and . . . and I'm so afraid, Aunt Marie. I'm so afraid." He buried his face in her bosom, sobbing, and she held it there, stroking his hair and rocking him gently in her strong arms. "Cry, my Nicky, cry. It is good to cry for it washes all the badness away and leaves behind a clean slate."

When he withdrew from her arms he turned his head, refusing to face her. She sat on his bed and with one finger lifted his chin until their eyes met. "See, it is better already."

Nicky nodded and attempted a smile.

"Yes, it is. Now let me tell you something, my Nicky. Once, a long time ago, I too was afraid. Not of life, but of death. And when it was decided that I should live I knew that the greatest gift of all is the gift of life. And that is the gift I am giving you. I promised myself that I would enjoy each day I was granted. I promised myself I would never look back. And I tried, Nicky, oh, how I tried. And that is all the legacy I can leave you, my son. The wish that you learn to live every day fully, and the need never, never to look back. Are you listening to me, Nicky? Do you understand what I am saying?"

"Yes. But I'm still afraid."

"You have made a friend... no, do not protest. I know you have."

"No, Aunt Marie. It was all a mistake. It wasn't me... it was...."

"Hush... I won't hear it. Whatever happened is in the past. It is dead and what is dead is best forgotten. It is a lesson I have learned well. The future is all that matters."

Nicky was being given the only thing he had ever wanted, his freedom, but to gain it he had to lose the man who had raised him as would a father and the woman who loved him like a son. And Tom, his only friend, was the most important reason for wanting to be free and he had lost him, too. "Let me come with you, Aunt Marie," he pleaded, trying to mask the fear in his voice.

She sat erect, her head held high and her manner as imperious as a queen's. "You will stay, Nicky, and you will succeed. And, my son, one day you will forgive me."

"Forgive you? For what? For giving me my life? It's I who need to be forgiven for not graciously accepting the gift."

Marie Romaine smiled. "But you have already accepted it in your heart and that is where all things begin. Now come, you must say goodbye to Alexis and then we will make our plans."

Arm in arm they walked down the dark passage, an old lady and a young man.

"I feel so old, Nicky."

"You are as young and as pretty as the princess in the fairy tales you used to read to me."

"And you, my Nicky, are a prince." The young man did not see the mischievous smile on the old woman's face.

London — 1955

Mrs. Eric Lindenhurst looked every inch the ambassador's wife and did not have to work at fulfilling the role. She was matronly, in the nicest sense of the word, kind, patient and pretty with nothing more than a trace of powder on her usually smiling face. Her speech and manner reflected her upbringing which was old guard, Boston. She was happy with her daughter's choice of husband but chagrined at not being given enough time to plan a more elaborate wedding.

"My debut was elaborate enough to last a lifetime and I think a fancy show in London right now would be in very bad taste," Erica announced.

Her father agreed and was proud of his daughter's sensitivity to the times. "And," Erica told her parents, "we want to go on a long honeymoon. Because of the war Tony and I never saw Europe and we want to explore every inch of it."

"Do whatever you wish," her mother answered, "but don't play too long. Your father and I want grandchildren."

Before the wedding Erica told Tony Hall everything without naming Alexis Romaine. "If you tell me who he is, Erica, I will gladly kill him."

"Just be honest with me, Tony. If you don't want to marry me say so and I'll go away by myself until this is over. I don't want you to marry me out of pity. I can live with what's growing inside me but I couldn't live with that."

"I'm marrying you because I love you and I hope you feel the same way about me."

"I do love you, Tony, very much. And I'll make it up to you, I swear I will. Can you ever forgive me what I've done?"

"We don't forgive people we love, we accept them as they are. And it's not for me to forgive; my glass house couldn't stand the retaliation."

The newlyweds did not disappear completely. They saw friends on the continent and even visited London on several occasions. When her condition became obvious Erica even tried to feel the joy her parents expressed over the coming event. The couple had decided to be abroad in February, the month the child was expected, and when it came and had been delivered to its rightful father they would announce that it had been born dead and their nightmare would be over. It was a deceitful but painfully simple plan.

"I want to keep it," Tony said as her time grew near. "I feel it's mine and it could easily be ours."

Erica thought of Alexis Romaine and shook her head. "That's not posible, my love, but we're young and have plenty of time ahead of us to have a family of our own."

Paradoxically, it was Tony Hall who was sterile and he and Erica were never able to have a family of their own.

At twelve noon on Christmas Eve, all office parties officially begin. Tom hated the ritual and each year vowed to break away as soon as he had had the obligatory drink with those above and those below his station at the bank, and each year the spirit of the vow succumbed to the weakness of the flesh. But this season, for sentimental reasons, he didn't mind the false camaraderie inspired by booze which always arose at these affairs between executive vice presidents and lowly mail clerks. He didn't mind the flirting secretaries and the instantaneous friendliness of junior executives. He didn't mind because he knew that in a few short weeks he would never see any of them again and he had suddenly realized they were not, after all, a bad lot.

So he joked with his boss, kissed his secretary and patted the ass of a junior executive whose ass he had long wanted to pat. For the first time in his career at the bank Tom got into the spirit of "office Christianity" and arrived home, slightly aglow, about four in the afternoon. He showered as usual, put on his robe and sat in his living room surrounded by dozens of brochures, collected from as many travel agencies, on the city of London. Tonight was Dicky and Amy's Christmas Eve party, a big annual event, and then those two would be off to Palm Beach to officially open the season, or so Amy liked to think, with their big annual New Year's Eve party.

"Well, fuck them," Tom thought as he changed his mind for the tenth time in a week and decided not to go to the Culvers' gala. He was sure he had been invited as odd man, and he was sure the odd lady he was intended to amuse was his bridge partner, Nancy Maron. When Amy found something she thought worked, she stuck with it. But Tom liked Nancy. She wasn't a bad sort and could be, he suspected, a lot of fun. "Well, maybe I will go."

He began to examine his brochures which made London look like a cross between Eden and Shangri-la. Surely the city must have some bad aspects and even if it had only half as many as New York it was in a lot of trouble. As he looked at the gaily colored photos he knew that travel brochures were not what he needed. He wanted concrete information on London, not a vacationer's guidebook to castles and cathedrals. Tom wondered if he could get into banking there and grinned at the thought. He didn't know a shilling from a pound from a quid. What the hell *was* a quid? Yes, he would certainly take the London banking world by storm.

And then, quite suddenly, the feeling that something was wrong came over him. He had seen something that had not registered on his brain at the time, but now it came back to him and he was damned if he could remember what it was. Did he have his wallet when he came in? He went to the bedroom and there it was, in the leather caddy he always put it in when he got home. His keys were beside it. Where else could they be? He had used them to get into the apartment. He went to the kitchen; the oven was off and all the gas jets were closed as was the refrigerator door. But he had seen something. What the hell was it? He started back to the living room, stopped, and with a flutter under his breast returned to the kitchen.

It wasn't something he had seen. It was something he had not seen. The bottle of champagne was gone. Had someone broken in and taken it? Nonsense. . . why would anyone want to break into an apartment and take nothing but a bottle of champagne? True, Tom didn't own anything of great value but he did always keep a hundred dollars in cash buried under his clean shirts. He went back to his bedroom and opened the dresser drawer. Five twenties, right where they should be. Any thief worth his salt would have sniffed them out in two minutes. No, no one had broken into the apartment. Someone had entered it with a key and then locked the door behind them when they left and that someone was Nicky Three.

"Well, fuck him, too," Tom shouted. A lousy bottle of not very good champagne and he had to sneak in like a thief to get it back. "Fuck him in spades," he shouted even louder. "And he still has my key. I want my fucking key."

Tom lit a cigarette — he hadn't had one since Nicky left — and puffed furiously on it. "I should have flushed that cheap wine down the toilet, that's what I should have done. And why the hell didn't he take his goddamned robe and undershorts? What does he think this is, a fucking hotel?"

After the explosion, and hating himself for even entertaining the hope, Tom opened the refrigerator. It was there. . . the bottle of champagne, properly on its side, cooling, and next to it a similar bottle but with a label that bespoke the very best in imported French champagne.

"Holy shit," the roaring lion whimpered like a mouse.

Tom sat and waited. What he wanted to do was dance, or sing, or get drunk, but under the circumstances all he could do was sit and wait. Nicky had been there and he obviously intended to come back. It could mean everything or nothing. Tom lit another cigarette and looked at his watch. It was six o'clock.

An hour later it was, of all things, seven o'clock, and still no Nicky. Tom decided to make a positive move. He took off his robe and got into a pair of jeans and a shirt.

By seven-thirty he felt certain that Nicky was playing some macabre game and had no intention of showing up. Tom went back to his "fuck him" attitude, built himself a bourbon and soda and changed his mind, for the twelfth time, about going to the Culvers'. Now, he was going. He should be there no later than nine but all he had to do was change his clothes and jump into a cab. That would take no more than a half hour. He sipped his drink and lit another cigarette.

It began to snow. His tree, moving gently in the winter wind, turned white before his eyes. From the street below the sound of sleigh bells drifted into the apartment. Tom, well into his bourbon and not fully recovered from the ones he had had earlier in the day, began to cry. A real old-fashioned crying jag. "No one should be alone on Christmas Eve. Shit. . . no one should ever be alone.

"I wonder if Nancy would marry me. If she lives in the Culvers' apartment building she must be rich. I'll ask her tonight. Engaged at the Culvers' Christmas party in New York and married at the Culvers' New Year's party in Palm Beach. It should make all the society columns."

The dream was interrupted by the sound of a lock bolt being turned with a key.

"A guy could get lung cancer waiting for you."

Nicky, his hair and raincoat wet, appeared in the doorway. "You didn't have to wait."

"How the hell can I leave when some creep comes in and out of the place juggling champagne bottles as soon as I'm gone."

"You could have changed the lock."

"You could have returned the fucking key."

Nicky walked into the room and Tom stood up. They came face to face and each hesitated a brief second before their arms encircled each other as their bodies locked in a tight grip. Two tall, lean figures swaying in the center of the room as they laughed and cried and swore, all at the same time. Tom kissed Nicky's lips and cheeks and hair. He squeezed Nicky's shoulders and back and behind. "I can't believe you're really here."

"I'll be black and blue before you're convinced."

"Christ, you're all wet."

"That's apt to happen to a person who's just walked twenty blocks in a snowstorm."

"Don't be a smart ass. Change your clothes and I'll fix us a drink. The champagne?"

"That's just what I want."

"The good stuff or the cheap?"

"Let's save the good one for midnight."

An hour later it was as if they had never been apart. They sat in the snug room, the snow falling outside and the television tuned to a station which, as it did every Christmas Eve, showed nothing but a Yule log burning in a fireplace as carollers filled the soundtrack. Nicky related the events of the past two days. "She left me some money, not much, about five thousand bucks. I think it was all she had." It sounded like a lot to Tom whose savings account was just about that much but had taken years to accumulate. "The apartment was rented furnished so all I have to do is pack Aunt Marie's things and ship them to her."

"And then?"

Nicky shrugged. "Sink or swim, I guess, and you know how well I swim."

"Before you start swimming you have to have a place to live. Have you thought about that?"

"I could get a small studio for under five hundred a month." It was more a question than a statement.

"You could also win a lottery for million bucks but I wouldn't hold my breath waiting for either. You're going to live right here."

Nicky, even if he had wanted to, could not hide the relief Tom's words offered. For the first time since entereing the apartment he relaxed completely, his body almost sagging before Tom's eyes. "You know I want you with me, Nicky."

"I know and. . . well, I'm sorry I walked out like I did."

"You never gave me a chance to explain."

"I was sorry the minute I did it."

"Then why the hell didn't you come back?"

"Pride. What else?"

"Do you know I walked up and down West End Avenue, looking for you, until I was almost arrested for loitering?"

Nicky laughed. "I'm glad."

"About that picture—"

"Not now, Tommy. . . look. . . it's almost midnight, open the other bottle."

Tom got out two crystal glasses and filled them with the Moët. "You know, this is the first Christmas I feel like. . . ." Tom hesitated, looking for the right word.

"Like you belong?"

"Yeah, exactly. How did you know?"

"Because I feel the same way."

"Merry Christmas, Nicky."

"Merry Christmas, Tom."

Tom Bradshaw was no longer alone in the world, alone in his room, alone in his bed. They lay side by side, listening to each other breathe as if the sound was as miraculous as the holiday they had just celebrated. "This is the first night I've ever spent without my aunt and uncle."

"And you're the first person to ever spend the night in this bed. Besides me, that is."

"Bullshit." Nicky could now say the word without a trace of embarrassment in his voice.

"Would I lie to you?"

"You would."

"If it wasn't Christmas I would toss your ass out in the snow."

"Christmas — and I don't have a present for you."

"I'll accept the Moët as the best Christmas gift I ever got."

"And what are you giving me?"

Tom took Nicky's hand in his and answered, "The best Christmas gift you've ever had. . . me."

107

"Santa Claus would never approve."

"What does he know about love?"

London — 1956

Alexis met Erica at Heathrow amid a crowd bundled in great coats and mufflers. The frigid temperture was all that prevented the lead-gray sky from unloading its burden of snow over half of England but the shivering Londoners knew it was only a matter of time before the predicted blizzard would whitewash the city and its suburbs.

"You look very big, my dear, but healthy," Alexis greeted her.

"And you look like the bastard you are."

Neither exchanged another word during the long drive from the airport to Alexis's country home. The only words he uttered in the car were, "We have arrived, Mrs. Hall," as he steered the car through an iron gate and up a drive that led to an old Tudor house.

Alexis's sisters, Tatiana and Marie, showed Erica to a comfortable room. "If you want anything all you need do is pull the cord." The one called Marie spoke and indicated an ornate bellpull near the large bed. "My sister or I will come at once." There was an air about these two women which reminded Erica of their brother and the mystique she associated with him. But Alexis worked and moved about modern London. His sisters spoke and acted like characters from a turn-of-the-century play. Theirs was a look and manner Erica thought had died with the first shot fired in the first world war.

"Have you always lived here?" Erica asked the women.

"For a very long time," Marie answered. "With my mother and father and another sister, Olga."

"Did Olga marry?"

"No," Marie told her, "she died of an illness several years ago. Our parents are also now dead."

The snow began to fall at dusk and Erica began her labor before dawn. Shortly after a local midwife came to attend her. "When will the doctor come?" Erica wanted to know.

"There'll be no doctor, dearie, but you needn't fear, I've delivered more young'uns than half the swells on Harley Street."

Erica's scream rang through the old house. "I hate him. I hate him. I hate him."

It was close to midnight when the midwife entered the dimly-lit parlor where the women and Alexis, called from London, were seated. She wiped her sweating forehead with the back of her hand as she announced, "It's all over. Mum and babies doing very well, indeed."

Alexis jumped out of his chair. "A boy?" he asked anxiously.

"Babies?" Tatiana cried.

"Yes to both of you. Two boys if you please and both as healthy an' pink as the Lord knows how to make 'em."

Alexis ran out of the room, pulling the midwife with him.

"Easy, sir," she protested, "I've had a hard time, I've had."

Erica was sound asleep, an infant nestled under each arm.

"Which was the first born?" Alexis demanded.

"The one on the right, sir. You see, I put a string on his tiny wrist. I know my job, sir."

The room was deathly still. Alexis moved toward the bed and carefully took the infant in his hands and lifted him high in the air.

"Careful, sir," the midwife cautioned. "You don't want to wake him now, what with his mum just getting her bit of peace."

Alexis did not hear the woman. He stared at the infant for a long time and then whispered, "Nicholas. Nicholas, my son. Nicholas the Third." The infant began to scream.

Erica tried to ignore the two tots who fed at her breast but her efforts were in vain. She grew to love them more every day. The boys' aunts, Tatiana and Marie, were constantly in and out of Erica's room, doting on the new babies as much, if not more, as did their mother and Erica was grateful for their company and compliments. The children had brought joy into the old Tudor house.

"They are identical," Tatiana said. "If it were not for the string on his wrist I would not know Nicky."

"Why is he called Nicholas?" Erica asked.

"We must buy two bracelets," Marie continued as if Erica had not spoken. "One gold and one silver. Two tiny, delicate bracelets."

"Why is he called Nicholas?" Erica repeated.

"It is an old family name," Marie answered and then, as if the question had recalled a nagging thought, she blurted, "You must not hate Alexis. If you knew the truth, you would understand."

"What is the truth?" Erica asked.

"She has said too much already," Tatiana answered for her sister.

Erica turned her back on the women and stared at the white landscape outside her window. "They are as crazy as he is," she thought.

The following weekend Alexis arrived from London with an armful of presents for the twins and an exquisite diamond and sapphire pin, in the shape of the sign Gemini, for Erica. "It's beautiful, Alexis, and appropriate."

"You see, I am a normal new father."

"And I am a typical new mother."

Erica had been thinking about this moment all week. She had rehearsed what she would say but she had not planned on performing this soon. She wanted more time to win Alexis's sympathy and understanding but seeing him now, with all those presents for two infants who wouldn't be able to enjoy them for months and months, he looked so happy and, as he had just said himself, normal. And the gift he had given her! He could not refuse her anything at this moment.

"I am sure you are, my dear." Alexis refused to meet her gaze.

"I want to keep the children." She could hear her heart beat as she spoke the words.

"That is not possible, Erica." His tone was not threatening and Erica took courage from this. "We made a bargain, remember?"

"You used me, Alexis, and now you must have some pity on me. I am their mother and I can't bear even the thought of having to give them up. Please try to understand."

"I do understand, but it is not possible." His voice was hesitant. He was afraid and Erica knew it.

She took a deep breath and said as calmly as possible. "If you don't let me have them I will expose them and you to the world."

Alexis smiled his sad smile. "So now it is you who threaten me."

"You told me once that without an heir your life was meaningless. Now you have two heirs and therefore twice as much reason to live. You're hiding something, Alexis. Marie as much as told me that today. She spoke about a truth she could not reveal. Now a scandal would hurt you as much as me. Perhaps more."

Alexis moved to the window and pretended to look out at the rapidly darkening winter sky. "Marie is foolish and you are still an over-imaginative child. A scandal would also hurt them," he said, indicating the crib where the two boys slept. "Have you thought of that?'

"They are young, they will survive."

"So the mother of my sons is a fighter. Good. . . I am glad." He left the window and moved across the room to the crib. His eyes reflected the activity going on in his mind. "Can we strike another bargain, Erica?" he said, looking at the sleeping infants and not at her.

"My father once told me the history of the civilized world could be related in terms of bargains."

"A very smart man, the Ambassador." He turned from the crib to face Erica. "There are two children and two of us. You have read Dumas?"

Erica was shocked. "We are talking about human life, not romantic novels."

"When you wanted to abort you were talking about human life, too, my dear."

Erica avoided his gaze. As intended, she had no answer for this.

"Think, Erica, a public scandal would solve nothing. Neither of us would emerge a winner." Now he came to her and touched her arm. "I never wanted to be cruel to you, my dear. Please believe that. And what I am suggesting now is just and fair. I will keep Nicky. The other is yours. Believe me, it is the only way."

⊠

Two months later Mr. and Mrs. Anthony Hall and their son, Eric, returned to the United States to make their permanent home in New York.

12

Tom Bradshaw never made it to London but thanks to Nicky he was transported, without moving an inch, to a magic land no travel brochure could offer. On Christmas Day they trampled across the virgin snow in Central Park, rented skates, and spent hours showing off to each other on the ice. Tom was surprised at how good a skater Nicky was and, as they cavorted like little boys, he began to realize how little he knew about the young man he had taken into his home as a friend and lover. Occasionally they clung to each other for support and the gesture held more meaning than just trying to keep afoot on the slick ice. Both friendless for so long, each now looked upon the other as a savior brought forth, as it were, on a very appropriate day.

Christmas Night, cold and exhausted, they showered together, ate hamburgers together, drank beer together and talked, sometimes vying for the floor, as if they had just been blessed with the power of speech.

"If I'm going to live here do I have any say in the decor?" Nicky asked.

"What decor?"

"For openers, the paper you bought for the bathroom."

"What's wrong with it?"

"It would take less time to tell you what's not wrong with it."

"My God, I'm harboring a fag decorator."

"Do you think I could become a decorator?"

"I'll let you know after I see the new wallpaper."

112

They packed Marie Romaine's belongings and shipped them off to England. They moved Nicky's clothes into Tom's apartment and Tom was awed not only by the quantity but also the quality of Nicky's wardrobe. It was all Saville Row and Fifth Avenue. "He treated you like a prince," Tom exclaimed.

"But I told you that."

The apartment off Central Park West was also the recipient of a television set, much better than Tom's, a stereo, infinitely better than Tom's, and a collection of books that almost amounted to a mini library. There were all the classics, of course, but more in evidence were romance and adventure novels and mystery thrillers. Tom knew they represented the vicarious life Nicky had lived until now and he wondered if he could make Nicky's dreams of an adventurous life a reality. Tom thought he could, and not only for Nicky Three but for Tom Bradshaw as well.

"Where's the porn?" Tom demanded.

"Never touch the stuff."

"Cut the crap. . . where do you keep it hidden?"

Nicky shook his head. "I used to buy them, read them and toss them. I was afraid they would see it."

"Did they ever go through your personal stuff?"

"Never, but I didn't want to take the chance."

"God, they must have known you had a sex life even if it was just between you and your fist. Didn't Alexis and you ever have a man-to-man?"

"I told you, no. That's what he paid tutors for. But once, in London, he asked me if I wanted to go to a. . . you know, a house."

"A bordello? Holy shit. And you refused."

"With Uncle Alexis supervising, would you?"

"Hell, no."

Tom was disappointed about the porn. Nicky's tastes in that area would have given Tom more insight into what Nicky Three was all about. But Tom was reasonably sure that there had been no strictly gay stuff, or very little of it, in Nicky's erotic reading. Nicky's jack-off hero was made of the same stuff as the heroes of his adventure novels: all macho on the outside and all heart on the inside. In short, about as realistic a picture of the male animal as the plots which evolve about them. However, that was the type that had introduced the young boy to sex and what has kindled the flame is usually what we stick to all our lives. Tom was secretly pleased. If this was what Nicky wanted, and Nicky had picked

Tom... well, it certainly said something about Nicky's image of Tom Bradshaw.

Tom had no complaints about Nicky's performance in the bedroom. On the contrary, he was delighted as he watched Nicky go from shy, inexperienced beginner, to apt, interested pupil, to demanding partner. Tom had the best of all possible sexual experiences wrapped in one neat package. Like everything else about Nicky Three it was unique.

Invitations to several New Year's Eve parties arrived and Tom showed them all to Nicky. "We spent our first Christmas together, alone, and I want to spend our first New Year the same way." Nicky happily agreed, and after that no longer hinted of wanting to meet Tom's friends or of going out more often. The reason, obviously, was that Nicky was frightened. He had just been cast out of a secure life situation and had no intention of having it happen again. He was an intelligent man who had recently learned that freedom, too, had its price; he wasn't as yet able to ante up.

After the holidays they settled down to a simple, domestic routine life. Tom worked and Nicky kept house. And Tom, of all people, liked it. He wouldn't admit the fact, not even to himself, but he liked it. None of his supposed friends contacted him after the rush of holiday parties to see what had happened to him and to inquire, for curiosity if for no other reason, if he were alive or dead. He told himself he didn't give a shit even though he did. Nicky, however, was more than enough balm to soothe the deepest of wounds and now that the euphoria of discovery had given way to the peace of acceptance, Tom once again began to make plans for his and Nicky's future, the blueprint of which contained no spot labeled "simple, domestic routine life." If dreams of bliss are one of life's blessings, then not knowing when one has come true is life's greatest curse.

▨

"I don't know what to say," Nicky sighed as he sat on the living room floor, looking somewhat pale, surrounded by Tom's collection of Eric Hall clippings and photos.

"I wanted you to see this because I want you to know everything. No more secrets, Nicky. It was because of this that I lost you once and I don't want it to happen again."

Nicky picked up one of the photographs of Eric. "I feel like I did the first time I saw him, sort of sick to the stomach. Christ, it's me. Every one of these photos looks like me."

"Now maybe you can understand how I felt the first time I saw

114

you at the Y. It wasn't a question of you or him, or of substituting you for him. You see now that I had to get to know you because I really thought you were Eric. I almost went off my rocker just thinking about it. When I got to know you I thought about Eric less and less, and you were all that mattered."

"Was it like you said? Were you and Eric just friends?"

Tom opened his arms in a gesture of despair. "I said no more secrets. If it wasn't like that I would tell you. Nicky, Eric Hall and I were worlds apart. If this country were a monarchy Eric would be the Prince of Wales. I just happend to sit next to him in one class and we became friends. . . and not very close friends. The idea of it becoming something more was in my head, and in my head only."

"How do you figure it, Tom? I mean the resemblance. The odds against it happening by accident are incalculable."

Tom shook his head. "But it did happen." He pointed to the photos. "There's the proof. Nature fucked up, I guess."

"Oh, Tom—"

"Why not? I mean why the hell not? Look, there are billions, maybe trillions of combinations of genes and once in a million eons a set falls into identical slots in two different wombs. Do you know the theory of the monkey and the typewriter?"

Nicky grinned. "Enlighten me."

"They say that if you sit a monkey at a typewriter and teach him how to punch the keys, and let him do it for a million years, he'll one day punch out a Shakespeare sonnet. There are just so many letters in the English alphabet, twenty-six to be exact, and just so many combinations that form words and the rest is obvious."

"Obvious," Nicky shouted. "The only thing that's obvious is that you can't sit the same monkey at the same typewriter for a million years so the theory can never be proved. Just like the gambler can't stand at a dice table for a million years until he finally throws a thousand straight passes in a row. Believe me, a lot of guys have died paupers trying to prove your theory."

"Don't be an asshole, Nicky."

"Me? You're the asshole."

"I'm a genius, and you just answered your own question. Genes have been around for millions of years and people have been combining them for millions of years. All shapes, sizes and colors of people. . . all the possible combinations. So why, after eons, couldn't two eggs and two sperms unite to turn out two of you?"

Tom had the uncanny knack of ingesting a little knowledge, mixing it with some imagination and spewing out a seemingly irrefutable statement.

Nicky, as intended, had no reply, but he wasn't fooled either. "I won't say it's impossible because nothing, I guess, is impossible. But I'm not buying the monkey and the typewriter." And before Tom had a chance to protest he added, "Or the eons of gene combinations. Shit, Tom, he's my twin but it's just not possible."

"I know... I thought the same thing a thousand times and came up with the same answer. It's not possible, even if you were both born on the same day and in the same year."

"What?" If Nicky wasn't already there he would have fallen to the floor.

"I forgot to tell you. Eric Hall would have been twenty-eight next month. The seventeenth."

Nicky opened his mouth but no words came out. He seemed to be struggling to breathe. "Are you okay?" Tom asked.

"No, I'm not okay. Tommy, there are no words to describe what I'm feeling. I mean... there are no words."

"Now you can appreciate how I felt when I discovered you."

Nicky laughed, a slight hysteria to the sound. "Discovered me? Like the source of the Nile or a cure for the clap. Jesus Christ, Tommy...."

Tom stood up. "You want a beer?" Nicky nodded a response and Tom went to the kitchen. When he returned, carrying two cans of beer, he found Nicky once again engrossed in the Eric Hall collection.

"He was a rich bastard," Nicky said to one of the clippings.

"Here's your beer."

"And a handsome one," Nicky continued.

Tom laughed. "Nice to have you back in our world. For a minute there I thought you were going to freak out on me."

"So did I." Nicky drank straight from the can. "It's just something I have to get used to, I guess. I have a twin and we're not related. How does that grab you?"

"I've had months to get used to it and, by the way, Eric Hall was not a bastard. He was documented for five generations back, on both sides of the family tree."

"Uncle Alexis told me we could trace our family back over a thousand years." Nicky seemed proud of the fact and it was the first time Tom had seen him exhibit this pose.

"Uncle Alexis was crazy."

"I wish you wouldn't keep saying that."

"Never again. . . I promise. Where were we? Oh, yeah, Eric and his money. When Eric turned twenty-one he came into a trust of fifty million dollars." Nicky appeared very impressed. "When the ambassador died a little more came his way."

"How much more can there be?'

"A lot, Nicky, a hell of a lot. If he had outlived his grandmother he would have gotten another fifty at least and when, had they both lived, his mother died he would—"

"Stop it. . . there's not that much money in the world."

"Oh, but there is, my friend, believe me there is."

"And where's all that money now?"

"Well, it's the old lady's but it gets tricky. You see, Eric's body and his mother's were never recovered. They were presumed dead but there was no corpus delicti, so their money was placed in trust for a period of seven years. . . that's when they'll be declared legally dead. . . and then it goes to old Mrs. Lindenhurst. . . including the interest." Tom spoke from dimly remembered newspaper accounts of Eric's and his mother's fortunes published at the time of their deaths.

Nicky stated, "You know an awful lot about him and his money, Tommy."

Tom waved at the Eric Hall collection which now cluttered the floor and answered, "The very rich are my hobby."

"Then what am I doing here?"

"You have sex appeal, and that's also a hobby of mine."

"I'd rather have the money."

"You can."

Nicky's head jerked upward and his eyes met Tom's. They stared at each other; one determined, the other uncertain. Neither wanted to be the first to avert his eyes but it was Tom who, with the slightest flutter, blinked first. "What did you say?" Nicky whispered.

Tom relaxed and, as if talking about the weather, answered, "I said, it could all be yours."

Now Nicky relaxed, smiled and then laughed aloud. "For a minute, I thought you were serious."

"About what?"

"Me, passing myself off as Eric Hall."

"I never said that, you did."

"Come off it, Tom. To get his money I would have to pretend to be him."

"And you could do it."

"Sure... here I am, heir to the millions, start shoveling it over."

"It wouldn't be quite that easy."

"I'll say it wouldn't."

"But it could be done."

Nicky sat up, raised his knees, and encircled them with his arms. "You know, this just didn't pop up out of the thin air. You've been thinking about this for some time." To Tom's relief Nicky sounded amused.

"No more secrets... yes, I have been thinking about it for some time."

"And it really is funny. It's too stupid an idea to be anything but funny."

"If you would listen to me for a minute you might find out that it's not a joke but a very viable plan."

"I'm all ears."

"Don't be a smart ass and wipe that shit-eating grin off your face." Tom sat forward in his chair and Nicky bent toward him, his blue eyes wide and alert and bright with glee. At least, Tom thought, he hasn't stormed out the front door. "Now," Tom began, "no one who knew Eric knows you."

"So that's why I was never allowed to meet your friends."

"I told you to shut up and listen."

"Am I right?"

"Yes, dammit, you're right, now just shut up." Tom once again tried to collect his thoughts. "No one in the city knows you, except me. It might even be safe to say no one in the world knows you, except me. Eric's body, as we know, was never found. You look exactly like Eric, and you can't argue that fact. So... you become Eric."

"Back from the dead, just like that." Nicky snapped his fingers at Tom.

"No, not just like that. We have to build a case, make all the pieces fit and then," Tom snapped his fingers at Nicky's face, "just like that."

"But I never knew the guy. I know nothing about him. Suppose they ask me something real tricky like my address or phone number or the color of my toothbrush? Pie in the sky, Bradshaw, forget it."

"I'll teach you everything you need to know."

"You? What do you know? These newspaper items...
Tommy, they're more bullshit than fact."

Tom, having rehearsed this scene a long time, remained calm
and was ready to counter any objection raised by Nicky. "I was at
school with him and I know his friends. I've done a little research,
as you can see, and all I want you to know is what I know. You're
not supposed to know too much."

Nicky hit his forehead with the palm of his hand. "Amnesia...
I should have known. Tommy, that plot went out with hoop
skirts."

"Suppose I told you your Uncle Alexis wasn't dead." Tom once
again got up and headed for the kitchen, speaking as he went.
"Well, what would you say if I told you Alexis Romaine wasn't
dead?"

"I would say it was a lie. I would say prove it."

"And suppose I did prove it," Tom called from the other room.
"How?"

"By bringing Uncle Alexis into this apartment, alive, and having you talk to him." Tom returned with two more cans of beer.
"Then what would you say?"

Nicky shrugged. "I would say he was still alive. What else
could I say?"

Tom settled back into his chair. "See? No matter what story we
hand out the end result will be you, Eric, standing before them,
alive and well. They have to believe it because there you are, in the
flesh." Tom spoke in earnest now. "You understand what I'm saying. Only the final fact, Eric alive, is relevant."

Nicky seemed to be thinking it over. "His grandmother would
certainly know her own grandson."

"Mrs. Lindenhurst is near eighty and senile."

"Aunt Marie is near eighty and sharp as a butcher's knife."

"Some people make it and some don't. Mrs. Lindenhurst suffered the loss of her entire family, all at once. She's mentally confused. All she wants is to have her family back and we're going to
give her her grandson. She'll welcome you with open arms. Christ,
we'll be doing the old lady a favor."

"You can rationalize anything, Tom."

"Well, what do we have to lose?"

"About twenty years of our lives. No, my life, you'd be out of it.
It's illegal, Tom. It's robbery, and worse."

"Only if we get caught."

The conversation was not going as Tom had intended. He was rambling, not presenting his case logically, in sequence, as he had so meticulously thought it out. This, he knew, was because of Nicky's constant interruptions and questions. But Nicky was fast becoming the plus side of Tom's initial proposal. For one thing Nicky had not bolted as Tom feared he might. For another, Tom couldn't help but notice not only Nicky's interest but, more important, the slight tinge of excitement in Nicky's attitude. Tom knew, in fact he had counted on it, that Nicky was doing what he had done all his life. Living, vicariously, the plot of one of his adventure novels. But now he was doing it actively, not mentally, and even had someone to share it with. He was one of the characters, indeed, the lead character, in what he must have thought of as the planning of a "caper." Nicky could not resist the temptation. Besides, he thought it was all in jest and, like his daydreams, would never come to pass.

"How did Eric survive?" Nicky was asking.

"It took fifteen minutes for the Coast Guard to reach the wreck. That's a long time, and more than enough time for a small craft to have spotted the yacht and reached it in time to save at least one of the passengers."

"So where's the rescuer? He saves the life of the richest kid in the world and keeps his mouth shut about it"

"You would too, if you were a smuggler."

Nicky pounded his fist into the carpet. "It's too fantastic," he responded, loving every fantastic minute of it.

"Is it? In the old days they used to smuggle liquor into the country and Montauk was one of the major seaports of entry. There are hundeds of small coves and inlets for a small boat to tie up in and unload. Now, they smuggle in marijuana and shit like that. The Coast Guard's had several stakeouts in the area." Nicky's excitement proved contagious and the director turned actor as Tom became increasingly animated as he spoke. He reached for the pack of cigarettes which usually lasted the two of them for a week but was destined to be totally consumed on this memorable evening. "You want one?"

"Yes."

Tom inhaled deeply and passed the lighted match to Nicky. "A smuggler would have a small boat and a fast one. If he happened to be near the scene of the accident he could have picked up Eric and gotten him well out of sight a good ten minutes before the Coast Guard arrived."

"And what did he do with him?"

"Took him to Block Island, where he lives."

"And Eric, a victim of amnesia, stayed there," Nicky concluded.

"And the smuggler, whether he knew who Eric was or not, kept his mouth shut. He had no choice."

"Not bad, but it does have its flaws," Nicky said.

"But it *is* possible," Tom countered.

"Oh, it's very possible."

"That's all I care about."

"Now how does Eric find his way into the arms of Thomas Bradshaw?"

"I'm working on that."

"Continued next week, music swells, fade, the end. You should write soap operas, Tommy."

"I can't figure you out sometimes, Nicky," Tom said. "I thought you would be sore as hell about all this and you're not."

Nicky grinned. "Why would I be sore?"

"You know damn well why. A few weeks ago you would have accused me of cultivating your friendship, to put it delicately, just so I could pull this off."

"You pulled off something else along the way." Nicky laughed at his own pun and then became very serious. "Yeah, I would have thought that because it's true. This is what you wanted me for." Tom tried to object but Nicky stopped him with a wave of his hand. "No secrets, remember. But what I know and you don't is that you want me, rich or poor, and not Eric, but you'll learn."

"You're pretty damn sure of yourself," Tom answered, wondering why Nicky's statement suddenly made him feel very uncomfortable.

"I'm surer of myself than you are of you."

"Will you do it?"

"Never."

"Will you think about it?"

"Maybe."

"We could start easy. I'll teach you everything I know about Eric Lindenhurst Hall."

"Fuck off, Tommy."

"Can I call you Eric?"

"Try it and I'll belt you."

"Or the Duke, that was his nickname."

"Duke? Why?"

"We used to watch old newsreels at school, you know, going

back to the thirties and forties and once we saw clips of the young Duke of Windsor and believe it or not he looked just like Eric. Just like you," Tom added, surprised at his own revelation. "So he got the name Duke and it stuck."

"Uncle Alexis hated the Duke of Windsor."

"Why?"

Nicky looked embarrassed. "Something about giving up a throne when others go begging for one."

Tom shook his head. "Uncle Alexis—"

"Don't say it, Tom."

"Okay, I won't."

13

Tom knew better than to push, but gradually over the following weeks he began to educate Nicky on the life of Eric Lindenhurst Hall. Tom, a born storyteller, and Nicky, an attentive listener, spent the long winter evenings practicing these talents. It proved to be a chore for neither; Tom liked nothing better than to expound on his favorite topic and Nicky always enjoyed hearing about people whose comings and goings were deemed important enough to be reported by the press.

Strangely enough, as they relived Eric Hall's life in bits and pieces, Tom and Nicky got to know each other more intimately than years of living together could have achieved. Tom spoke of Eric in the light of his own experiences and often compared Eric to himself in order to make his point. Nicky, in turn, interpreted Tom's words and responded to them as could only one who had been raised in such a unique manner. They were analyst and patient, with Eric playing the part of a Rorschach inkblot in which each saw himself.

"It was never the money that I envied Eric," Tom said, "It was the security. When I was small I thought my grandmother was very, very old and I think I worried about what would happen to me if she died. Once I came home from school and she was asleep on the couch, something she had never done, and I was petrified. I stood over her, staring down, not even realizing that she couldn't be dead because she was breathing. No, I had to shake her and wake her up before I was convinced. Then I had diarrhea for two days and couldn't leave the house."

"I never felt insecure," Nicky responded. "Just lonely. I guess we each focus in on our most obvious need. God knows I should have felt insecure. At least your grandmother was a flesh-and-blood relation; I had no one."

The lessons, if they could be called that, were never formal occasions. They arose naturally, in general conversation, and Tom allowed them to take whatever direction interested Nicky at that given moment. Tom's tests were more a joke, a game whose rules only they knew, than an accurate measure of what Nicky was learning. Walking through the park on a chilly Sunday morning Tom would suddenly ask, "Who did you room with at prep school?"

"The first year, Ken Brandt and Dicky Culver. Then we went two to a room. Dicky and me, Ken and . . . I don't remember."

"Neither do I, if I ever knew. Who did you date when you were at Yale?"

"Everyone."

"Who was your special girl?"

"Ronnie, for Veronica, Attwood, with two T's."

"Did you have an affair with her?"

"I never discuss my sex life."

If Nicky was disinterested one wouldn't know it from his answers. He was becoming as much an expert on Eric Hall as was Tom Bradshaw. And then one day they crossed the park to the East Side and Tom felt like a general taking an inexperienced recruit on a reconnaissance mission. They were in enemy territory and at any minute one of the enemy could materialize. Tom was becoming as childishly excited about his caper as he had induced Nicky to become. "Don't get upset if I suddenly wrap my scarf around your face."

"Try it and I'll kick you in the balls."

"For one raised by British tutors you certainly have a colorful vocabulary."

"What the hell are you talking about? I was raised on East Ninety-second Street by my parents, grandparents and a Scotch nanny."

Tom put his arm around Nicky's shoulders, hugged him, and held him like that as they marched up Fifth Avenue and turned east on, naturally, Ninety-second Street.

They stood across the street from a mansion that had been built at the turn of the century when the very rich could indulge themselves in townhouses that rivaled the châteaux of France. Its width was that of four New York brownstones, at least, and it was five stories high. Red brick, casement windows and two oak doors replete with brass knockers completed the picture of elegance as gleaned by the robber barons of the nineteenth century.

"What do you think?" Tom asked.

"It's a castle."

"If you knocked on that door and the old lady who lives there opened it she would faint on the spot."

"I don't think I want to do that to an old lady."

"You're right. We've got to use a more gentle approach."

"Let's get out of here."

"What's the matter? Don't you like your house?"

"Come on, she might be looking out the window."

Now why didn't I think of that, Tom pondered as Nicky dragged him back toward Fifth Avenue.

One night during dinner Tom cautioned Nicky, and not for the first time, on the one kink he feared would upset all their plans. "Dicky Culver," he exclaimed. "That's the bastard we have to worry about."

"You really dislike him, don't you."

"I don't dislike him, Nicky, I hate the fuck."

"Why?"

"Because his pomposity is second only to that of his wife. They think they're Mr. and Mrs. King Shit whom the world should stop and bow to whenever they walk by. Have you heard how rotten the weather has been in Palm Beach? I'm so glad."

Nicky suppressed a smile. "What you mean, Tommy, is that they spotted you for a four-flusher from day one and you can't stand it."

"Not they... her. Dicky doesn't have two brain cells that mesh. You see, Dicky thought Eric was his private property and off with the head of anyone who trespassed."

"And you trespassed."

Tom let out a sound that was something between a moan and a grunt. "Eric liked me. We had a few good times together. We went to a movie once and had a few drinks on very rare occasions. Christ, Culver thought I had married the guy."

"So he started calling you names." This was Nicky's meat-and-gravy-type talk. He loved hearing about the episodes in people's lives that showed them interacting, especially in the heat of passion, with other poeple. For him it was the page of a novel come to life.

"He would have, if he had known what names to call me, but

125

all he could do was sizzle like a lit fuse connected to nothing. Then Amy came up to the campus one weekend, met me, and told Culver I was social shit. Almost ten years later she still hasn't changed her mind."

"From what you've told me about Eric I'm surprised he was so buddy-buddy with someone like Dicky Culver."

"I don't think Eric ever saw that side of Dicky. Hell, he had no reason to. But they were buddy-buddy, from the first grade till ever after. Listen, it was once hinted around school that they knew each other in the Biblical sense."

"Do you think they did?"

"Maybe some friendly jack-off sessions when they were kids but nothing after that. Shit, Eric had taste."

"I think we should be more worried about Amy than Dicky," Nicky suggested.

"How right you are. They've always reminded me of Sherlock Holmes and Dr. Watson and you know which one is Sherlock. Christ, when she starts on the trail of something she's like a fucking bloodhound. Did I tell you how she started to give me the needle about not knowing a single girl I had an affair with? You would think every woman in town had to call Amy the minute they spread their legs for someone."

Nicky was really enjoying himself. "She suspects you're a closet case, Tommy, and she's going to sniff you out. Do you know what a bloodhound could do if it ever got its teeth on your nuts?"

"You are getting to be the most verbally graphic bastard I have ever had to listen to and I'm not a closet case, you know what I think of them."

"What did Shakespeare say about the gentleman who doth protest too much?"

"I think Shakespeare had his own problems."

"That reminds me, I had a real bad nightmare last night."

"Really, do you remember it?"

"Do I ever. I was in this strange room with a monkey who was sitting at a typewriter, pounding away, and I walked up to him to see what he was writing. . . ."

Tom was rocking with laughter. "And what was he writing, smart ass?"

"I've been sitting at this fucking machine for a million years and I have to take a piss. HELP!!!"

Tom was laughing so hard he could hardly speak and when he

126

did the words came out in short gasps. "Nicky... I... love you...
I really do."

"And I feel the same way about you, so why don't we cut this
Eric Hall crap, chuck the hundred million and live happily ever
after in blissful poverty." Nicky spoke with such sincerity that
Tom almost... almost... conceded to the plea.

"But why can't we have the money *and* each other?"

"Why? Because Eric Hall won't live here, that's why. He'll live
in that mansion across the park. And from what I understand Eric
Hall will be lionized by a sweet old lady and a hundred friends, not
to mention lawyers and bankers, so he won't be able to come and go
as he pleases. Tom, I'll be right back where I fucking started from."

"But it won't last forever. Just until the old—"

Nicky nodded. "Go on and say it. Just until the old lady dies. I
don't want a relationship predicated on someone's death. I got my
freedom because Uncle Alexis died and I still feel guilt about that."

"Well, don't. People die, especially old people, that's a fact of
life. Get used to it, Nicky, and grow up."

And so it went, give and take, and Nicky Three gave as much as
he took. *You can't say he doesn't try.* Tom had once used those
words to describe Nicky and now he realized how true they were.
Nicky Three was a fighter and whether this came to him from he-
redity or was the result of Alexis Romaine's upbringing Tom didn't
know but he certainly felt, on more than one occasion, the thrust of
this side of Nicky's nature. Tom was streetwise; Nicky intelligent.
Tom was clever and Nicky was shrewd. Were they enemies Nicky
would have won the battle of wits hands down, but they weren't
enemies, they were friends... and more. Nicky, above all else, was
a romantic. He was the hero of his novels and movies: steel on the
outside and butter on the inside. Tom had merely to appear offended and the steel bent. Tom had merely to touch the nape of
Nicky's neck and the butter melted. The intellect is slave to the
emotion. Tom would win.

"What about the newspapers and television and all those tabloids I see on the newsstands," Nicky began on another occasion.
"They'll cover the Eric Hall saga as if it were the second coming and
they won't let it alone until they ferret out every detail. Heir Re-
turns From The Grave. Rich Kid Rises From The Waves. And one of
those buggers will say I've been living in the belly of a whale for the
past two years."

"You should have been a copywriter, Nicky."

127

"And you should have been committed."

"The media is going to be our number one ally. Have you ever watched the news on television? It's ten percent fact and ninety percent show biz. Two pretty guys and a gal; one black, one white and one yellow, bringing you live soap opera every night at six and eleven. Babies falling out of windows, cancer patients being denied medical treatment, slumlords raising rents, everything but Uncle Tom and Little Eva sweeping out the cabin. Of course they'll cover the Eric Hall story and play it for all it's worth, but they won't toss Eric back into the Atlantic. Their audience wouldn't stand for it. What they're handing out is "there but for the grace of God go I" and hope. You will be their hope item for two days, and that's it, two days. The news does not do reruns. Then you'll be as forgotten as last year's Washington scandal."

"Suppose they want to interview me?"

Tom answered with a sigh, "You're going to be Eric Lindenhurst Hall. What they want doesn't mean shit. Mrs. Lindenhurst can pick up the phone and instantly be connected with the president of this nation. They can ask for an interview but they won't get one and if they get annoying the old lady will make that phone call and believe me, they will annoy no more."

"But what about the people who know me now?" Nicky tried a different approach. "The doormen at the apartment on West End Avenue and some neighbors I used to say a few words to when we met."

"Nicky, when Eric Hall drowned his picture made the front page of every newspaper in New York and, I'm sure, most of the papers in the United States and Europe, not to mention the television coverage. Has anyone, besides me, ever told you you look like Eric or asked you if you were Eric?"

Nicky was genuinely surprised and impressed. "I never thought of that. No, they haven't."

"Of course not. People don't memorize press photos or images they see briefly on television. That's what advertising and public relations are all about: constantly bombarding the public with a product or its name until the customer does become familiar with it. Even movie actors don't get recognized on the street after one film. Hell, it takes years and a lot of press before they do. If your doormen or your old neighbors see you in the newspapers or on television they might say he looks like someone who used to live here, but I doubt even that."

Tom had a point and Nicky knew it. "Maybe you're right."

"Not maybe. I am right. Let me show you something I've been saving just for this moment." Tom went into the bedroom and came back holding a press phot. He handed it to Nicky. "What do you see?"

"A man... about our age, give or take a few years. Curly hair, glasses, wearing a t-shirt... that's what I see."

"Who is he?"

"Hell, I don't know. Should I?"

"You should if you think the few people who know you will recognize you as Nicky Three when you appear as Eric Hall. This, Nicky, is a photo of Laurance Rockefeller, as rich as Eric Hall and from a family even more celebrated than the Lindenhursts. His father also happened to be the governor of this state for a dozen years. He was lost in the jungles of New Guinea and never found. This picture made the front page of every newspaper in the world."

"I remember when it happened," Nicky said, "so I must have seen that picture."

"I'm sure you did and so did most of the people in this town, but show it to any of them and I'll give you a hundred bucks for every person who knows who he is and you won't make a penny. Fleeting images, Nicky, fleeting... no one remembers because no one gives a shit. Now are you convinced?"

"Christ, you've thought this out," was all Nicky would say. "You've researched it to death."

"No, Nicky, I researched it to life. Remember that, we're going to bring Eric Hall back to life."

"But why, Tommy. Tell me why and no bullshit."

"Because I want us to have it all. A bastard and a recluse by accident of birth climbing right to the top of the heap. It was thumbs down from day one for us and I'm going to take that thumb and stick it straight up... straight up Dicky Culver's ass."

"You've got an axe to grind and you're using me as the wheel."

"Come here, Nicky, come sit next to me."

Nicky made himself comfortable on the couch and Tom took Nicky's hand into both of his. "When I was little," Tom began, "and when I was not so little, I used to dream or fantasize about this faceless person, strong and all powerful, who was always there when I needed him and he never let me down. He was my personal angel, but a sexy one, if you know what I mean."

"Why didn't he have a face?"

"I don't know. I tried to give him one a few times but I never liked the end result. It just wasn't him and I knew it. Does that sound crazy?"

"Nothing we think is crazy, it's only crazy when we start acting out the weird stuff that goes on in our heads."

Tom nodded in agreement. "I always thought he would one day show me how to get everything I've always wanted. I didn't know how or when but I knew that sooner or later it would happen. When I saw you that first time, and even after I got to know you, I still didn't know that the time had come. I told you what Dicky told me about Mrs. Lindenhurst being a little senile, but even then the plan didn't occur to me. I thought of it gradually, fits and starts mostly, and always when I was alone or getting ready to go to sleep.

"I had wanted Eric and I want you and I suddenly saw a way to have you both. Try to understand this, Nicky; a totally impossible desire became as obtainable as a hot dog at a ball park. Then I knew, I was certain, that it was the omen I had been waiting for all my life. The chance for the impossible dream to become a reality. If I turn my back on it my faceless superman will turn his back on me."

The emotion of Tom's words was transmitted through the vise-like grip in which his hands held Nicky's. They sat quietly for several minutes, not looking at each other but each more aware of the other than they had ever been. "And where do I fit in?" Nicky finally broke the spell.

"Maybe you're the man without a face."

"Did you ever pin Eric's face on your hero?"

"Yes."

"And it didn't work, did it?"

"No," Tom admitted.

"Then mine won't either; it's the same face."

Tom dropped Nicky's hand and turned from him, speaking to the single lamp which illuminated the quiet room. "If you don't want to do it we'll just forget the whole fucking thing."

"I think you can't see his face because you're afraid."

"Afraid of what?"

"Of finding that you're looking into a mirror."

◻

Nicky gave Tom a bottle of Moët for his birthday, a cashmere sweater and a Superman doll with a tiny paper bag covering its head. Tom was delighted. "The story of my life. Thanks, Nicky, it's the best birthday I've ever had.

"But that's only the beginning." Nicky was in high spirits.

"More? What is it?"

"For dinner: onion soup, frog's legs, your choice of wine and chocolate mousse for dessert."

Tom was flabbergasted. Nicky's culinary skills to date fell in the general category of boil and broil. "You made that? How?"

Nicky held up one finger. "I dialed the best French restaurant in town and made a reservation for eight o'clock, so shower and dress, Mr. B., we're going on the town."

"But—"

"No buts, ifs, or whys. I don't give a shit who sees me, in fact I think it's about time I was seen. It's your birthday and I'm going to celebrate."

It was the first time outside their bedroom that Nicky had asserted himself and Tom knew better than to object. After all, he was doing it for Tom and the chances of running into friends of Eric Hall's on just one night out seemed very remote. The best French restaurant in town? Tom tried hard to look as if he were about to enjoy a happy birthday celebration in his honor.

But he did enjoy it. Tom's luck in keeping Nicky Three a secret held firm because Nicky's idea of the best French restaurant in New York hardly coincided with that of Tom's friends. It was a small, family-run place on the West Side which Nicky and Marie Romaine had sometimes frequented and, if it wasn't the best it was by no means the worst... in fact, it was very good. Tom enjoyed watching Nicky as much as he did his dinner. He reminded Tom of the boy who had left Nebraska for the green pastures of Yale... it now seemed like a hundred years ago. It was one of the few public places Nicky had been to and was somewhat familiar with, a fact that caused him to act like the man-about-town he was not. He had obviously memorized the very small menu and ordered without referring to it. He asked for the wine list but here Nicky knew just what he was doing. Alexis Romaine had not taken Nicky to the better places but he had brought the best into Nicky's life. The wine was superb, and very expensive.

"You're not still mad at me, are you?" Nicky asked, lighting a cigarette. He had actually bought his own pack and this, more than anything else, told Tom that he was witnessing a new Nicky.

"I wasn't sore at you."

"You could have fooled me."

"It's just your thick head that makes me mad."

Nicky held up his hand. "We won't discuss it. A moratorium

has been declared on the resurrection of Eric Hall. He'll remain between this world and the next until further notice."

"Don't say that," Tom shuddered, "it gives me the creeps."

"I wish it would give you some sense."

"You're getting to be a cocky bastard.'

"It's a new me, Tommy, and I'm going to show you just how cocky I can be."

Arriving home they opened the Moët, carried it into the bedroom and drank while they undressed. They sat on the bed, each holding a wineglass while Nicky poured their refill. "Some for you, some for me and some for. . . him." With an air of abandon and his blue eyes dancing in this head, he poured the expensive champagne on himself.

"What the hell are you doing?. . . No, Nicky. . . no. . . no. . . ."

"Yes, Tommy. . . yes. . . yes."

"It's my birthday for God's sake, I'm the honored guest."

"You gave me yours for Christmas and I'm returning the favor, although you must admit I know how to wrap a present."

"You're crazy."

"And you love it." Nicky raised his glass. "Cheers, Tommy."

Tom saluted in return but before he had a chance to take a sip Nicky removed the glass from his hand. "The glasses are for me," Nicky stretched out on the bed, "and this is for you."

"I'm not interested," Tom said, looking more interested than Nicky had ever seen him look before.

"Then why is that little fellow staring at the ceiling?"

"Little? Ha. I don't have to feed it wine to make it grow." Nicky beckoned with his fingers. "Come on, Tommy."

"It's my fucking birthday."

"I know. . . so go on and blow out the candle."

They lay in perfect bliss in the dark room. From somewhere a million light-years away the sound of traffic moving up and down Central Park West drifted over their heads. Nicky stirred, reached to the foot of the bed and pulled a blanket over their naked bodies. "It's freezing in here."

"I think I found the bottom of the pit," Tom whispered.

"What?"

"Nothing, Nicky, nothing at all. Is there any more champagne?"

"No. You poured the rest of it on my—"

"Shut up and come closer, I'm freezing."

"Is this close enough?"

"Hmm. Christ, you must have been saving it for a week."

"A week and a day, exactly. That's when you stopped talking to me."

"You mean I have to wait a week and a day before it happens again?"

"Give me a half hour."

"I'm counting."

Two days later, on Nicky's birthday, Tom arrived home from work empty-handed. Nicky tried not to look disappointed but didn't manage it very well. "Aren't you going to ask me where your present is?"

"It's better to give than to receive but. . . since you mentioned it, where's my present?"

"Tomorrow morning, at ten sharp, you will go down to Bleecker Street and accept graciously," Tom gave a courtly bow, "my present."

Nicky covered his heart with his hands. "Oh, Tom. . . the Dukedom of Little Italy, it's what I've always wanted."

"Now he's a stand-up comic. You're going to like this one, Nicky. You're going to like it a lot."

"Bleecker Street? What's there?"

"A job, Nicky, and it has your name on it."

Nicky was too stunned to react. He stared at Tom with his mouth slightly ajar and a suspicious look in his eyes. "You're kidding?"

"No."

Then he reacted by jumping up and down like a two-year-old. "I have a job. How, who, where, what. . . everything, tell me everything."

"Relax and fix us a birthday drink. I'm going to wash and then I'll tell all."

"Now! I want to know now," Nicky shouted.

"Let me get comfortable," Tom said, starting to march into the bedroom and pulling off his tie as he went. "The Dukedom of Little Italy. You're a shit, Nicholas, a shit."

Nicky had been begging Tom since the first day of the new year to help him find a job. It was an obsession that had replaced his longing to meet Tom's friends. Tom kept putting him off, telling Nicky that it wouldn't be easy to find an opening for someone who had never worked a day in all his twenty-eight years and the excuse did have some merit. However, he was really playing for time: time to construct the final phase of his plan, the discovery of Eric Hall, and to place Nicky in a position that fit the scenario. But from the first day Nicky had insisted on paying his own way, out of the money left to him by Marie Romaine, and he had contributed one-half of the rent, food bills, utilities and everything else it took to live in New York. Tom accepted the arrangement because to do otherwise would demean a very proud young man. The situation gave Tom more spendable income than he had ever had before but they both knew that it couldn't go on forever. In fact, the way Nicky spent money, the end of the line was closer than the coming of spring. Hence, a job for Nicky was of prime importance.

And even here Tom's luck held firm. A restaurant owner had come to the bank seeking a business loan and Tom had gotten in on the negotiations. He told the owner a little something about Nicky and asked if he would take him on as a waiter.

Nicky sipped his drink. "You conned him, Tom. You made it sound like no job for Nicky, no loan from the bank."

"Would I do that?"

"You would, and for once I don't give a shit. I have a job. A real job. Happy birthday, Tommy."

"No, Nicky, it's your birthday. Christ, you're going ape."

"If that means I'm ecstatic then I'm going ape."

"You don't mind being a waiter?" Tom asked timidly.

"Why should I? It's an honest job. Uncle Alexis told me most of the Russian nobility became waiters in Paris and New York after the revolution."

"Uncle Alexis had a one-track mind."

Nicky was too excited to care that Tom had once again zapped Uncle Alexis. "I'm going to work," he kept repeating. "I'm going to speak to more people in a day than I've probably talked to in my whole life!"

"You're going to be a waiter, not an analyst. Don't push, Nicky."

"Do you think I can do it, Tom?"

"What's to do? They'll show you the ropes, which will take all of two hours, and then you're on your own. I told him you were inexperienced."

"And what did he say?"

"He said he never met an experienced waiter."

"What should I wear?" Nicky's question was directed more to himself than to Tom.

"Black pants, white shirt, black tie and not your damn Gucci loafers. You're going to be a waiter waiter, not a Russian nobility waiter. People don't tip waiters who can afford Gucci loafers."

"Tips? Christ, I forgot all about tips. I'll be making money."

"That's the general idea, now go find your birthday present."

"Where? I've been searching the apartment all day."

"Try the hamper in back of the bedroom closet."

"What did you get me, a pair of dirty jockey shorts?"

"No... but I should have."

The following evening Tom came home to an empty apartment. It was a strange feeling; Tom had lived alone practically since he had left Nebraska yet now, after two months of living with Nicky, he couldn't imagine going back to his solitary existence. For the first time he fully realized the implication of Nicky's major complaint about becoming Eric Hall. Nicky would be living in the mansion on Ninety-second Street and not in the one-bedroom apartment off Central Park West. But why did Eric have to live with his grandmother? He was a big boy and a rich one, he could live any place he wanted to live and with a roommate if it pleased him. Tom's spirits rose. Every problem had a solution when money was no object.

Nicky got in at midnight, exhausted and radiant with joy. "I did it. I did it," he announced. "The owner loves me and so do the customers." Nicky was literally gushing. "They think I'm Italian because I can speak it."

"You can speak Italian?"

"Sure. And French."

"How much did you make?"

Nicky pulled a wad of bills out of his pocket and some loose change. Together they counted the take. "Fifty-four bucks," Tom exclaimed. "I don't believe it. How long did you work?"

"I did dinner. Six to eleven."

"Fifty-four bucks in five hours, tax-free? For a five-day week that's two hundred and seventy bucks a week and no Uncle Sam. What the hell am I doing at the bank?"

"And Terry said it was a slow night. Wait till the weekend."

"Who's Terry?"

"One of the waiters. He sort of trained me and he's not always a waiter. He's an actor."

"Nicky, nine out of ten waiters in this town are actors and the other one is working his way through medical school. Is he handsome?"

"Who?"

"Terry, who else?"

"No. . . he's beautiful."

"Did he put the make on you?"

"Shit, it's an Italian restaurant in Little Italy, not a fucking gay bar."

"Little Italy be damned, it's the heart and balls of Greenwich Village, and you didn't answer my question."

"I don't even know if he's gay."

Tom rolled his eyes skyward. "An actor who's working as a waiter and you don't know if he's gay. Is a priest who works for the Pope a Catholic?"

"I think you're jealous and I like it."

"I'm looking out for your interests. You're a baby."

"The bartender is looking for a roommate and he asked me to audition."

"Screw the bartender."

"That," answered Nicky, "is what he has in mind."

"Tell him to fuck off."

"The bartender? Never. The bartender is the waiter's best friend. He makes the drinks, fast and strong, and the drinks are what ups the bill and the bigger the bill the bigger the tip."

Tom moaned. "He's a fucking professional."

14

The first tiny buds appeared on their tree, the heartier joggers shed their sweatsuits in favor of shorts, those who had previously fled the city for points south began to trickle back, and Tom took the first step toward breathing life into his male Galatea. He called Dicky Culver.

"Missed you in Palm Beach," Dicky said after a slight pause which shouted "Tom who?" and always preceded Dicky's initial response to a phone call from Tom Bradshaw.

Savoring the sweet taste of revenge, Tom allowed the cut to go unnoticed. Without inquiring after Amy he plunged from drawing board to execution without a backward glance. "I have to see you, Dicky."

Again there was a pause in the conversation but this time because Dicky was taken completely by surprise. He had expected a flip and thinly disguised insult from Tom and had gotten what sounded like a pleading request. Something told Dicky to tread carefully and weigh each word he spoke. "Why?"

"I can't explain it on the phone but I have to see you and . . . and show you something."

"Bradshaw, if this is your idea of a joke forget it. We've been back in town a few days and I've got a lot to do and seeing you is not on the top of my priority list."

Tom took a deep breath, swallowed hard and forced himself not to slam the phone back in its cradle. "Look, I don't like you any better than you like me and if there was anyone else I could share this with I would, and gladly." It was the first time either of them had declared the hostility that had long existed, and the sudden open declaration of war acted as a precursor to their first truce.

Dicky answered in a tone that was less arrogant and more concerned than he would care to admit. "Are you in trouble?"

Having never heard Dicky express such emotion, Tom immediately interpreted the concern as hope and happily informed Dicky that he was not in trouble but.... "Something happened a few months ago... well, happened is not the right word.... Dicky, I have to see you and what it's about is as much concern of yours as it is mine. Christ, I'm telling you it's something unbelievable." Tom delivered his lines with just the right amount of pathos, fear and awe as to render Dicky speechless. Tom had never considered a career on the stage but now, as the smile on his face belied the tremor in his voice, he wondered if he had not missed his true calling. He imagined Dicky on the other end of the line adjusting his glasses or running his fingers through his thinning hair, looking desperately about for his wife.

"But what is it?"

"Can you meet me tonight?"

Reluctantly, Dicky admitted he could. "Amy's gone to her parents' place and I don't expect her until tomorrow." This bit of information was more luck than Tom had ever hoped for. Amy was out of the way and he could get to Watson without Sherlock sticking her nose where it was not wanted.

Dicky, never known for his sharp wit, was torn between demanding to know what Tom was talking about and fearful of missing out on something he would later regret. Tom made the most of Dicky's half-hearted acceptance by immediately setting a date for that evening. "Do you know the Casa Maria on Bleecker Street?"

"No, and I don't think I want to."

"Bleecker, just off Seventh, I'll meet you there after work, about six. It shouldn't be too crowded at that time."

"I don't want a pasta dinner," Dicky groaned.

"We're not going there for the cuisine, Culver, we're going for the floor show. Just be there. Casa Maria, Bleecker and Seventh. " Before Dicky could change his mind Tom relieved his frustration by disconnecting the line and wishing he could erase Dicky Culver from the face of this world with the same ease.

He then dialed the apartment and got Nicky. "We're on. Six o'clock tonight."

"Are you really going through with this?" Nicky asked, slightly bored.

"You can't back out on me now."

"I won't."

"Do you remember what you have to do?"

"Sure. All I have to do is nothing."

"Right. I'll see you later. . . and, Nicky, thank you."

"For doing nothing? Thank me when you have a reason."

What Nicky had consented to was a compromise. He would allow Tom to "exhibit" him to Dicky Culver in a setting prearranged by Tom. If Dicky didn't truly believe that Eric Hall had returned from the dead then Tom would forget his plan and no mention of it or the name Eric Hall would ever pass his lips again. If Dicky fell for the charade then Nicky would consider — nothing more — going through with step two: meeting Mrs. Lindenhurst. Both secretly felt they had made a good deal. Nicky was certain that no one but Tom would believe a young man worth millions and presumed dead was in reality suffering from amnesia and working as a waiter in an Italian restaurant in Greenwich Village. If the idea wasn't so funny, it would be sad. Nicky knew he looked like Eric, the photos of Eric he had seen proved that, but only one with Tom's zealous imagination, especially where money was concerned, would swear that they were the same person. That was strictly an illusion of Tom's, an illusion born of two basic human emotions: sex and greed. It was time Tom got his comeuppance.

But there was another reason Nicky accepted the compromise. He had long wanted to meet Tom's friends and now he was going to do it — and no less a friend than the famous Dicky Culver. Nicky had the idea that once the ice was broken in this direction and he became visible to Tom's crowd with no after-effects Tom would resume his social life and Nicky would become a part of it.

Nicky was more than ready to branch out socially. His job at the restaurant had proved a roaring success; in just three months he had become as close to a maitre d' as the likes of the Casa Maria would ever possess. The owner adored him, the customers liked him and the bartender was still trying to make him. As he gained confidence he began going out on his own. A late night drink with some of the other waiters, Sunday dinner with the owner of the Casa Maria and his family, and occasionally he would wander into one of the Village's many bars all alone. From these latter expeditions Nicky learned two things. One, he was a very desirable young man and two, he was never tempted because he was very hung up on Tom. First it was Uncle Alexis and now Tom. "I'm a born inmate destined to love my jailer." But as Alexis Romaine had provided a gilded cage so Tom now offered an exciting one. Nicky was content.

After the compromise was agreed upon Tom insisted, as part of the deal, that Nicky was not to have his hair cut for at least one month. When it was longer than Nicky had ever worn it Tom made an appointment for Nicky with a well-known hair stylist and wanted to accompany Nicky to the salon to oversee the trim. Here, Nicky drew the line. "I'm a big boy and I can get my own damn hair cut without Mother Hen giving directions."

Tom loved it. "Uncle Alexis should hear you now."

"As a matter of fact I might just keep it this way. Tony the bartender told me I look dashing."

"Fuck Tony." If Tom knew how to raise Nicky's ire by bringing up Uncle Alexis then Nicky knew how to respond in kind.

Again they compromised. Nicky took a photo of Eric Hall to the stylist and told him to cut and shape his hair "the way I used to wear it." The stylist looked at the photo and did what his client asked. Nicky spent an anxious half hour in the barber's chair because the barber never doubted that his customer and the man in the photo were one and the same person.

When Tom saw the final result he stared at Nicky for a full minute and then announced, "Dicky Culver is going to have a coronary arrest at the fucking Casa Maria."

⬚

"Now what do you want to tell me and what the hell did you mean about coming here for the floor show?" Dicky was in high gear. He kept adjusting his glasses and looking about as if he expected to be gunned down by the Mafia at any minute.

Like elephants, Tom was thinking, Dicky and Amy never forget. A question mark was insufferable to the perfectly matched couple. They stalked until they erased the annoying punctuation from every thought that entered their head and every situation they encountered in their dull lives. Tom would lay any odds in favor of Dicky having called the Casa Maria and asking if they had a floor show. The amusing thought did little to counter the anxiety that was rapidly engulfing Tom. Dicky would never fall for it. . . and if he did Amy would return tomorrow and pull the rug from under all of them.

"I'm talking to you, Bradshaw."

"I hear you loud and clear. Just relax and let's have a drink."

"I called this place after I spoke to you and they don't have a floor show."

Dicky, as usual, was making Tom furious and it was what Tom needed to boost his courage. "But they do, Dicky."

"Really? When does it start?"

"Right now," Tom answered, pointing.

Dicky's eyes followed Tom's finger and. . . .

Before Tom's eyes Dicky turned a deathly white. He couldn't speak and his breathing became audible. For a moment Tom thought his prediction of a coronary arrest was about to happen. "Easy, Culver. . . easy," Tom cautioned.

Dicky began to stand and Tom quickly grabbed his belt and pulled him back down. "Not a word, Dicky, you understand. Not a fucking word. Just let me handle this."

The waiter was now standing over their table. He nodded at Tom. "How are you?"

"Fine. . . just fine."

"Are you eating?"

"Just a drink for now. I'll have a bourbon over ice and. . ." He looked at Dicky who was staring at the waiter and literally panting. ". . .and a scotch and soda for my friend."

The waiter turned to go and Dicky suddenly called out. "Eric?" The waiter froze and the look of surprise and fear on his face was not part of any act.

"Go on, get our drinks," Tom ordered, "he's. . . he's not feeling very well." The waiter fled.

"I told you not a fucking word," Tom hissed.

"It's Eric," Dicky whined. "It's Eric."

"Lower your voice," Tom whispered, "and calm down. It's not Eric, that's impossible. It's someone who looks like Eric."

"Don't tell me it's not Eric. And what the fuck do you know? I was Eric's friend. I knew him before you —"

"Listen to me and listen hard. Lower your voice and if you say one word to that waiter I'll knock your fucking head off your skinny neck. We'll talk later." Dicky knew that Tom meant every word he had just said and looked as if he were going to suffer a stroke as the waiter once again approached the table with their drinks. He glanced quickly at Dicky as the waiter put their glasses before them and then once agin made a hurried retreat.

"Drink," Tom ordered.

Dicky gulped his scotch so quickly a small amount escaped his lips and ran down his chin. He then did something Tom had never seen him do before. He wiped the spill with the back of his hand. "Now are you ready to listen?" Tom asked.

Dicky nodded. "It's Eric. Don't try to tell me it's not, because I know it's Eric."

"I'm not telling you anything, Dicky, except the facts. I came here a few months ago with some people from the office and I saw him. I know how you feel because I felt the same way the first time I saw him. But I was with acquaintances, not friends, and I had no one to lean on." Tom got in the dig but it bounced right off Dicky.

"Why doesn't he know me? What in God's name is going on? I feel sick to my stomach."

"Have some more scotch, slowly this time, and try to listen to what I'm saying. He doesn't know you because he's probably not Eric. He can't be Eric because Eric is dead. We all know that."

"How can you say he's dead when he's standing right over there? I'm going to talk to him, right now." Again Dicky tried to rise and again Tom pulled him back into his chair.

"If you talk to him you'll blow the whole thing. He'll beat it out of here and we'll never see him again."

"But why? I don't understand."

"If you'll give me a chance I'll explain. Just listen to me and stop staring. I'm telling you he'll hightail it out of here if you keep looking at him like that." Dicky forced himself to turn toward Tom. "Now... that first time... I told him I wanted to speak to him but he wouldn't have any part of it. I offered to pay for his time and he almost hit me. He thought I was trying to hustle him."

Dicky blanched. "Eric Hall a hustler in a Greenwich Village bar. Jesus H. Christ, Tom...."

"I kept coming back and gradually, very gradually, he warmed up. I told him very frankly that he looked like someone I used to know. I asked him his name and he said 'They call me Nicky.'"

"'They call me Nicky'?"

"He's a very sick and frightened man." Now that Tom was in the thick of it nothing could stop him from moving forward at a constantly accelerating pace. His anxiety left him as stage fright is forgotten by an actor in the passion of performing. He had rehearsed for nine months and was now giving birth to a fully-grown man, complete with a hundred million dollar bank account. Tom was looking into the eyes of his most demanding critic and what he saw was a hit even before the lights had dimmed on the drama's first scene.

"This is as much as I could learn in the past few weeks." Tom continued. "About two years ago Nicky woke up in a fisherman's shack on Block Island. He didn't know how he got there and he didn't know who he was. He still doesn't. He was sick, physically and mentally, for a long time and the fisherman took care of him but he didn't tell Nicky shit. When Nicky was well enough to get about and see what was going on around him he learned that the fisherman wasn't a fisherman but a narcotics smuggler. Nicky was confused, to put it mildly, physically and mentally ill and scared shitless of the fisherman who told him he would have him killed if he breathed one word of what was going on in the hut on Block Island. Nicky was a prisoner. He had no money and even if he did he had no place to go, so he stayed put. Then, right after the new year, the fisherman took his boat out but this time he didn't come back. Nicky waited a week and the guy never showed.

"He was scared before but at least he had the fisherman. Now he was completely alone and petrified. He took whatever money he could find in the hut, got a ferry to the mainland and thumbed his way to New York. He got this job because he had worked as a waiter in a small hotel on the island last summer. He has a room some-place in the Village and stays in all day and comes here at night. I repeat, Culver, he's not well and afraid of people. He keeps looking over his shoulder for that fucking fisherman."

Dicky stared at Tom for a long time and then breathed what Tom thought was a sigh of relief. Tom tensed and Dicky whispered, "He's Eric." Now Tom breathed a sigh of relief.

"Don't be an asshole. He can't be Eric. It's just an uncommon resemblance. That's what I brought you here for."

"Don't call me an asshole," Dicky fired back. His fury accentu-ated his effeminate air and Tom had to suppress a giggle. "You're the asshole. It *is* Eric and it all figures."

"What figures?"

"Block Island, asshole, is in Long Island Sound, between Mon-tauk Point and Martha's Vineyard." Dicky was triumphant.

"You're kidding?" Tom was shocked.

"Where did you think it was, off the Jersey shore?"

"As a matter of fact, yes."

Dicky covered his face with his hand. "I don't believe you, Bradshaw. He was rescued. . . somehow he was rescued and ended up in that hellhole on Block Island." Dicky started to rise for the third time. "And I'm getting him out of here right now."

Tom gripped Dicky's arm until the latter winced. "Try that once more and I'll tell Nicky you're one of the fisherman's people and you'll never see him again. Never! He's my friend, not yours, and don't forget it. Any contact you want to make is through me or no dice." Tom's tone left no room for a rebuttal and Dicky sank back into the chair sporting a red face and a quivering lower lip. Certain he had Dicky where he wanted him, Tom mellowed. "I told you, repeatedly, he's not well and very afraid of strangers. All you have to do is take his hand and say 'let's go' and there's no telling what he'll do."

Dicky looked miserable. "What am I going to do?"

"We," Tom replied, emphasizing the pronoun, "are going to discuss this calmly and in private and then decide what has to be done."

⊠

When Nicky arrived home he found Tom sitting with a glass of champagne in one hand and a cigarette in the other. Tom raised the glass to the newly arrived. "You went out there an unknown and you return a star."

"Did you see the look on that guy's face?" Nicky fell into a chair. He looked at me as if I was a fucking ghost."

"I expected nothing less. And you should have heard him. He's going ape, Nicky. . . the guy is going ape. Now are you convinced?"

"I'm convinced all right. I'm convinced that this crap is coming to an end right here and now. No more, Tommy. . . no fucking more."

Tom had expected a reaction but certainly not this one. Nicky looked as pale and shaken as the day Tom discovered him staring at the photo of Eric Hall. Tom put down his glass and leaned forward in his seat. "You promised—"

"Nothing. I promised nothing. I said I would consider and I've considered. The answer is no."

It went on till the sky grew light over Central Park and the sparrows in tree in front of the limestone building began competing with the furor raging inside the aparment. Tom pleaded. Nicky remained adamant. "We'll never get away with it. No one will ever believe us."

"Not us, Nicky. . . him. . . Dicky Culver. I denied you were Eric three times and three times he insisted you were." Tom held

144

up the appropriate number of fingers to stress his point. "He said you were rescued and taken to Block Island... not me. We're free and clear and on our way to the bank with Dicky Culver's compliments."

"Semantics, Tom, and bullshit and you know it. You fed him every cue and he answered with the obvious."

Even in the heat of argument Tom couldn't help relishing his victory. He smiled broadly and then laughed aloud. "You should have heard him. He thought he had made a remarkable discovery. Christ, I wish you were there."

"But I was there. I was the object under discussion, remember? I thought he was going to bore a hole right through me with his eyes."

"You were sensational, Nicky."

"Were, is the correct word. Just keep it in the past tense, because what I did I'm not going to do again."

All the old reasons, arguments and counter-arguments were brought up and raked over the coals once agin. But it was no longer theory that was being discussed, it was hard fact. And Tom, having exhausted all other approaches, presented his Galatea with the hardest fact of all. "Dicky Culver saw you... there's no turning back."

Nicky's shoulders drooped and he looked at his friend with a mixture of fear and determination. "I can leave town."

"Without me?"

The steel was bending; the butter melting. "I don't want to leave you, Tommy."

"And I don't want to live without you."

Without me — or without Eric Hall? Nicky wondered. He was still as far from an answer as the first time he had posed the question. "Then why do you want to do this to me?"

"Not to you, Nicky. For you."

Exhausted almost beyond endurance, Nicky was overwhelmed with the eerie feeling that he had lived this scene in the distant past or perhaps in another life. He was a little boy and he could see Aunt Marie, standing erect over a seated Alexis Romaine, shaking her finger at her brother and shouting, "Charles did nothing to us, Alexis, he did it for us... for us... for us...."

"There's no turning back." The full implication of those words swept over Tom as he sat in the Culvers' den the following evening. The room looked like the headquarters of an army preparing a major invasion at dawn. Maps were strewn all over the place. There were road maps and nautical maps in all shapes and sizes and drawn to a variety of scales. There were old newspaper clippings and official-looking documents whose nature Tom could only guess at. Sherlock and Watson had had a very busy day and, as expected, had left no stone unturned in their quest.

The invitation to the Culvers' had come to Tom that morning at his office. "Dicky told me everything," Amy began.

This had come as no surprise to Tom. In fact it was what he wanted, but only after Dicky had been convinced that Nicky was Eric Hall. "And what do you think?" Tom had replied.

"It's Eric. There's no doubt about it." Amy, as imperious as ever, sanctioned Tom's con in one sweeping statement. "Can you come to the apartment tonight?"

So Tom sat in the Culvers' den, completely relaxed, sipping a bourbon and watching with amusement the Keystone Kops antics of the bespectacled couple. Dicky and Amy had taken over the re-surrection of Eric Hall, and Tom knew how much it must be irking the pair to have Tom included in what they certainly considered the triumph of their existence. But what choice did they have? Tom was their only link to "Eric." Tom had made that clear and Dicky had obviously passed that fact on to Amy. Tom sank deeper into the comfortable chair, took another swallow of the expensive liquor and bit his lower lip in an effort to keep from laughing out loud.

"This," Dicky was saying, pointing to a penciled X on the largest nautical map, "is where the yacht went down." Tom rose and joined the generals around the campaign table. "And here is Block Island." Dicky's finger drew a line that represented many watery miles to the west and south of the X.

"Do you think he swam?" Tom asked.

"Don't be a fool, Tom," Amy snapped. "He was picked up and taken to the island."

"Who picked him up?"

Amy sighed and exchanged a meaningful look with her husband. "You mean you haven't figured it out yet?"

Tom shook his head and continued staring at the map. "I'm still not sure he is Eric."

"Not sure?" Dicky screeched, sounding like a frustrated old maid about to lose her last chance at the brass ring. Even Amy looked embarrassed and Tom wondered, as he often did, what the Culvers' sex life consisted of. "You saw him and you can say he's not Eric. Why did you call me and show him to me?"

"Because of the striking resemblance, naturally. The fact Eric might possibly be alive never entered my mind," Tom shouted back.

"Quiet, both of you," Amy came between them. "This is getting us no place. Tom, I think I know what happened. It was the smuggler who rescued Eric. He must have been right there when the yacht went down and managed to pull Eric out of the ocean. Then, for obvious reasons, he didn't hang around for the Coast Guard to arrive. He would have to show identification, his boat license at the very least, and only God knows what he was carrying on board at the time."

Tom looked at Amy with great admiration and it wasn't all an act. She had always been jealous of her husband's friendship with Eric Hall and now that young man was about to re-enter her life. True, there were certain compensations. Amy was a snob and Eric Lindenhurst Hall was a big, big name: She didn't mind having her husband's close association with the Lindenhurst-Hall name rub off on her. Dicky might not be the best lay in town but he did have the right credentials and if Amy had to choose between the two she would surely pick the latter. Did Tom see a little of himself in Amy

Culver? He shrugged off the annoying thought. Besides, *he* did have the perfect sex partner and he would soon have the social standing. In fact he was grand slamming Amy and couldn't be more pleased with himself for doing so.

"You know, Amy, I think you must be right."

"I'm sure I am. The man might have been a smuggler but he wasn't a murderer. He saved Eric because it was the humane thing to do. Look how he cared for him all those months. What he did to Eric later he did to survive. There was no other way." Dicky nodded his agreement as Amy continued to flesh out Tom's plot line. Tom helped himself to more bourbon thinking that he must remember to send the Culvers a bottle as soon as his ship, now clearly visible on the horizon, came in.

They talked, amid the maps and documents, for many hours until Tom found himself slightly bored with the entire affair. He was like a teacher, superfluous because his class had learned their lesson too well. He began to envision life as the consort of Eric Lindenhurst Hall. A penthouse on Fifth Avenue in the Sixties. . . no, the Eighties. Was anything available in Jackie Onassis's building? Well, he could always check that out. A house in Southampton. . . no, East Hampton. Southampton was getting too commercial. Of course they could dock the boat off Fire Island or P-town some weekends. Even the very rich had to let it all hang out on occasion. He wondered if Emily Bradshaw was alive. Maybe he would buy her a church. . . she would like that. Her very own church with a huge crematory for her to burn the collected works of all the great authors who had ever transferred a thought to the printed page. Perhaps he would hire a platoon of beautiful hustlers and send them to the West Side Y.M.C.A. as a gift for the regulars. They could wear little signs on the pouch of their jockstraps. . . FREE/COMPLIMENTS OF THOMAS BRADSHAW (CONSORT).

Yes, Tom would be generous to all the deserving. He might even forgive the Culvers for flinging shit in his face for the past ten years. After all, it was they who were right now plotting to open the portals to Eden for him and Nicky.

"I'm going to see Mrs. Lindenhurst tomorrow night." Tom came crashing back to earth with the speed, if not the commotion, of a comet. "I called her today and made the appointment," Dicky announced.

Appointment. . . but of course. . . one just didn't knock on Mrs. Lindenhurst's front door even to announce her grandson's return from the land of the dead. One made an appointment, and Tom was beginning to get the feeling that Sherlock and Watson were up to no good. "Do you want me to come with you?" Tom asked, knowing in advance what Dicky's reply would be.

"No. . . I don't think that's necessary." Dicky avoided looking directly at Tom and Amy was busy rolling up maps.

Tom was all smiles on the outside and seething on the inside. The editors had bought his scenario but, true to form, they were already making subtle changes in the plot. Well, let them rewrite all they want, Tom thought, the final chapter will remain intact. I own the goose and it won't lay one fucking egg unless I tell it to. No, he would not forgive the Culvers. His first edict as consort would be to rain shit on Dicky and Amy for forty days and forty nights.

"Whatever you think, Dicky."

The Culvers exchanged a fleeting look which said, "That was easy."

Tom rose, took Dicky's hand and thought, *I'm gonna tie your little prick in a knot before this is over,* and said, "We'll be in touch."

"Sure. I'll call you as soon as I've talked to Mrs. Lindenhurst."

On his way home Tom made a firm decision. If he did not hear from Dicky Culver by ten tomorrow night, Nicky would never show his face at the Casa Maria again and Eric Hall would once again disappear from the face of this earth. Then let Dicky make another appointment with Mrs. Lindenhurst and explain that to the lady. "I have you by the short hairs, Culver. Win, place, show or run last, I have you by the short hairs."

🔲

The phone rang at eight. "She wants to see you." Dicky's voice gave no indication of what was going on at the mansion on Ninety-second Street.

Tom could feel beads of water breaking out on his forehead and a sudden urge to relieve himself surged through his bowels. The panic button had been pressed and he didn't know why. "Is. . . is she all right?"

"Fine. But she wants to see you." It was now obvious that Dicky was making the call in Mrs. Lindenhurst's presence.

Why, Tom wanted to scream, why, why, why? "Can you come right over?" he heard Dicky say.

"Sure. It'll take me about fifteen minutes."

For the first time since he had put the plan into operation Tom was scared. This was not Eric's old friend and Tom's old enemy that he was coming up against. This was Mrs. Eric Lindenhurst, the legend and the grandmother of Eric Hall. Would she cross-examine him? Call him a liar? Have him arrested? Perhaps the police were already there. Maybe some had been dispatched to the Casa Maria to pick up Nicky. It would be just like Dicky to have him walk into a trap. And tonight, of all nights, the city was almost void of traffic. His taxi literally flew across Central Park and in minutes was tearing up Madison Avenue. They made every fucking green light. If he had almost shit at the summons, what would he do when he came face to face with the lady herself?

"The Ambassador taught me many things," Mrs. Eric Lindenhurst smiled, "most of them long forgotten, but one has remained with me. Always get the story first-hand. Thank you for coming so promptly, Mr. Bradshaw."

Tom was bedazzled. He had anticipated anything from a cordon of men in blue to being verbally attacked by a ranting old hag. What he did not expect was a beautiful old lady, perfectly calm and serene, whose demeanor was so overpowering as to put everyone in her presence in that same blissful state. Her white hair was perfectly coiffured, her simple black dress impeccable, her manner regal without the slightest hint of condescension. But should he have expected less? Here, seated before him, was the legend.

Mrs. Eric Lindenhurst had lived through two world wars; during the second her husband had been one of the most important members of the President's cabinet. Together they had traveled between Washington and London in the most precarious days of the nineteen forties. She had survived the blitz, dined with kings, become a dear friend of a reigning queen, entertained heads of state both friendly and hostile, become widowed and suffered the loss of her remaining family in a tragic accident. Why did Tom think this great lady would fall apart at the news Dicky had just imparted to her? Never would Mrs. Lindenhusrst allow herself to act like anything but what she was: a lady, and all that the word implied.

"It was no trouble at all, ma'am. Any help I can be to you would make me happy."

"You're a very handsome man, Thomas Bradshaw."

Tom actually blushed. "Thank you, ma'am."

"Were you a friend of Eric's?"

"Yes, at school. We didn't see too much of each other after.

150

We. . . ." Tom left the thought unfinished.

"You traveled in different circles," Mrs. Lindenhurst finished for him.

Tom grinned. "You might say that, yes, ma'am." He glanced at Dicky who was sitting on the other side of Mrs. Lindenhurst, contemplating his hands.

"Would you like something to drink, Mr. Bradshaw?"

"Tom. Please call me Tom. Yes, I would. Is bourbon possible?"

Mrs. Lindenhurst smiled her serene smile and replied, "Anything is possible, Tom, that's why you're here tonight, isn't it?"

Tom felt a sharp pain in the area of his heart. What the hell was that supposed to mean? Did she suspect? Was she playing with him? Why the hell didn't Dicky say something? Mrs. Lindenhurst turned to Dicky Culver. "Would you mind playing host, Dicky?" He jumped to attention like a puppet being manipulated by an invisible master. Tom watched him walk to what appeared to be a sideboard, pull down the panel and expose a complete bar set-up. But that wasn't all he observed. From the moment he had entered the house, and in spite of his nervousness, Tom tired to absorb as much detail as possible under the circumstances.

They were seated in what was obviously a family room in the rear of the mansion where tall, majestic windows overlooked a garden that was well tended and softly lit on this early spring evening. The room was dominated by an oil of the ambassador, Eric Lindenhurst, placed directly over the fireplace. He had been a very handsome man, here posed rigidly erect with a decorative ribbon of state cutting a diagonal across his black dinner jacket. Tom could feel the man's piercing eyes staring down at him and was more than grateful for the drink Dicky now handed him.

Mrs. Lindenhurst accepted a sherry and Dicky went back to his chair carrying a glass of scotch. "Now, Tom," Mrs. Lindenhurst said, "would you tell me in your own words how you found my Eric."

Found my Eric? Tom took a healthy swig of the bourbon and didn't even feel the whiskey go down his throat. Then he looked directly at Mrs. Lindenhurst and told his story as simply and clearly as possible. No embellishments for the lady. . . just the facts. His tale was met with a respectable silence and then Mrs. Lindenhurst said, "I see."

Her grandson had returned from the grave and she says, "I see?" Tom was beginning to doubt his own sanity.

151

"You're wondering at my calm acceptance of all this," she said, as if reading Tom's mind.

"Well...."

She brushed aside whatever he was going to say with a wave of her hand. "I never believed my Eric was dead. You might think that the ranting of a senile old lady, but I tell you in my heart I never believed he was gone. I knew Erica was, and Tony. But not Eric. No, not Eric. Do you know I had the area searched for almost a year after the accident? I did. But not Block Island." She laughed, the sound a tiny silver bell in the still room. When she continued to speak she looked not at Tom and not at Dicky but at some distant point across the spacious room.

"Last January Milly Russell came to visit me. You know Milly, Dicky, or at least your mother does. I think they were at school together. Makes no difference. Milly had been to the opera, a Saturday matinée, and came on Sunday ostensibly to tell me about the performance but I knew from the moment she arrived that *Butterfly*, or whatever it was, was the furthest thing from Milly's mind. I've known Milly since the day she was born and she's never been able to stop her face from saying what's on her mind.

"I let her talk, knowing sooner or later she would let it out, and sure enough, after boring me for almost an hour she suddenly jumped out of her chair and said, 'Mary, I saw Eric yesterday,' and then the poor thing burst into tears."

Dicky adjusted his glasses and Tom raised one foot as if about to cross his legs and then changed his mind. The opera house was a few blocks from the apartment off Central Park West. Tom suddenly longed for his apartment. Longed to be there, waiting for Nicky to come home, to count the dollar bills and silver, to have a quiet drink together, to talk about the day that was coming to an end, to go to bed, to make love, to wake up and find that this was all a nightmare.

"Her car got caught in traffic and while the driver idled she looked out the window and saw Eric walking on the street. He was carrying what appeared to be a bulging pillow slip."

Good grief, the laundry. Nicky had been taking the laundry to the laundromat on Columbus Avenue.

"Well, then I knew what I had always thought was true. But if Eric were here, in the city, and hadn't come to me, then I also knew that something was frightfully wrong. I called my solicitor, Jack Goodwinn, and he told me that Milly Russell had seen Germans behind every bush in the park in the nineteen forties and a communist under her bed in the fifties. True, Milly was always a little. . . impressionable, but she had seen Eric. I never doubted it for a moment. The only advice Jack gave me was not to advertise or say anything to the press. I would be overwhelmed with pretenders and, of course, he was right. I called my friend Henry Kissinger and enlisted the help of the FBI."

Tom suppressed a groan and asked, "Do you mind if I smoke?"

"Not at all, Thomas. I used to, you know. So did the Queen, but never in public." Tom silently thanked the Queen and lit a cigarette.

"They did what they could," the old lady continued, "but to now they have had no luck locating my Eric."

Because they never looked, Tom thought. A grand old lady, more or less in her dotage and wishing for the impossible, had been placated by the FBI. Respect her as they would, they owed it to her, but search for her dead grandson they would not. Suddenly Tom was flushed with elation. He was going to bring back her grandson. He was going to show those fuckers that this sweet old lady was right. The bastard was going to stick it to Mr. Goodwinn and the entire Federal Bureau of Investigation.

Tom leaned forward in his chair, exhibiting the courage he thought had deserted him outside the front door of the mansion on Ninety-second Street and said, "I think I found him, Mrs. Lindenhurst."

"I know you have, Thomas. I know you have." Mrs. Lindenhurst began to cry.

Dicky looked embarrassed and made a futile attempt to take charge of the situation. "Everything is going to be all right, Mrs. Lindenhurst."

"I'm sure it is, Dicky." Then she turned to Tom. "Do you have his confidence, Tom? Does Eric trust you? I realize how ill he's been and I don't want to upset him."

"Yes, ma'am, I think I do. I told him he looked like someone I knew and he's asked me about that several times. I. . . I didn't want to do or say anything until I had spoken to Dicky. . . and you."

"You're a very wise and sensitive boy, Thomas. I will call my physician in the morning and then. . . ." Her entire face lit up. "And then I want you to bring my grandson to me. I want you to bring my Eric home."

Walking toward Fifth Avenue Dicky still looked slightly

shaken and a little chagrined. Tom walked like a man who owned the world. "Do you want me to come with you tomorrow?" Dicky asked.

"No, I don't think that's necessary," Tom answered.

16

The whirl of activity that had begun when Dicky saw Nicky and culminated with his and Tom's visit to Mrs. Lindenhurst had no effect on the person who was the cause of all the speculation, planning and plotting. Years of listening to his aunt and uncle discuss his situation and their individual hopes for his future without consulting their young ward had conditioned Nicky to accept whatever destiny satisfied his mentors' desires. He had not defied Uncle Alexis because, as Nicky often noted, he owed his life to Alexis Romaine; he would not now defy Tom Bradshaw who had come to his rescue when he had been left adrift in a somewhat leaky boat.

But Tom had done more than just rescue Nicky. He had fulfilled Nicky emotionally and physically and had given him, however briefly, the independence Nicky had long desired. What had never occurred to this young man almost bereft of ego was that he was giving Tom as much, or perhaps more, than he was getting. But Nicky had had a taste of that independence and he gave in to Tom's wishes reluctantly. He had always known what he did not want but now he knew what he did want.

"My own restaurant. I was going to open my own restaurant. French. That's the cuisine Uncle Alexis knew best and taught me to appreciate."

"When you meet her, Nicky, you're going to love her. She's the nicest and grandest lady it's ever been my pleasure to know and you're going to make her so happy."

"What the Village needs is a good French restaurant and I

wouldn't be taking any customers away from the Casa Maria. I wouldn't want to do that to them. They taught me the business from the ground up. Mine would have a very different ambience."

"Oh... in three months you know the business from the ground up?" Tom finally decided to mesh his conversation with Nicky's.

"In another year I would have been ready."

"For what?"

"The Chez Nicky."

"Christ...." Tom doubled over and looked as if he were about to lose his dinner. "For originality you take the prize. Why not the Left Bank or the Red Mill?"

"I like the Chez Nicky."

"Do you know how much it costs to open a restaurant in this town?"

"I still have some of the money Aunt Marie left me."

"Twenty-one hundred bucks. Ten times that wouldn't get you off the ground."

"I would borrow from the bank."

"Not my bank. I would turn you down flat."

"Because you're a prick."

"Nicky... Nicky... come on, let's talk," Tom pleaded with open arms.

"We are talking."

"In circles... avoiding topic number one. Tomorrow is the big day."

"Your big day... and Culver's. I'm just going along for the ride."

"You're the fucking star."

"No, Tommy, I'm the patsy."

"Did you hear what I said about the old lady?"

"I did, and the thought of making a fool of her makes me sick but it doesn't seem to be bothering you."

"When you meet her you'll change your mind. Nicky, you're going to feel like a hero."

"Whose hero?"

"Mine, dammit. Don't you like me, Nicky, even a little?"

"Don't start that shit. It always ends up the same way... in the sack, and then I do whatever you want me to do."

"A compromise?" Tom offered.

"I agreed to one last week and look where it got me."

156

"One more... come on, Nicky... one more."

"Let's hear it."

"You meet Mrs. Lindenhurst tomorrow and, if for any reason, you don't want to go through with it you can tell her who you really are or tell her anything you want and walk out."

Nicky looked skeptical. This was too good to be true. "And what will you do if I walk?"

"Wash dishes at the Chez Nicky."

And so on the eve of the resurrection the star fell asleep clutching a straw of hope. Tom had offererd him a way out and this made Nicky's heart a little lighter. Was Tom saying he was not certain he wanted Nicky to go through with the charade? Nicky thought so, but he wanted Tom to admit it to himself and not leave it to Nicky, like the toss of a coin, to tell Tom what he truly felt. If Tom refused to realize that he wanted Nicky in the flesh and not Eric Hall in spirit then Nicky would lose no matter what he did. If he stayed in the mansion on Ninety-second Street he would lose himself. If he walked out he would lose Tom. Ever the romantic, Nicky dreamed that Tom would offer him a reprieve in front of the double oak doors of Mrs. Lindenhurst's home.

Beside the sleeping Nicky, Tom lay wide awake. He had just wagered one hundred million dollars on Nicky's soft heart and his friend's inability to walk away from a sobbing old lady. One hundred million bucks! Why had he made the offer? Nicky would do anything for Tom. Why had he given him an out? Christ, he wasn't trying to get rid of Nicky, he was offering him the world. He wanted Nicky... but with Eric's money. A hundred million bucks... Christ! Tom finally drifted off into a restless sleep counting stacks of dirty dishes piled high in the tiny kitchen of Chez Nicky.

Amy Culver thought of what tomorrow would bring in terms of her social standing. Certainly things would improve. She didn't need anyone to tell her that since the sun (Eric) had gone out of their lives, she and Dicky were not quite as popular as they used to be. Now they would be in the eye of the hurricane which would herald Eric's return and thereafter they would be an important satellite revolving around the heir to the Lindenhurst millions. After all, her husband was Eric Lindenhurst Hall's closest friend. Amy turned uneasily in her oversized single bed. Would she once again be relegated to the position of indulgent wife, pretending to be having such fun while her husband followed Eric around like a puppy dog? Would she once again flirt with any man who appeared interested only to see Dicky yawn at the sight while he turned livid over anyone, man or woman, who came near Eric? She had never forgotten Dicky's reaction to Tom Bradshaw... Tom Bradshaw.... Again Amy tried for a more comfortable position.

She trusted Tom as far as she could throw him and she trusted her husband, where Eric Hall was concerned, about the same distance. Without telling anyone she had journeyed down to Bleecker Street and entered the Casa Maria as if looking for someone she knew among the diners. She found someone she knew among the help and almost fainted on the spot. Tom had not lied and Dicky had not been misled. Eric Hall was alive. And how queer that Tom Bradshaw, of all people, had discovered this fact. Yes, all things considered, queer was the perfect adjective for any situation involving Tom Bradshaw.

Dicky Culver, in his oversized single bed, wondered why Mrs. Lindenhurst had excluded him from tomorrow's interview. He, of all pepole, should be present at Eric's homecoming. And Tom, the bastard, kept insisting that Eric was his friend. Just what the hell did he mean by that? The waiter was Tom's friend but tomorrow the waiter would become Eric Hall and as soon as Eric came to his senses he would tell Tom Bradshaw to go take a flying shit.

But suppose Eric felt indebted to Tom? So indebted that he would turn his back on Dicky in favor of Tom? No, that was impossible. Dicky and Eric went back a long way together and Tom Bradshaw was not one of *us*. All it would take was a little time and then everything would be just the way it had been before the accident. He couldn't wait to get Eric on the squash court. Damn, how he had missed his friend.

Mrs. Lindenhurst had very little to do to prepare for her grandson's return. Indeed, she had been preparing for it since the day Eric had "left." His room, except for being scrupulously cleaned every week, remained untouched. Even the chocolate mints Eric so loved were on hand in the kitchen pantry. Tomorrow he would be with her and this house would no longer be a museum but a real home once again. Eric laughing and talking aimlessly, the telephone always ringing and every night company for cocktails and dinner. Yes, every night, lots and lots of young people would once again fill her life. Her eyes clouded with tears as she looked up at the imposing portrait of her late husband. "He's coming home, my love, our Eric is coming home. But that's no surprise to us . . . we always knew he would come back."

The couple employed by Mrs. Lindenhurst to run her home, Olga and John, had been with her for over twenty years. Naturally, when the entire family had occupied the house there were many more servants to see to their needs and wants. Tony and Erica Hall had been very social and were known for their fun parties and intimate dinners where the guest lists ran the gamut from politicos to maestros to the latest Hollywood bombshell or heartthrob. When young Eric had reached his majority he began to imitate his parents' style so that before long the mansion became known, to the cognoscenti, as the Grand Hotel. And, like that hotel of fiction, it took a great deal of help to keep the management and guests happy.

But since the death of her husband and the tragic accident which had swept away the remainder of her family, Olga and John were all that Mrs. Lindenhurst required. The day after the accident the Grand Hotel had closed its doors, prematurely but permanently, and its vast rooms were never again to be filled with the glitter and chatter of those who lived in the limelight. Olga cooked and did some light cleaning. Her husband was butler and jack-of-all-trades which included tending the garden, polishing silver which was now never used and chauffeuring a limousine which had not left its garage in months. They were a self-sufficient little island plunked smack in the center of the largest metropolis on earth.

For almost two years Olga had tried to get her mistress to go out more or have friends in on occasion. This began when, after a respectable period of time, Olga had hinted that perhaps Mr. Eric's clothes should be given to a worthy charity as had been done with the belongings of Eric's father and mother and even the Ambassador's. "You know how he hates to have us fuss with his things, Olga, and I'm sure Mr. Eric will want to keep some of them. Why, he practically lives in that old corduroy jacket."

After this conversation Olga immediately consulted her husband. "She's balmy," John announced. "It's all been too much for her and she's gone off the deep end. Should I call Goodwinn?"

"It might be temporary," Olga mused, "and besides, she ain't doing no harm. All the poor thing has is her memories and dreams, so let her keep them."

So the loyal couple continued to indulge their mistress. "These mints are stale, Olga, and the chocolate's melting. You know Mr. Eric likes them crisp and fresh." So fresh mints were ordered and when they went stale and the chocolate once again began to melt they were tossed out and mints were once again placed on the shopping list.

After Tom and Dicky's visit Mrs. Lindenhurst had rung her bell to summon Olga from the kitchen and announced, "Mr. Eric will be here tomorrow. Please tell John to get his room ready and make sure we have everything we need in the kitchen. And liquor, Olga, tell John to check the liquor. Mr. Eric does like his cocktail although I've always thought he drank a bit too much."

Olga had run in search of her husband to report this latest development. "Should we call Mr Goodwinn?"

John gave the question a moment's thought. "Don't see that it's anything different than what we heard from her before."

Olga straightened her back. "You don't? Before she was dreaming, now she expects the dream to come true. Tomorrow. What'll happen tomorrow?"

"Nothing," John reassured his wife. "Either she'll forget about it or else tomorrow she'll say to expect him tomorrow. I saw a movie where an old dame went dotty just like that. Everything was always gonna happen tomorrow only tomorrow never comes." John returned to his coffee and sweet roll and dismissed his wife.

But tomorrow did come and John was the first to be informed of the fact. It was he who answered the young man's ring, opened the front door and. . . "Mr. Eric!" John backed away from the apparition. Olga, who was just descending the stairs which faced the door saw who was standing on their threshold as her husband retreated.

"Mother of God," the poor lady screamed. "Mother of God, it's him." She ran to her husband, took a firm grip of his waist, and peered over his shoulder. The young man stepped into the house and the couple, moving like one, took another step backwards.

"Is Mrs. Lindenhurst home?"

"It's really you, boy, isn't it?" John whispered and his wife, taking this as a cue, ran from the room shouting, "It's him, ma'am, it's Mr. Eric. He's come back."

She had promised herself she would not allow the moment to be reduced to a maudlin spectacle. Eric was ill and he needed attention, not to be frightened out of his wits by a hysterical old lady. All her life, at the Ambassador's side, she had dealt with crisis after crisis, from the momentous to the petty, and had never lost her head. She would do so once again. But when Eric walked into the sitting room with Olga and John hovering in the doorway, the legend was reduced to the status of mortal.

Her heart swelled in her chest as she let out a sob and, stand-

ing, she ran to her grandson, enfolding him in her arms and squeez-
ing his firm body again and again as if to assure herself that he was
indeed solid flesh and blood and not the mirage she had seen on
more than one occasion in the past two years. "Eric... Eric...
Eric...." She wept as she repeated the litany.

He was embarrassed beyond words. His arms felt like bars of
lead as he raised them to encircle the fragile old woman. He patted
her back and tried to gently free himself from her grasp. "Please
don't do this... please don't."

"You're back," she sobbed. "My Eric is back."

"Yes," he said in an effort to calm her, "I'm back and everything
is all right now. Eric has come home."

17

In the offices of Goodwinn, Barr, and Goodwinn, Russell Good-winn, unannounced, invaded the office of Henry Barr and without preamble exclaimed, "She's taken some kid off the street and is calling him her grandson."

Mr. Barr took off his rimless glasses and began polishing them. "Who?" he asked.

"Mary Lindenhurst. Who else? I've been afraid this would happen since Eric drowned and now it's happening. She's even had a doctor, a psychiatrist, talk to the... the imposter."

Mr. Barr returned his glasses to their rightful place. "What did the doctor say?"

"He said Eric — Eric, mind you — was in fine physical shape but suffering from severe memory loss due to a traumatic experience. Ha! How do you like that for a medical diagnosis of a corpse?"

"Perhaps it is the boy."

"Hank, you're getting as senile as the old lady. Eric Hall is dead."

"Mary Lindenhurst might be a little senile but she's not blind. If this boy weren't her grandson, surely she would know it."

Mr. Goodwinn pounded his thumb against his chest. "And so would I. I've known Eric since he cut his first tooth and I'm on my way there right now."

"And what are you going to do?" Mr. Barr asked, once again removing his glasses.

"I'm going to kick the bastard out on his ass, that's what I'm going to do."

162

Mr. Goodwinn did nothing of the sort. "It's Eric," he announced on his arrival.

Mrs. Lindenhurst stretched out her arm to the young man who had just entered the room. "That's exactly what John and Olga keep saying," she said. "You didn't believe me, Russell, did you?"

Mr. Goodwinn continued to stare at the young man who, prompted by Mrs. Lindenhurst, now sat beside her as she put her arm through his. "You are Eric," Mr. Goodwinn stated, not sure if he believed his own words. "You are Eric Hall."

"He's not always this way, Eric, he's really a very competent lawyer. His name is Russell Goodwinn and he's an old family friend as well as our legal advisor."

"How do you do, sir," Eric said.

"You. . . you don't know me?"

"Of course he doesn't know you, Russell, and he doesn't know me either. Now snap out of it and get your wits about you. There's a lot to be done." Eric winked at his grandmother and she winked back. "Tell Russell your story, dear, and try to pretend he isn't staring at you as if you had two heads."

Eric spoke and Mr. Goodwinn listened. When Eric had finished Mr. Goodwinn shook his head and sighed. His very logical mind told him he had just heard the plot of an Agatha Christie novel while his legal training pointed to the evidence, exhibit A, seated not five feet from him. "I think you had better get Russell a drink, dear."

Eric went to the sideboard and opened the panel. Mrs. Lindenhurst let out a sharp cry and Eric froze. "You knew where the bar was," she cried. "You remember. . . you're starting to remember. Oh, I knew it would all come back to you."

Mr. Goodwinn sat forward and, picking up Mrs. Lindenhurst's enthusiasm, asked, "Do you remember what I drink, son?"

Tom didn't tell me that, Nicky thought. In fact he didn't even know you existed. "No, sir, I don't."

"It's scotch, and you used to call me Russ."

"Scotch it is, Russ. Straight up?"

Mrs. Lindenhurst beamed. This was her Eric.

It was decided that the offices of Goodwinn, Barr and Goodwinn would announce the return of Eric Lindenhurst Hall. They would issue a fact sheet, and that was all they would issue. They would not answer questions and there would be no communication whatsoever between the press and Eric. "Let them make of it what they will." Mrs. Lindenhurst added in lieu of an amen.

And what they made of it was a three-ring circus. It was all that Tom had said it would be, and more. The bold, black headlines, the "we interrupt this program" radio flashes, the television coverage tracing not only the career of Ambassador Lindenhurst but the debut and wedding of Eric's mother and, of course, the tabloids' "Back to Life" and "She Never Stopped Hoping" feature stories. Mrs. Lindenhurst exercised her considerable influence at City Hall and the cordon of men in blue that Tom had envisioned appeared in front of the mansion on Ninety-second Street. The telephones inside the mansion were turned off and one phone, with a three-digit number, was temporarily installed. Nicky was awed at the power of the Lindenhurst name and actually started to enjoy himself. It was going just as Tom had said it would go but the master planner wasn't on hand to view his creation. Twenty-four hours and Nicky already missed Tom. He wondered when he would be allowed out of this newest and grandest of his gilded cages.

The day after the story broke the people who had aided, fed, clothed and assisted the heir to the Lindenhurst fortune on his way back to the bosom of his beloved grandmother came forward. Their number was legion. In fact, if all the drivers who claimed to have given the boy a lift from New London, Connecticut to New York City had been on the New England Expressway at the same time, the Lindenhurst heir would have been caught in the most colossal traffic jam of the twentieth century. The more brazen reported their deed to the press, the modest only told their story to family and friends. The boy had been fed, according to vendors en route, enough hamburgers and hot dogs to feed, and give indigestion to, a small army.

No less than three hotel owners on Block Island claimed to have employed the Lindenhurst heir during his stay on the island. Photographs of their establishments and their toll-free reservation phone numbers made it into a surprising number of newspapers and the story aired on several local TV stations. It was going to be a lively summer on Block Island.

A regular at the West Side Y.M.C.A. whispered to friends that he had tried to put the make on Eric Hall in the Y's shower room.

The number of smugglers who gave themselves up was nothing short of ludicrous. One, with a black bag covering his head, was interviewed by a respected investigative TV reporter who should have known better.

A television crew rented a boat in Montauk and, assisted by the Coast Guard, took viewers on a wave-by-wave tour of the route of the Lindenhurst yacht, stopped at the scene of the accident and then continued along the "rescue route" to within a short distance of Block Island. "And that," said Robert Evans McBride, "is where Eric Hall was taken after being dragged from the sea and held captive for almost two years." Cut to a long-shot of the Block Island coastline and then back to McBride standing on the prow of the boat, his blond hair waving in the breeze. "This is Robert Evans McBride reporting for WXYZ-TV. Thank you and goodnight."

If the city of New York could have been silenced for one minute and all ears turned in the direction of a certain limestone building just off Central Park West, the population would have been treated to the sound of laughter emanating from the belly of Thomas Bradshaw. He laughed until his sides ached and the tears rolled down his cheeks. He had done it. The bastard from Nebraska had given the finger to the entire world and the entire world was licking the digit that had goosed it. If only he could share this moment with Nicky — they would fall into each other's arms and roll across the floor with glee. They would open a bottle of champagne and toast their success. They would. . . Christ, he missed Nicky. Only two days and he missed his friend.

In an obscure cemetery in England an old gray-haired woman stood in the pouring rain, holding a black umbrella over her head. She lingered before what was obviously a family plot, five graves marked by a single monument which bore the name Romaine. Was she crying or was it the rain, driven by a strong breeze, which created the illusion? But she was speaking to the silent, wet mounds of earth. "He has found his way home. Our Nicky has found his rightful place in life. I don't know how it happened and I don't care to know. It is enough that I have lived to see justice done. And, Alexis, he is a prince. Nicky is a prince and as rich as all the czars of Russia."

In New York, Eric called Russell Goodwinn and insisted that the Casa Maria be acknowledged, officially, as the place Eric Hall had found love and comfort upon his arrival in New York. And so, with Mrs. Lindenhurst's approval, Goodwinn, Barr and Goodwinn issued a second, and final, statement. The Casa Maria became an overnight success. Their regular customers were aghast at the uptown "carriage trade" which suddenly usurped their home away from home. Limousines became a common sight on Bleecker

Street as the Casa Maria became the new "in" spot. Its owner repaid Tom's bank in record time and repaid its former waiter by papering its walls with framed photos and clippings of the Eric Hall saga.

Tom was also clipping those same newspaper accounts of the life and times of Eric Lindenhurst Hall to add to his vast collection. The one he liked best concerned an old lady, living in Baltimore, who had actually called the Associated Press to tell them that Eric Hall was in reality her nephew, the Grand Duke Nicholas Alexievich, the czarevich of Russia. It was also reported that the lady had claimed, for over fity years, to be the Grand Duchess Anastasia, daughter of the last czar of Russia and had fought and lost a number of court battles in Europe for the right to be recognized as such. And, the article added, the lady was now quite old and quite senile.

Tom had to remember to show it to Nicky. He chuckled to himself and thought, "How Uncle Alexis would have loved that one."

Almost a week later Tom still had not heard from Nicky but he did hear from Amy and Dicky Culver daily. Amy called after each new press release and TV newscast to congratulate herself on piecing together the story of Eric's ordeal in a matter of hours. Tom acknowledged her brilliance. Then she announced she was going to open the Southampton season with a big "welcome home Eric" party. "Everyone will be there, Tom. Everyone." Except Eric, Tom thought, and he proceeded to tell Amy that in view of the fact that Eric was not well and had returned from the grave and not a tour of duty in the service of his country, he thought the idea in the worst possible taste. Amy was miffed but stood her ground. A party she would have and, come to think of it, she had no intention of inviting Tom Bradshaw.

Dicky called, rambled on about nothing and ended up asking. . . . "Have you heard from Eric?"

"No, Dicky, I have not heard from Eric. Does that make you happy?"

Jim Carr wanted to know if it were true that Tom had found Eric. Tom assured him it was. "But I didn't read anything about it in the papers. Not a single mention of Tom Bradshaw."

"Fools' names, like fools' faces," Tom quoted to Jim, "always appear in print and public places."

The mansion on East Ninety-second Street was the calm port about which the storm raged. Each day Mrs. Lindenhurst and Eric sat and talked and became acquainted with each other. Eric loved the grandmother he had recently acquired and Mrs. Lindenhurst adored the grandson she was getting to know for a second time. "I'm twice blessed, Eric," she told him. "Most people have the pleasure of watching their grandchildren grow up only once and here I am living that joy all over again."

She told him all about his family, recalling details of the past as only the very old can, and the young man still liked nothing better than to listen to the continuing saga of the human condition. And what a saga it was, crowded with names and places and events he had only read in the dull pages of history books. "Was I born in this house or in a hospital?" Eric asked his grandmother.

The old lady giggled. "You were born in Switzerland."

"Switzerland?"

"Of course. Your mother and father took the longest honeymoon in history and didn't settle down until after your birth someplace high in the Alps."

Wait till Tom hears this, Nicky thought.

"My God," Mrs. Lindenhurst suddenly put a hand to her lips. "Do you know your birth date, Eric?"

"February 17," he grinned.

"You do remember. Oh, I'm so glad."

"It was the one thing, Nana, I never forgot."

After three days the Eric Hall story moved from the front pages to page three. In a week it was a dead issue. "If there are no new angles," feature editors declared, "forget it." Now the society and gossip columnists waited with baited breaths and sharpened pencils for the Lindenhurst scion to make his first public appearance. They would have a long wait.

Tom heard the sound of the radio coming from his apartment before he had even put his key into the front door lock. His heart danced in time to the music as he rushed to get in, shouting his greeting before the cause of all this merriment became visible to his eyes. "Nicky... God, am I glad to see you."

"Please," Nicky bowed, "the name is Eric. Eric Hall."

Tom, grinning from ear to ear, bowed back. "If the name displeases thee, may I call you love?" A slight alteration, but a clever one, to the Shakespeare line.

"You, sir, are not Romeo."

"And you, thank God, are not Juliet. Now shut up and let me look at you."

They embraced for a long time, saying nothing for there was nothing to say. Genuine emotion cannot be verbalized, only experienced, a fact they were both delighted to learn.

"Christ, how I've missed you."

"I don't see why. My picture has been staring at you from every newspaper and television screen in the city."

"We did it, kid. We really did it," Tom beamed.

"Do you want to hear all the glorious details?"

"Not now, I have more important things on my mind." Tom inserted his hand between their tightly pressed bodies. "I think you have the same things on your mind."

"As I recall the bedroom is in that general direction?"

"For one suffering from amnesia you do remarkably well in the remembering department."

168

"Get your ass in there."

By some unspoken agreement they resolved to go slow, to make it last. But if absence makes the heart grow fonder it also makes the fuse grow shorter; in ten minutes they were satiated, content and at peace with themselves and each other. Encouraged by an early evening breeze their tree applauded their performance.

"The tree is all fresh and green," Nicky said, as if in response to the rustling leaves.

"Just like you. Do you want a cigarette?"

"No. I've given up the weed."

Tom lit one for himself. "Well, tell me all about it."

Nicky shrugged. "It worked, but you know that. What else can I say?"

"What about the old lady," Tom blew smoke into the air, "is she everything I said she was?"

"And more. You know, Tommy, I feel. . . no, I can't explain it."

"Go on, try. What is it? Do you think she suspects something?"

"No," Nicky was astonished at the very thought. "Nothing like that. It's just that. . . I have this feeling that she's not a stranger. That I know her and that. . . dammit. . . that she really is my family." Nicky was embarrassed and Tom's eyes followed a smoke ring from his mouth to the bedroom ceiling. "Maybe it's because she reminds me of Aunt Marie. Do you think I'm nuts?"

"No, but I do think you're beginning to believe your own publicity. It's been the downfall of many a star, baby, so watch it."

Nicky glanced at the clock radio. "I've got to go." He sat up and Tom tried to pull him back down.

"Shit, you just got here."

"We dine at eight and to bed at eleven."

"Then what do you do?"

"Read, jack off and go to sleep. Not necessarily in that order."

"Every night?"

"What? Read?"

"No, jack off."

"Just about."

"Wait till the press hears about that. Millionaire wacks wong nightly."

Nicky laughed. "Rich kid beats his bat."

"Polishes his diamond?"

"Jiggles the family jewels?"

And then an uneasy silence. Nicky got up and began getting into his jockey shorts. "I think those are mine," Tom said.

"I know. Do you mind?"

"Christ, he comes into a million bucks and goes kinky on me. It's all that self-abuse, it's driving you balmy. Next thing I know you'll be shaving the palm of your hand. Some people just can't handle great wealth."

Nicky zipped up the fly of his pants and stuck his hand into a side pocket. "That reminds me. Here." He drew out a wad of bills and laid them on the dresser.

"What the hell is that?"

"Ten one-hundred-dollar bills. For a banker you don't show me shit."

Tom crushed out his cigarette and sat straight up on the bed. "I don't want that," he cried.

"You don't want it?" Nicky shouted back. "I thought *it* was the only reason for this whole fucking mess we're in."

"I make you the richest bugger in the world and you call that a mess? And I don't want you coming over here and tossing me a . . . a . . . a . . . ."

"Quickie, I think is the word you're looking for."

"Yeah, a quickie and then leaving me a goddamned thousand-dollar tip like I was your whore. I'm your lover, remember."

Nicky, about to step into his loafers, almost fell over. "Your what? Did I hear you say the secret word? You've certainly come a long way for a guy who not too long ago told me he wasn't sure if he were gay. That was right after you told me how you dicked every unsuspecting traveling salesman who ever booked a hotel room in this town."

"I think I told you too damn much."

"And I didn't tell you enough."

"You're sure as hell making up for it now. Money has turned you into a bitch."

"No, Tommy, it's turned you into my lover."

Tom reached for another cigarette. "Thanks for the kick in the balls. What other funny lines do you know?"

Nicky sighed and sat on the bed, his hand gripping Tom's knee. "I'm sorry."

"No, you're not. But it's just as well. . . . I deserved it. Don't you know I felt that way about you before you became Eric Hall?"

"Why didn't you tell me?"

170

"Because then you wouldn't have become Eric."

"You're mad, Tommy... MAD... do you heard me?"

"I think the joggers in Central Park can hear you. Why are we fighting?"

"To avoid facing reality." Nicky looked very sad.

Tom covered Nicky's hand with his own. "You've said it all."

"Christ, Tom, it's like being back with Uncle Alexis. She wants me next to her every minute. This is the first time I've been out of the house in almost two weeks. It's getting to be the fucking story of my life."

"Where did you tell her you were going?"

"Here. I'm a man and I'm sick and tired of lying about where I go and what I do and I'll be damned if I ever do again."

Tom looked at Nicky with a great deal of respect. "You're right. You don't have to lie and shouldn't. What did she say?"

"Give Thomas my regards."

"She is a sweetheart," Tom smiled. "How did you get here?"

"I walked through the park. Why?"

"Just wondering. Did your fans mob you?"

"Are you kidding? The only thing that acknowledged my existence was a pigeon. It shit on my head as I crossed Central Park West."

"Our pigeons can always spot a piss-elegant East Sider. Good for the pigeon."

"What are we going to do, Tom?"

"Nothing. Just play it as it lays and take it one day at a time. The way I see it everything is going just fine. In a little while the newness of it all will wear off, Mrs. L. will ease back and you'll start living your own life... with yours truly at your side."

"You always make the improbable sound so easy."

"And you always make the easy sound impossible. Come on, Nicky, cheer up."

"Don't call me Nicky. The name is Eric."

"I can't call you Eric. You're Nicky... my Nicky."

"This gets better all the time. Bradshaw, you trained me for the role for six months and now you can't call me Eric. Well, learn, and fast. If you call me Nicky in front of people someone'll get suspicious."

"People? What people? I haven't seen a soul in almost two weeks, but the Culvers call in daily. Dicky thinks you and I are about to elope."

171

"You're coming to dinner tomorrow night."

"Who invited me?"

"Me. It's my house. And the Culvers will be there, too."

"Every cloud has a black lining."

"It's my semi-official debut."

"Are you going to wear white lace and have Kenneth do your hair?"

"Fuck you, Tom."

"Take off my underpants and you got yourself a deal."

"They feel loose. I think you're gaining weight."

"Not me, friend. Must be the guy who wore them last night. I rent, haven't you heard?"

Nicky liked that one and laughed hysterically. "I needed this. . . now I can face anything and tomorrow I'm going to need the courage of Alexander the Great and the patience of three saints. Lunch with the Culvers, at the club would you believe, followed by squash with Dicky."

"You poor kid. All that and a semi-official debut, too?"

"When I go, Bradshaw, I go all the way. You know, I don't even know what a squash ball looks like."

"Cut off the ones hanging between Dicky's legs and bat them around. I would love it. . . come to think of it, so would Dicky. How, may I ask, did you get involved with the Culvers for lunch?" The green monster raised its ugly head.

"He called, that's how."

"I read that all your phones had been temporarily disconnected."

"Except for one very private line and Dicky's mother. . . ."

"Got the number. . . I might have known. Do me a favor, Nicky. . . tell the pansy you came to visit me today."

The peacock spread his feathers. "Maybe I will and maybe I won't. Right now I have to go."

"Take your money with you."

"I don't want it."

"Neither do I."

Nicky sat on the bed once again. "Look, Tom, I think you had better begin to understand the enormity of our situation. I can walk into any store in this town. . . in this world. . . and charge anything from a fancy tie to a Rolls Royce and walk out with the merchandise. I can do the same in any restaurant.

"The bills are sent to our accountants and are paid on sight. . . no questions asked as long as the signature is mine. It's going to

172

take Goodwinn, Barr and Goodwinn a hell of a long time to straighten out the money situation and until they do I'm getting — thanks to my grandmother — a thousand bucks a week walking-around money... pocket money... piss-it-away money. A grand a week, Tommy... how does that grab you?"

Tom covered his genitals, not out of a sudden fit of modesty but more to feel the comforting reassurance of an old friend while listening to a new one. "I don't want it," he stated flatly. "I feel like a criminal."

"So do I, Tommy. See you tomorrow."

Tom picked up the money and counted it. Ten one-hundred-dollar bills. Or thirty pieces of silver... what the fuck was the difference. He had gotten a thousand bucks, just like that, and there was a lot more where that came from but Tom Bradshaw was alone in the world, alone in his room, alone in his bed. Had he traded Nicky for this? Nicky had come to see him today and Nicky had made love to him today, but, by God, it was Eric Hall who had just left the apartment. Would he ever see Nicky again?

The small dinner party was an unqualified success. Everyone, especially the host, was in rare form. "Thomas, it's so good to see you again." Mrs. Lindenhurst offered him her hand and Tom held it for a brief moment.

"I'm delighted to be here. Thank you so much for having me."

"But it's not my party, it's Eric's."

Tom nodded at Eric. "Dicky... Amy... good to see you. How have you been?"

"Right now exhausted," Dicky said. "Eric ran me ragged on the squash court."

"Don't believe him, I couldn't hit the broad side of a barn. But Dicky is damn good." Eric smiled at Dicky and Dicky looked as if he were about to purr.

"We're going to play every week, Eric, just like the old days when you used to beat the pants off me."

"Do you remember—" Amy began and then suddenly stopped.

"That's all right," Eric smiled graciously. "Please don't pretend I'm the same Eric you used to know. I'm not and it'll be some time before I am. What did you want to know, Amy?"

Cool, Tom thought proudly. I wonder if he's wearing my jockeys under those beautiful tuxedo pants. He suppressed a grin.

"Well," Amy began, "it has been a trying day." Dicky shot her a

173

nasty look. "I mean, one doesn't know what to say."

"Say what's on your mind," Eric told her.

"I was going to ask if you remember how to play bridge."

"As a matter of fact," Eric answered, "I do."

Amy clapped her hands. "Good. I'll get up a game. We beat the pants off Tom the last time around."

Tom acknowledged Amy's smile with a smug bow in her direction. "Which reminds me, how is the beautiful Nancy?" Tom asked.

"Why don't you call her and find out?" Amy responded.

Sweet Amy... dear, sweet Amy... how Tom would love to light a firecracker under her ass... or a bomb. Tit for tat, Ms. Culver, and here goes. "By the way, Eric, you left your belt in my apartment yesterday."

"His belt!" Dicky almost jumped out of his seat. "How did he come to leave his belt in your apartment?"

"Oh, it's a long story, Dicky, and it would only bore you." Tom winked at Eric and Eric grinned.

Dicky began to pout. Amy looked mortified and Tom thought, *That ought to hold her for a few hours. If you haven't realized we're playing a different ball game, Ms. Culver, you're going to know it before this night is over.*

"But how did you leave your belt?..."

"Oh, shut up, Dicky," his wife hissed.

Mrs. Lindenhurst smiled radiantly. It was so good to hear polite conversation again and be surrounded by such pretty people. But the young did speak a language all their own. Indeed, it was very difficult for her to follow their chatter but there was really no need to. It was so good just to hear their voices and see Eric having such a good time. And didn't he look handsome? He was by far the handsomest man in the room. Well... that Tom Bradshaw was devilishly good-looking. Yes, Mrs. Lindenhurst was having a fine time, too.

"We're drinking champagne," Eric announced, "unless someone wants a proper cocktail."

"I think champagne is the proper cocktail," Tom answered.

"How would you know?" Dicky asked.

Eric opened the bottle with a loud pop just in time to prevent Tom from asking him when he could expect his underpants back.

Eric poured and made the toast. "It's good to be with friends again. Especially my oldest friend of all," he added, touching his grandmother's glass with his.

"You're making me cry, Eric," she sobbed.

"And spoil my party? Never. . . come on, Nana, let's give them a song."

"No, Eric, no," she laughed.

"Yes. We've been practicing all week. Are you ready?"

"Well, I'll try."

"One. . . two. . . three. . ." And together they raised their voices in pure Cockney and belted out. . . "Underneath the arches, someone waits for me. Underneath the arches. . . ."

Tom, Dicky and Amy were awed by the performance.

After a very good dinner Amy said, "I'm trying to talk Eric into coming out to Southampton next week. We're opening the house and I'm giving a little party. Everyone will be there, Eric."

"Thank you, Amy, but the everyone scares me. I'd rather feel my way around here for a while before I take the big plunge."

"But they're all people you know, old friends," Amy insisted.

"No, Amy, I don't know them."

"I think Eric is right," Mrs. Lindenhurst spoke up. "When you feel ready, dear, we'll open the beach house and then you can see whomever you want."

"What about our squash games, Eric? I thought we would continue playing out there." Dicky looked somewhat hysterical.

"We'll have to put that off for a while, Dicky, but I'll practice every week. I promise."

A perfect ending to a perfect evening, Tom thought as he raised his champagne glass. "I used to know someone who did the craziest thing with champagne."

"Like what?" Amy asked.

"I can't tell you in polite company," Tom answered.

"I'll be by to pick up my belt tomorrow, Tom."

"Good. Should I chill a bottle of the bubbly?"

Eric was laughing openly now. "Depends on what you intend to do with it."

Dicky Culver looked positively ill.

19

In the weeks following his semi-official debut, Eric and his grandmother drew closer and closer to each other. Although she kept a tight rein on his activities, his "illness" being the excuse to keep him at her side, it wasn't long before the patient began rehabilitating the nurse. Like encouraging a baby to crawl before teaching it to walk, Eric at first took an interest in the garden and slowly got Mrs. Lindenhurst to accompany him to the backyard to oversee John's work. This led to lunch in the delightful oasis on more than one occasion.

"Do you know, Eric, my garden was once photographed by a well-known gardening magazine and used to be included on a city garden tour sponsored by the mayor's office."

"And it will again, Nana," he told her.

The old lady laughed. "I'll not live to see it. It takes many years to cultivate an award-winning garden and we've let this one go far too long."

"I think John's done a pretty good job," Eric answered looking about the area.

"But he's not a gardener, dear. He's not even a very good butler. But I've never known you to take such an interest in our backyard."

Eric looked a little uneasy and began picking the tiny leaves off a hedge that had just begun to fill in. "Could I ask you not to think of me in terms of the old Eric?"

"Beg pardon?"

"What I mean, Nana, is I'm not the person you used to know. A lot has happened to me and it's made a great deal of difference in the way I think and feel. You can understand that, can't you?"

"Of course, Eric. Have I been upsetting you?"

"No, you've been more than kind. What I'm trying to say is that I don't want to become the person I used to be when I would be more comfortable being the person I've become. I don't think the new me is too bad, do you?" Eric gave her his most winning smile.

"That is so well put, Eric, and how much you remind me of your mother. Erica was a very strong-willed girl, like her father I always thought. So..." she patted his hand, "no more chatter of the past. From now on we look to the future. And I think the new you is the best of all possible worlds."

From the backyard they ventured the few blocks into Central Park. The intense heat of summer had not as yet settled in and the days were perfect for strolling and people-watching. They made a pretty picture, the petite old lady on the arm of the very handsome young man. An enterprising photographer, recognizing the pair, snapped them unawares on one of these walks and sold the photo to a wire service. It received a big play in the national press and even made it onto the television screen. It was to become something of an American classic, a modern symbol of hope and, as one of the tabloids captioned it, "The Power of Prayer."

One astute commentator compared the photo to one of the late Queen Mary and her son David, then Prince of Wales. "Has anyone besides myself noticed the striking resemblance between Eric Hall and the young Duke of Windsor?"

Aside from this incident they were relatively untroubled by the media. There were the usual number of requests for interviews, feature stories, appearances on TV talk shows, an offer of a Hollywood contract for Eric to portray himself in a mini-series based on his life story and every publisher in town wanted his name on the dotted line for an autobiography. None of these requests got past a junior clerk in the offices of Goodwinn, Barr and Goodwinn. The society and gossip columnists, tired of waiting for the heir to go about socially, contented themselves with speculating as to where and with whom he would go once he had begun to resume his old lifestyle.

For their first big night out Eric decided on dinner at the Casa Maria and included Tom in their party. It was a very sentimental event for the new Eric Hall and a slightly embarrassing one for his former employer and co-workers. Mr. Carluccio, the owner of the

Casa Maria, almost fell over himself greeting his distinguished guests. Tony, the bartender, and Terry, the waiter, tried to treat Eric as if he had just returned from a brief vacation but instead came off like two disobedient subjects facing a displeased monarch. "I used to pat his ass," the bartender whispered to Terry as he passed a drink order over the bar. "A hundred million bucks worth of ass."

Eric sensed their unease and felt miserably isolated from his old friends. But some of the Casa Maria's regular customers who were in the room smiled and waved; a few even stopped at Eric's table to shake his hand and, being true Villagers, said things like, "When are you coming back to work?" Eric immediately felt better and ordered a far larger dinner than he or his guests could possibly consume.

"Waitering," Mrs. Lindenhurst observed, "is a very honorable profession. Certainly it's more thought of in Europe, where they have raised it to the status of an art, than here. I get the impression that you were very good at it, Eric, and your customers obviously miss you."

"Their loss is our gain," Tom quipped.

"I *was* good," the usually modest Eric admitted, "and if things had turned out differently I was going to open my own place." He looked directly at Tom as he spoke.

"Really?" His grandmother seemed very interested. "Our ancestors, Eric, were in commerce."

"Shipbuilding in New England two hundred years ago is a little different than the restaurant business," Tom reflected.

"I agree, Thomas," Mrs. Lindenhurst quickly answered. "With the restaurant business one is always assured of eating a good meal every night."

Eric grinned at his friend. "More pasta, Tommy?"

And so the long, hot days of a New York summer began and for Eric Hall and his grandmother they were spent in idle tranquility, doing what they wanted, when they wanted to do it and paying scant attention to the world about them. It reminded Eric of life with Uncle Alexis and Aunt Marie except that now he was free to come and go at his leisure — but with Tom working all day, he had no place to go and nothing to do when he got there. Eric was learning that obscurity and great celebrity have a great deal in common. Many of Eric's old friends called, some out of genuine concern but most out of curiosity, and a few of them even came to the house on Ninety-second Street to visit with him. Eric handled them exactly as he had handled his peculiar situation to date: "I am not the person you used to know, but I am very happy to make your acquaintance." They respected this not only because it made sense but even more because the rich have a great deal of respect for the super-rich.

The new Eric had no interest in cultivating these people. Indeed, he had no interest, as he had told his grandmother, in becoming "the Eric they used to know." Because fate, over which he had never had a firm grasp, had endowed him with Eric Hall's face he had become Eric in body, but he would be damned if he would become Eric in spirit. "As the Bard said," he told Tom, "what's in a name?"

"A hundred million bucks, that's what."

"You're full of crap, Bradshaw. You care as much about the money as I do. What do you do with the money I've been giving you?"

"Adding it to Aunt Marie's nest egg. You want an accounting?"

"Spend it, dammit."

"On what?"

"What about those Gucci loafers you were always mooning over?"

"I bought a pair and they hurt my feet. I have very peasant feet, Nicky."

"Eric, blockhead. Eric."

"I liked you better when you were a waiter," Tom lamented.

"And I liked you better when you were a swimming instructor at the West Side Y."

Gradually, Tom became a more and more familiar sight at the Lindenhurst mansion. Mrs. Lindenhurst liked him and, exercising her own particular charm, soon had Tom relating to her the story of his life. "You're a very courageous young man, Thomas, and I think the Ambassador would have liked you." She looked at his portrait as she uttered his title. "I also think your grandmother should be proud of you."

Tom shook his head. "I was an embarrassment to her."

Mrs. Lindenhurst nodded sympathetically. "I know the type. My lord, I've known all the types there are to know. I remember a very royal lady was so upset by her son's homosexuality that she pretended not to know what the word meant, let alone that such romances have existed since Eve did in Adam... and the whole human race, come to think of it." Tom and Eric sat enraptured, like two little boys at the knee of a great teacher.

179

"Well," she continued, "one evening at a dinner party in Buckingham Palace the talk turned to gossip and someone mentioned that a certain general and his aide-de-camp were extremely close, so to speak. 'But,' another stated, 'we all know the general is homosexual.' Well, this great lady raised her head and said, 'Is that so? The King of Spain has the same thing but the doctors are now able to control the bleeding.'"

Her audience roared their appreciation. Tom, clapping his hands, cried, "It's not true. I don't believe it."

"Oh, but it is true, Thomas. It is indeed true."

Tom and Eric went to the films or the theater at least three times a week and Tom was soon spending his weekends at Eric's home. A gossip columnist finally picked this up and mentioned that "Eric Hall was in the constant company of his discoverer."

"How does she know you found me?" Eric questioned. "It was never mentioned publicly."

Tom rubbed the palms of his hands together. "The lady is a great friend of Amy Culver. Can you add two and two? And please note that my name was not mentioned which makes me certain Amy the Sweet got a call from the scribe who, in twenty-five words or less, told Amy that she had seen us about and asked Ms. Culver if she might know who I was."

"And Amy," Eric continued, "said she would tell her if she promised not to mention your name, only mine."

"Give the man a cigar. Good old Amy, with her for a press agent I wouldn't get an obit if I paid for it."

"Stupid," Eric said, tossing the paper aside.

"Stupid, yes, but not funny. You can expect a call from Southampton."

"What?"

"Dicky now knows that you and I are an item, as they say in gossip-land, and the little weasel must be adjusting and readjusting his eyeglasses, pulling what few hairs he has left out of the top of his head and driving his wife up a fucking wall. I repeat, you're going to get a call from Southampton."

Eric got a call from Southampton. Dicky pleaded with him to come out for a few weeks. One week? A lousy weekend? Well. . . then Dicky would come into the city. He had some business to attend to anyway. "Lunch and squash, Eric, I don't want you getting rusty on me."

Eric was not in the least bit rusty. In fact he had improved a great deal since his first match with Dicky and rather enjoyed his afternoon with Tom's nemesis. The new Eric felt at ease with Dicky. He had heard so much about the man from Tom that he now felt as if he had indeed known Dicky all his life. And Dicky, always solicitous of his beloved friend, was now even more so. Like the first time they had been alone together Dicky was once again nervous, at a loss for a topic of conversation, and appeared to be relieved when Eric took the initiative along these lines.

It was all perfectly understandable but Eric still wondered what the true relationship had been between Dicky and the former Eric Hall. Was it an intimate one and was Dicky now wondering if his friend remembered, would rather forget, wanted to resume...?

"Have you seen anything of Tom?" Dicky finally asked.

"Now and then. A movie, things like that."

"You never cared much for him," Dicky suddenly exploded. It was obviously what he wanted to tell Eric since their first reunion. "He's not one of *us*, Eric."

"Who are *us*?"

"You know what I mean."

Eric shook his head. "No, I don't."

"Do you remember that Tom Bradshaw is a bastard. I mean a real one. He used to brag about it."

Eric smiled. "No, I didn't remember but Tom told Nana and me all about it."

Dicky was shocked. "Your grandmother?"

"Yes." Eric leaned across the table as if betraying a confidence to his lunch partner. "It seems I have a few ancestors who were born on the wrong side of the bed, as she so quaintly put it."

It was just possible that Dicky Culver would close the season in Southampton without a hair left on his head.

Tom had scheduled his vacation for the last two weeks in August and that time was rapidly approaching. "You could take the rest of your life off," Eric told him.

"I intend to do just that, but not right now. How the hell would it look? You return from the dead and I grow rich. We've been very lucky so far, but let's not push it."

"I think you're developing a guilt complex about being a kept man."

"Wait, and I'll prove how wrong you are. Can you get away for a couple of weeks?"

"Not to the Hamptons, I can't. According to Dicky if I sat on the beach or in any pub I would see my life pass before me."

"I know," Tom said, "and I have no intention of sharing you on my vacation. I was thinking about the Jersey shore. I once went to one of those small towns on the ocean where the only celebrities they know are the local volunteer firemen. Can you swing it?"

Eric discussed it with his grandmother. She was a little hurt, hid the fact and said he certainly deserved a vacation and should go wherever he wanted. "I also wanted to talk to you about the future," Eric continued the conversation.

"Yes?" she asked.

"Well, I'm very happy here, you know that but I would like to get a place of my own."

She nodded slowly. "I can understand that. You're not a little boy any more and if our lives had taken a more normal course you would have left home a long time ago." There were tears in here eyes as she spoke but she held herself rigidly erect and smiled her pleasant smile.

"Not far, Nana," he quickly added. "I would never want to be too far from you. Someplace in the Seventies or Eighties. . . only a few blocks from here, but my own place. Do you understand?"

Her face brightened. "Of course I understand, my dear. A man, especially a single one, needs room to breathe and can't be expected to spend his days and nights with an old lady."

"You are not an old lady and I'm happiest when I'm with you."

She waved away the compliment. "Nonsense. I'll tell Russell to—"

"No, Nana, please. . . no. I want to find my own place and rent it and furnish it. This means a great deal to me."

Now the tears which again appeared in her eyes expressed joy and not sorrow. "I'm so proud of you, Eric. You could so easily fall back on all our money but you insist on doing for yourself. You know the joy that comes from personal achievement. Just like your grandfather, Eric, you are just like your namesake."

"Now don't start pushing me out. I intend to be right here for Christmas and then, after the first of the year, I'll start looking around."

"I want to have a real old-fashion Christmas, Eric. . . and we'll have a party. The grandest party New York has seen since your mother's debut."

20

From the moment they boarded the bus they were Tom and Nicky... a junior bank executive and a former waiter on a two-week hiatus. Nicky's sparkling blue eyes and Tom's boyish good looks charmed everyone on the bus. Tall and slim... both clad in jeans that fit to perfection and knitted shirts that had seen better days, they presented a picture of the great American dream on the move.

"What would they think," Tom whispered, "if they knew we had just pulled off the biggest heist in recorded history?"

This struck Nicky as very funny. "We did do that, didn't we? Has anyone ever done it before?"

"I don't know, but I doubt it. How does it make you feel?"

"Sexy."

"You're kidding."

"No... look...." Nicky pointed toward his lap.

"Christ, it's standing straight up."

This was to set the tone for their two weeks on the Jersey shore. Tom had rented a garage apartment behind a very impressive house just one block from the ocean. One bedroom, a small kitchen and even a postage-stamp view of the Atlantic. Their landlords in the manor house, as it was immediately labeled, were a craggy old man and his very nervous wife. "I'm so glad your friend is not a woman, Mr. Bradshaw. Some of our neighbors have had trouble with... well, cohabitating, if you know what I mean."

Once inside the apartment they squared away the few changes

of clothing they had brought with them and Tom asked, "Do you want to go for a swim?"

"After. . . right now I want to cohabitate." This became another label that was to remain with them for their two weeks in the sun.

"Are 'we' up again?"

Nicky shook his head. "'We' never went down."

In three days they were tan, more handsome than ever, and the talk of the beach. They spent their days swimming and basking, then home for a quick shower and out for a simple dinner before going back to the tiny apartment to sip wine or beer, talk and cohabitate. They lay naked on one of the twin beds, a cool breeze coming through the wide open window, the sound of the surf just audible and a bottle of beer precariously balanced on each firm, flat belly. "The first one who spills it is a shit," Nicky announced.

"I'm going to laugh."

"Better not. . . you'll drown your little friend."

"Remember the night you poured champagne. . . ."

"Your birthday. . . did you like that?"

"I like you without embellishment better."

"Better than Moët?"

"Much better."

"That's the nicest compliment I've ever had."

"Give Dicky a chance. . . he's just warming up to the new you."

"You know, Tom, I sort of like Dicky."

Tom drowned his little friend.

▨

One day at the beach two girls who had beens staring at them for days finally got up the courage to approach them. "Are you Eric Hall?" one of them asked.

"Yes, I am."

The girl giggled. "No, you're not."

"But he is," Tom said.

"I told you he wasn't," the other girl said, pulling her friend away.

"But I am."

Giggling and embarrassed the two young things fled.

"Cute, but nuts," Nicky observed.

"No," Tom answered, "just human. If you had said you weren't Eric Hall they would have believed you were. That's how we got

184

away with it Nicky. I never said you were Eric."

"And neither did I. Everyone told me I was."

One evening they walked the boardwalk, watching the young lovers strolling hand in hand and avoiding the fact that in a few days their idyll would be over. They stopped to look at the ocean, lit only by the moon and a starry sky. The air was clear and almost chilly. They were surrounded by people but very much alone. "If I never have anything else in my life, I've had this," Nicky said.

"That's the nicest compliment anyone's ever paid me," Tom answered.

Their hands touched for one brief moment, but because of its clandestine brevity it was more thrilling than any overt display of emotion.

"What's going to happen to us, Tommy?"

"I don't know. I thought the Lindenhurst money and the Lindenhurst name could make me legitimate. Why did you do it, Nicky?"

"Because I thought it would make you happy."

"I want Nicky Three back."

"It's too late. It's not just us anymore. . . it's her, too. I love her, Tommy, I love her as if she truly were my grandmother and I won't let her lose Eric a second time."

"I burned my ass and now I'm going to have to sit on the blister."

"A hundred million bucks makes a nice cushion, Thomas."

"Then let's make it work, Nicky. Let's sit on that cushion and turn it into a magic carpet. Come on, smile. We've done our homework, passed the exam with flying colors and now we're going to have some fun."

"I must be crazy."

"Why?"

"Because I believe you."

21

Eric Hall's friends were drifting back into the city from their summer retreats and the town was once again revving up for its annual spurt of energy. The year was winding down and New York would tick off its remaining days in a manner similar to a rocket launch countdown. Target date: December 31.

Feeling he had had enough time to acclimate himself to his return to life, as the press had described it, old friends, casual acquaintances and perfect strangers invited Eric Hall to everything from theater openings to intimate dinners for two. With Tom's help he separated the genuine from the phony, responded to the cream of the crop, and soon found himself living the life Nicky Three had thought only existed in novels and films. The people he had vowed not to cultivate he now found not only likable but interesting and diverting company. It was amazing how few of them referred to "the old days"; they treated Eric not so much as a new friend but as the friend of an old friend.

They had all reached that time in life when the door was finally closed on prep school and college and opening on a future which involved careers and the starting of families. The new Eric had arrived just in time to join in their march forward. However, when talking to or dancing with one of the many pretty girls or the wives of his new friends Eric couldn't help but wonder if he had slept with any of them. It was an interesting, and not unexciting, bit of speculation. He also looked over their husbands and entertained the same thought, though in this form it was even more interesting. When he started meeting people who had never known Eric Hall he considered this to be the best aspect of his new life.

It became an unwritten rule that Tom Bradshaw be invited to all these functions and in short time Tom began to feel like one of the *us*. "The Eric Hall name smiles upon everything it touches," Tom noted.

"Not true, Tommy. They always liked you but you never gave them a chance. They're accepting you now because you're finally learning to accept yourself."

But there was one home in which Tom Bradshaw was still not readily accepted. His absence from Dicky and Amy's more intimate functions was noted and this slight proved to be the Culvers' undoing. Their crowd, always very socially conscious, put the Culvers and Tom Bradshaw on the "do not invite to the same party" list and when it came to a toss-up between the Culvers or Eric and Tom the latter were chosen nine times out of ten. If the close friendship between Eric and Tom made Dicky upset, those invitations that so often failed to arrive made Amy furious. War was officially declared with Amy firing salvo after salvo at Tom every chance she got and Tom answering the challenge with a condescending smile. Never had he been so polite to Amy Culver. Eric, caught in the middle, cared nothing about any of it and neither did anyone else.

It was under these circumstances that Tom received the first indication that a dark cloud was forming on the horizon, but because of the hostility that had erupted between them he refused to heed the messenger's warning.

"I don't think he's Eric." Dicky's voice came across the telephone wires like a preacher announcing the end of the world.

"What the fuck are you talking about now, Culver?"

"I don't think he's Eric, that's what I'm talking about."

Tom took a deep breath. "No, friend, what you're saying is that Eric has not re-dubbed you his number one gentleman-in-waiting so you've decided to throw him back to the fishes. Well, it won't work, Culver, so fuck off."

"It's not, Tom, I swear it." Dicky began to wax soprano. "It's a feeling I've had for a long time and I never said anything about it, not even to Amy, but the idea won't leave me. I have to talk to you about it, Tommy."

It was the "Tommy" that did it. Never had Dicky used that endearing diminutive with Tom and it made him think that Dicky had finally lost his mind. He was reasonably sure that Dicky was doing nothing more than regurgitating sour grapes but still something had to be done about it.

There had not been one breath of gossip insinuating that Eric was not the true Lindenhurst heir and this had been the most important factor in facilitating their charade. Eric had been accepted, on sight, by his grandmother and oldest friend and that had been more than enough proof for all concerned. Should there now be even a hint of gossip to the contrary the sand of Eric's castle would begin to crumble. It wasn't Mrs. Lindenhurst or even Goodwinn, Barr and Goodwinn that worried Tom. It was the press. One word of foul play and they would take a hard, cold look at that survival story and begin to see themselves as the dupes they were. And then some clever investigative reporter would begin to. . . Dicky had to be stopped, right now.

"I'm sorry, Dicky," Tom literally purred. "It's not been easy for any of us. Now, what's the matter?"

"I don't know, Tom," Dicky began in earnest. "I just can't rid myself of the idea that Eric is not Eric."

"Can you prove it?" Tom could feel his pulse quicken.

"Yes. . . I mean, no, I can't. I mean I could if I could put my finger on what it is that's bugging me."

"What's bugging you is that your. . . our. . . friend is not the Eric we used to know. You were closest to him so you're more aware of this than the rest of us. A lot has happened to the man, Dicky, and you've got to realize that he'll never be your boyhood friend again." Now grow up, he wanted to add, but held back.

"It's more than that," Dicky moaned. "It's something that struck me like lightning and then was gone just as quickly and I can't bring it back."

Now Tom was convinced that Dicky, like a little boy, was crying over a lost toy. "Promise me one thing," Tom cautioned. "You won't talk about this to anyone else. That type of rumor could prove very harmful to Eric and Mrs. Lindenhurst."

Dicky was shocked. "Christ, Tom, what do you think I am?"

"You're one of *us*, Dicky." Tom couldn't resist the sting but it washed right over Dicky. "Look, let's have a drink together and talk it over. Would that make you feel better?"

"Thanks, Tom. It would."

Now, more than ever before, Tom had to pacify Dicky because if Amy ever got wind of this. . . Tom shivered at the thought.

Meanwhile the magic carpet carrying the two soldiers of fortune continued to soar in the seemingly cloudless sky. Eric began scanning the real estate section of the *Times* in search of his own apartment. He circled whatever he thought sounded good, called and viewed the flat and learned that what you read is not what you get; but he was having a great time trying. "I don't want you to ever give up your place," he told Tom.

"Why not?"

"Sentimental reasons. Besides, I can well afford to keep up two apartments." He had really become Eric Hall.

Mrs. Lindenhurst was going full speed on preparations for her Christmas gala. Guest lists were drawn up daily, edited, discarded and recomposed. Caterers were contacted and consulted. "But, Nana, it's only October," Eric reminded her.

"And hardly enough time for all I've got to do," she replied, completely missing his point. "I've decided not to invite the President, my dear, it always makes people nervous." A line was drawn through that illustrious name. "Should I call London? Andrew they say is very social and your contemporary."

"Andrew who?"

"Eric, really."

Mr. Goodwinn carefully explained Eric's financial situation to the young heir. "You see, Eric, when you and your mother died, so to speak, simultaneously, her estate left by your grandfather reverted to your grandmother and taxes were paid on that money. Now that you've... come back, so to speak, we have to put in a claim with the government to get that tax money refunded and hand the estate over to you, intact."

Eric nodded. "And then pay the tax on it."

Mr. Goodwinn seemed pleased. "Exactly."

"So why not tell the government to keep what they already took and call it square."

Mr. Goodwinn looked displeased. "It doesn't work that way, Eric. However... er... if you need anything or want to get your hands on some ready cash... er... without your grandmother knowing it, so to speak, just say the word and I'll arrange an advance with the bank."

Eric didn't need a thing but curiosity got the best of him and he asked, "How much cash could I get my hands on, Russ, in the event that something... er... came up, so to speak?"

Russell Goodwinn raised his eyebrows. "I could transfer a million to your account on a half-hour's notice."

Eric thought it prudent not to relate this story to Tom.

Tom was busy making his own plans. He had decided to leave

his job right after the first of the year. What bothered him was finding a title for his new position in life. "Companion" brought to mind a male nurse in charge of a semi-invalid old man. Besides, there was a well-known millionaire, whom Tom had met at the Culvers, who employed companions by the dozens. They were all eighteen and looked sixteen; tough and illiterate, they were, according to their employer, working their way through medical school. No, "companion" wouldn't do. "Social secretary" wasn't bad but it sounded rather demeaning. He had visions of getting flowers or cheap perfume from Eric on National Secretary's Day. But what the hell difference did it make? In six months everyone would know the story and pretend they were deaf, dumb and blind.

But what Tom was really concentrating on was an itinerary. Travel. . . that's what he wanted to do and so did Eric. Not for two weeks or even two months, but for years. "I want to explore every corner of this world," Tom often stated and Eric would always respond with, "And I want to meet everyone on it." The Lindenhursts had a townhouse in London. Tom recalled the time he had thought about settling in London and had wondered if he could get into banking there. He would get into banking all right, on the withdrawal line, every day.

Eric Hall received a tremendous amount of mail. Most were pleas for money from both charities and individuals. Many were offers of marriage, photo enclosed, and some were just plain crank letters. "We met on Block Island. Now I'm pregnant so what do you intend to do about it?" He was so unused to the phenomenon that he insisted on reading them all. John delivered piles of mail to his room and Eric devoted at least an hour a day to this pastime. He seldom looked at the envelopes but simply tore them open, read them, saved the good ones to share with Tom, and tossed the remainder. He read the contents of the one he was now holding twice before its meaning registered on his brain. "Marie Romaine entered this hospital on September 15, 1983 and died, peacefully, on October 1, 1983. Upon admittance, she listed your name, at the address stated, as next of kin. Miss Romaine was buried according to her written instructions with money provided by her. To the best of our knowledge she left no will, however should you wish to make inquiries regarding this matter you may contact. . . ."

He stuffed the letter into his pocket and ran blindly from the house. Outside it was cold and damp, the sky gray and threatening, but all he felt was a burning sensation behind his eyes. He crossed Fifth Avenue, completely ignoring the traffic signal, and was greeted with the blast of car horns and the curses of angry drivers. Once in the park he began to walk rapidly, paying no attention to where he was going, only knowing that he had to keep moving or explode. He heard nothing but her gentle, comforting voice; saw nothing but a casket being lowered into the cold earth with not one mourner to offer up a prayer, to weep, to lay a single flower on the fresh grave.

He walked until he was exhausted, his brain numb. Like a wounded animal guided only by instinct he finally returned to his lair. Tom found him sitting in the living room, staring at their tree which was beginning to announce, in glorious color, its doom.

"Christ, you look like you've been hit by a truck."

Without saying a word he took the crumpled piece of paper from his pocket and handed it to Tom.

Tom read and then sank onto the couch. "I'm sorry, Nicky. I'm so sorry."

"Alone. . . she died all alone. . . the sweetest, kindest woman in this world. . . my mother, Tom, my mother. . . put into the ground by strangers."

Tom put his hand on Nicky's shoulder. "Cry, Nicky," he urged.

The flood he had been holding back for hours ruptured the dam. His face buried in his hands, he sobbed out his anger, his sorrow, his frustration. Tom cradled him in his arms, touched his hair and wept for the mother he had never known, the grandmother who could not love him and the friend he had sold for thirty pieces of silver.

The room had grown dark. Tom turned on a lamp. "Some pair we are."

"Thank you, Tommy."

"For what?"

"For sharing it with me."

"Thank you for sharing it with me."

And then they were both embarrassed and refused to look at each other. "You're going to spend the night here," Tom said, standing. "I'll make us something to eat. I take it you haven't put anything in your stomach all day."

"Now that you mention it, I haven't, and I'm starved. I'm going to shower and. . . Tom, nothing frozen, please."

"Go look in the kitchen, pal."

"What for?"

"To observe, firsthand, that it does not contain an Olga and John."

191

"Frozen?"

"Frozen!"

After supper they sat, sipped wine, and talked. Like people who are comfortable with each other they acted as if life in the apartment off Central Park West had gone along placidly and uninterrupted since the day Nicky had moved in. Nicky spoke of the Romaines and Tom listened patiently, knowing that talking, like crying, is good for the soul.

"She knew you had become Eric and even went to the trouble of getting Eric's address," Tom said, looking at the official letter once again.

"There are newspapers in London, Tom, and Aunt Marie was an avid reader."

Tom shook his head slowly. "That's not the point. Wasn't she curious as to how you had done it? How you could possibly have become someone else? She was like your mother, so how could she accept the fact that you had assumed a new identity, and a rather well-known one at that?"

Nicky shrugged. "I don't know. In fact the thought never occurred to me."

"I can understand that. You were upset. But now, what do you think about it now? And she never tried to get in touch with you to see what the fuck was going on."

"She was old, Tom, maybe the whole thing never really meshed in her mind."

"Bull." Tom reached for a cigarette. "You told me she was as sharp as a ten-year-old, so if you had become Eric Hall she would immediately realize that you had to be Eric Hall's double. That must have struck her as rather strange."

"Maybe she dug up some old photos of Eric from the newspaper morgues. . ." Nicky began weakly.

"Maybe she knew, and had always known, you were Eric's double," Tom cut in. "Christ, I don't think she was very surprised when she read her newspaper last spring."

"I don't know what to tell you, Tommy, I really don't." He looked and sounded like the fawn Tom had discovered so long ago. "And now I guess we'll never know."

"There's a lot about Mr. and Ms. Romaine that we'll never know, Nicky. A hell of a lot."

22

Tom thought his tree would lose its leaves in the prime of its autumnal splendor. The storm clouds, which had been gathering in the heavens over New York all day, began to unload their burden in the early afternoon. By five, when commuters were making their weary way home, the downpour was torrential. By six, when Tom arrived at his apartment, a wind arose that caused the word "hurricane" to be tossed about by everyone except the weather forecasters who were sticking to their "light rain, clearing by evening" prediction.

Tom was soaked to the skin. He got out of his clothes, took a hot shower and wrapped himself in his terry robe. He brewed a pot of tea and laced it with bourbon as a precaution against the flu. It didn't work but neither did anything else, so why not a pleasurable hoax as opposed to a dismal one? He had everything in the house he needed, including a steak and a brand new mystery novel. He made dinner, declared it superb and settled down with his book. While the storm raged without, Tom was as snug as an unborn in its mother's womb.

A keen observer of modern civilization once noted that the telephone is the sole basis of all neo-frustration and anxiety. It is always there, ready to jar us out of whatever pleasantness we are engaged in to bring us the worst possible news from any corner of the globe. Or, when awaiting news, it sits, silent and dumb, refusing to utter even a single ring until it has been completely abandoned. . . and then it screams, in vain, its presence.

193

Tom was halfway through the second chapter of his mystery when his telephone began to ring with great agitation. He thought, naturally, that it was Eric wanting to know if he had been caught in the storm. People who are constantly sheltered like to inquire after the less fortunate. One imagines them in another life peering over the gate of hell and shouting things like, "Is it hot?"

"Hello."

"I know." Dicky Culver. Christ. . . not now. . . not tonight of all nights.

"Dicky, I thought we had settled all that," Tom almost pleaded.

"Forget all that shit we talked about, Tom. I know and there's no question about it. He's not Eric." There was not a hint of a falsetto note in Dicky's voice. A very bad sign, indeed.

"What is it, Dicky?" Tom wasn't condescending. He knew Dicky like every smart man knows his enemy and the enemy was on to something.

"I've written her a letter."

"Good God," Tom shouted. "Who? Mrs. Lindenhurst?"

"She has to know she's being made a fool of." Dicky began to sound like a drag queen doing Bette Davis. Tom's hopes rose at once. "We've been taken in. . . assholes. . . we're all assholes."

"You didn't mail the letter, did you? This can be explained, Dicky. I'm sure it can be explained."

Dicky began to laugh — or cry; without seeing Bette how was Tom to know? "You try to explain this one. Oh, I can't wait to hear you explain this one."

"What the fuck is it?"

"Come over here and read the letter. I want to hear you bullshit your way out of this one."

"What the fuck is it?" Tom repeated.

"Come and find out. I want to see your face when I tell you."

"Does Amy know?"

"She's at her mother's on the island and can't get back. The expressway is washed out for a change."

It sounded serious but with Amy out of the way he had a fifty-fifty chance. "There's a fucking hurricane going on out there," Tom said in one final try.

"Nothing to the hurricane you're gonna see when this letter gets delivered." Dicky was enjoying this.

"I'm on my way and don't you do anything stupid before I arrive."

"Me? I don't have to do a thing. It's your pal 'Eric' that should have done something before he started playing this game."

"He didn't do a thing, Culver. You told him he was Eric and don't you fucking forget it." Tom slammed down the phone.

If anything the storm had gotten worse. There wasn't a cab, or hardly a car, on the streets. Tom waited an eternity for a crosstown bus and when it finally came it practically had to wade across the park. At Sixty-eighth and Madison he got lucky. Someone got out of a cab and Tom jumped in and headed uptown. When he got to the Culvers' he was soaked to the skin for the second time in less than three hours.

"Do you want a drink?" Dicky asked.

"No, I don't want a drink and this had better be good, Culver, because if it's not I'm gonna toss you out of a fucking window."

Dicky was grinning from ear to ear. "Good? It's better than good, Tommy. Tommy, isn't that what 'Eric' calls you — Tommy?"

Tom's hair was plastered to his head. Water dripped from his nose and chin. His raincoat clung, like a wet towel, to his body. He was totally drained. "Jealous, Dicky? What's the problem, doesn't the new Eric let you blow him on a regular basis? You miss your bottle, baby?"

Dicky began to laugh. "Oh, that's rich, Tommy. That's really rich. You're having an affair with that phony, aren't you? Amy always said you were queer but I never believed her."

"She thinks you're queer, too. Do you believe that?"

"I don't care what Amy thinks, or what you think, or what anyone thinks. I only care about putting that phony bastard in jail. Do they let queers visit inmates, like wives?"

"You're a comtemptible bastard," Tom hissed and turned to leave.

"Don't you want to read my letter?"

"Wrap it around your dildo and shove it up your ass."

"But you came all this way in the pouring rain. Come on, Tommy, don't cut off your nose to spite your pretty face." Dicky walked to the desk, picked up a piece of paper and handed it to Tom.

Shaking with fury but unable to resist, Tom took the letter from Dicky and began to read. When he finished it fell from his hand, his knees began to buckle beneath him and he actually allowed Dicky to take his elbow and lead him to a chair. Tom, his eyes wide open, stared at nothing. His jaw sagged as he began to

mumble incoherently. "I thought of everything... everything...
doubles... perfect doubles...everything.. how could...."
Dicky put a bourbon, straight up, under Tom's nose. "Here,
you need it."
Tom drank what was offered, not even tasting the liquor, and
continued to stare into space.
"Start explaining, Tom. If it's good, I'll tear up the letter."
Dicky, triumphant, was more swish than ever. This seemed to re-
vive Tom. He looked at Dicky and then buried his face in his hands,
his shoulders heaving with emotion.
"Come on, Tom, it's not that bad. You and 'Eric' can...
Tom?... Tom? He's not crying. He's laughing. *The crazy fucker is
laughing,*" Dicky screamed and actually hit a high C.

23

He finished reading the letter and looked at her. There wasn't a trace of fear or shame in his clear blue eyes.

"I was going to destroy it," she said. "Pretend Dicky had never written it. He gave me that option."

"I never tried to—"

She held up her hand. "Please don't. Let me say what I must. I was going to destroy it but then I thought that wouldn't be fair to you, would it?"

"To me?"

"Yes. Because then you would never know who you are, and you don't know who you are, do you?"

"I don't. I swear I don't."

She smiled. "You don't have to swear, I'm a very good judge of character."

"And I never told you I was Eric," he continued.

"I know that, too. It was I who told you you were Eric. You look so much like him and I wanted so much to believe... don't worry, I won't cry."

"I hate it when you cry."

"Then I shan't cry. I owe you that much."

"Owe me? My God, you don't owe me anything."

"Oh, but I do. I'm eighty-four years old... eighty-four... and I thought I knew all that there was to know about this life we are given and told to live as best we can. When my family was taken from me I locked myself in this house and turned my back on the

197

world. I lived only in the past and for the past, and that was very wrong. When you walked through those doors I thought the past had returned and I began to enjoy my life once again. But the past hadn't returned. I only thought it had. It was all an illusion but that made no difference to what I felt. You taught me that life is whatever we choose it to be. Fate deals out the cards blindly but we, not she, play out the hand. You're never too old to learn, and don't you ever forget that, young man."

"I love you so much and if I could become Eric for you I would gladly give up my life in exchange for his."

"No more giving up lives," she protested, "living life, that's what we have to do. I want you to live your own life and not the dream of a foolish old lady."

"Oh, Nana, I. . . I can't call you that, can I?'

"I don't see why not. There's not another person in the world I would rather hear it from and I have grown so fond of the way you say it. Now I think it's you who's crying."

"I'm so sorry. Oh, I am so sorry."

"Don't be. We entered each other's lives at just the right time and gave each other a boost. You taught me how to live again and I—"

"You gave me the only grandmother I'll ever have."

She took his hand in hers and whispered, "Stay. . . please stay. . . no one need ever know and we can go on just as we were."

"We would know, Nana, and after a while what we have would turn sour. Living a lie, even for the sake of love, is wrong. I want to keep what we have, not destroy it."

"And you're still teaching me. Oh, Eric. . . I. . . ."

He smiled. "They call me Nicky. Nicky Three."

"Nicky. Nicholas. What an aristocratic name. What will you do, Nicky?"

He blushed and it didn't go unnoticed by the old lady. "I called Tom. Tom Bradshaw. I'm going to live with him."

"You like that young man, don't you?"

"Very much. He's a little. . . nutty. . . but we get along."

"And will you have time for an old lady?"

"Twice a week, I promise. We have a lot of unfinished business. The garden, your daily exercise, and we'll go out. I don't want you mooning around this house."

She looked at him very closely. "Eric's money doesn't mean anything to you, does it?"

He shook his head. "No, it doesn't."

Now the tears filled her eyes. "How I wish you were my grandson. How I wish you truly were my grandson."

"I told you, you're the only grandmother I'll ever have. And the money, my allowance, I'll give it all back to you."

"You will not." He tried to speak but she stopped him. "You told me once you wanted to open a restaurant. Well, do it, Nicky, and I'll be your partner. This town could use a good restaurant."

"Fifty-fifty?" He held out his hand.

"Fifty-fifty." She took his hand and then they were in each other's arms. He held her, very close, for a long time. "And I'm going to have my Christmas party," she sobbed.

"Of course you are."

"And you are going to be by my side on the receiving line."

"What will people say?"

"I'm as rich as Midas, Nicky, so people will say 'she's a queer old bird' and then trip over themselves trying to please me. Now let me teach you something. Don't you ever worry about what people will say. Do what you know is right for you and the only thing others will be is jealous."

"But I'll be Nicky."

"You call me Nana and I'll call you Sonny. That should make them all happy."

He laughed wildly. "You sound like Tom Bradshaw."

"Is that bad?"

"No, Nana, it's good. It's very, very good."

24

Nicky arrived home carrying only a small overnight bag. "The prodigal returneth."

"For the second time," Tom greeted him. "Maybe we should write our own bible."

"Are you sore?"

Tom shrugged and waved a hand in the air. "What's a hundred million, more or less, to a man in my position?"

"Are you sore?" Nicky repeated.

They looked at each other from across the room, unblinking, uncertain, each waiting for the other to make the first move.

"Come here," Tom finally said.

Nicky, still staring at Tom, shook his head. "You come here."

"A compromise?"

They both took a step forward and then rushed toward each other, colliding rather than meeting, and embraced warmly. "You dumb shit. Am I sore? Of course I'm not sore... I'm just happy to have you back. Put down that stupid bag and let me look at you."

"You saw me yesterday."

"Like looking in a store window at something you can't have. Now you're mine."

"I'm not Eric, and now we know I never will be... again." Nicky laughed.

"Eric who?"

"You're crazy, Tommy."

"But charming... don't ever forget that."

"I don't even have a job, Tom."

"Well, you had better get one. I got a notice yesterday that the rent's going up."

"On this rat's nest? I had a dressing room that was bigger than this whole fucking place."

"Had, baby, that's the operative word. . . had."

"We gave it the old college try, Tommy. Shit, we actually pulled it off."

"We did, didn't we? We really gave them a run for their money. Come on, let's have a beer."

And then they talked and laughed and laughed and talked. They relived every moment, thrilling to their own daring, complimenting themselves on their cleverness, mimicking the reactions of others and finally winding down to a peaceful silence.

"Our tree is almost bare, Nicky. A whole year down the tube."

"And what a year it was. We squeezed a lifetime out of it."

"Let's do it every year."

"Every other year, Tommy. I'm tired."

They were alone in the world, alone in their room, alone in their bed. They lay naked, a beer bottle balanced on each hard, firm belly.

"The first one who spills it has to lick it up," Nicky redefined the rules of the game.

"I can't reach that far."

"You might get some on me."

"Christ, are you still into that? I thought they would teach you some manners on the other side of the park."

"They taught me a lot," Nicky reflected.

"I can't believe she's letting you keep the allowance. That's a lot of bucks I put in Aunt Marie's nest egg. We could do some traveling, Nicky."

"It's for my restaurant. . . and hers. Besides, I don't want to leave her alone."

"You act as if she really is your grandmother."

"I think she is."

"What?"

"Nothing."

"Maybe she'll leave you something in her will. Maybe all of it, Nicky. All of it. . . just think. . . ."

"Easy, you almost spilled it."

"If I do it'll be on me alone."

"You're no fun anymore, Tom."

"Remember that lady in Baltimore?"

"What lady?"

"The one who said you were the Grand Duke something or other."

"Yeah, that was something, wasn't it."

"Should I contact her?'"

"What the hell for?"

"Well, if we play it right we can get her to acknowledge that you're. . . ."

"Go to sleep, Tom."

"Listen, I read once that there's a hundred million in gold, *gold*, mind you, in a bank in England, just waiting for a legitimate heir to the last czar of Russia."

"Go to sleep, Tom."

"We can do a little research. . . I'm good at that. . . and then. . . ."

"Tom, shut up and listen to me."

"I'm listening."

"If there is one thing I do not want to be, Tom Bradshaw, it is the czar of Russia."

DICKY CULVER'S LETTER TO MRS. ERIC LINDENHURST

Dear Mrs. Lindenhurst:

I am writing because, quite frankly, I do not have the courage to confront you with the disquieting news I feel compelled to relate. I know what I have to say will greatly distress you, however I feel it is my duty and obligation to inform you of what I know and your prerogative to act upon this information in whatever manner you choose. My only confidant in this matter is Tom Bradshaw and I can assure you that, after writing this letter, I will not speak of it or its contents to anyone now or in the future.

For some time I have felt that Eric is not your grandson and my old friend. His physical resemblance to Eric is so great that I refused to believe or dwell upon this thought which persisted in the back of my mind. But persist it did.

I confided in Bradshaw and he, predictably, reminded me of all

Eric had been through, his illness, etc. and concluded that such an experience could change any man. And, again, no one could deny that physically he was Eric.

I knew my first doubts began the day Eric and I renewed our Wednesdays at the club. There was nothing in Eric's new personality that caused my doubt because I had already geared myself to deal with this aspect of my friend's return. So it had to be something physical which was the one thing that made us all certain he was Eric. This evening, as so often happens, while thinking of other things I suddenly realized what I had subconsciously known all these months.

Indeed, what supposedly happened to Eric could cause him to change in many ways. But there is one change no outside force, short of a miracle, could bring about. Eric could not have grown a foreskin which had been removed in infancy. The man living in your home and calling himself Eric Hall is an imposter.

Sincerely,
Richard Culver

AUTHOR'S NOTE

In 1923 Dorothy Sayers published a Lord Peter Wimsey mystery entitled *Whose Body*. The plot revolved about the discovery of a nude body in a bathtub. The body is identified as that of a rich, Jewish industrialist. Lord Peter realizes in minutes that the body is no such person because the corpse is an uncircumcised male. Sayers' publishers were shocked that such a means of identification would be utilized in the book and (I think) twice as shocked that a female writer had thought of it. The publishers forced Sayers to rewrite and in the printed version of the book Lord Peter uses a somewhat contrived and rather unconvincing means of identification involving the dead man's haircut and manicure.

To the best of my knowledge Sayers' original idea has never been used in the myriad of books published wherein the plots hinge upon mistaken identity, imposters, pretenders, etc. Like the blood test used in paternity suits this physical attribute can prove that one could be. . . or, as in the case of *The Prince and the Pretender*. . . that one could most certainly not be. Hence my dedication and tribute to a writer who was indeed years ahead of her time and who, I am sure, would be happy to know that her smashing "clue" has finally won out over prudery.